# KEEP YOUR DOORS LOCKED

## A CAPTIVATING PSYCHOLOGICAL DOMESTIC THRILLER YOU CAN'T PUT DOWN

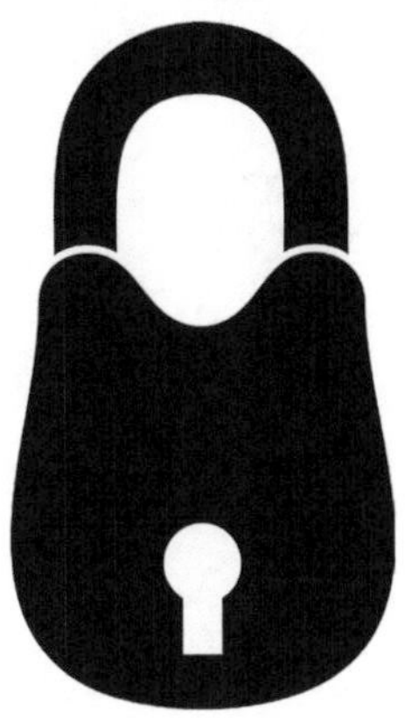

By Becki Willis

Special thanks goes to my 'inside expert' for proper usage of terminology and procedures. You know who you are.

Cover design by Anelia Savova
Editing by SJS Editorial Services

ISBN: 978-1-947686-98-4

KEEP YOUR DOORS LOCKED

# Chapter 1

## Sara

"Breaking news from the Channel Five News Center. This just in, an inmate has escaped from the Roscoe Unit of the Texas Department of Criminal Justice prison system. Details are still forthcoming, but it is believed Thomas Ramon Bernard, 47, sneaked aboard a delivery van to exit the facility. Once beyond the gates, Bernard overcame the driver and hijacked the van, abandoning it some forty miles away. He was last seen on foot near the rural community of Maypole in Apple County.

"Residents in the area are instructed to stay in their homes with their doors locked and to alert authorities if they see anyone or anything suspicious. Bernard is described as a five-foot, seven-inch male with a slender build and dark hair, wearing prison-issued white pants and shirt. Do not approach him. Presume he is armed and dangerous. Again, do not approach. Bernard is currently serving life in prison on multiple convictions, including capital murder, attempting to carry out a plot to commit murder, and kidnapping. Stay tuned to this channel for further details as they become available."

Pausing as she diced vegetables for her dinner, Sara Jennings watched the broadcast with a frown. She remembered hearing of a similar breakout in one of the Midwestern states about a month ago. Didn't they use locks in prison anymore? How were these people breaking out so easily?

She scooped up a handful of chopped carrots and potatoes and eased them into the bubbling broth. There was nothing like a pot of beef stew on the first chilly evening of the season. Fifty-eight wasn't cold enough to break out her winter jacket but considering that last night had been twenty degrees warmer, it almost felt like it. She would settle, instead, for a small pot of stew and a pan of cornbread. There would be enough leftovers to have for days, something she would appreciate while she worked overtime on her big project.

Sara had planned to eat outside by the fire pit, enjoying the warmth of the fire and the orange hues of the sunset while wrapped in a lightweight blanket, but in light of the special bulletin on the news, perhaps she should eat indoors. Technically, her address was Maypole, even though the town itself was several miles to the east.

With a sigh, Sara reached into her spice cabinet and started pulling out containers. She added a few shakes of this, a dash of that, and a healthy portion of black pepper. She blew on a spoonful of the hot broth before sampling.

"Needs something," she decided aloud.

She opened the refrigerator to forage inside its depths. She was always amazed that the vintage appliance still worked. It had come with the house when she bought it. Sara tolerated the white monstrosity, thinking it couldn't possibly last much longer, but a year later, it was still running strong.

And loud. Sara gave the appliance a gentle shove, knowing the floor was just uneven enough to cause an irritating vibration. The foundation of the house was solid—she had it checked before purchasing her first home, of course—but the wood floor sagged a bit beneath the hunk of steel. She had once attempted moving the appliance to clean behind it but quickly decided a little dust wouldn't cause permanent harm. Breaking her back might.

Satisfied when she found leftover brussel sprouts and a stray stalk of celery, Sara prepped the celery and dropped both vegetables into the stew. That was one of the good things about stew, she thought with a smile. It helped clean out the fridge.

Another dash of salt, and all it needed was time to simmer.

Reducing the heat on the stove, Sara gathered ingredients for her cornbread. She was always a sucker for comfort food, and with this project for work looming large in her mind, she needed all the comfort she could get.

At thirty-four, Sara was self-employed by her own software development company. She normally preferred small jobs, creating very specific programs for mom-and-pop businesses and small offices, but this upcoming project was more ambitious. She was designing a multi-faceted program for a large company's flagship store in Dallas. If the software worked as planned, they would implement the same system in six other locations. The project could make or break *SJ Innovations.*

Sara's mind wandered as she stirred baking powder, salt, and a small portion of sugar into the cornmeal and flour mixture. Imagining how the software would perform, she turned the oven on to preheat before returning to the refrigerator for milk, butter, and an egg. As she absently slathered the baking dish with melted butter—the same way her program would grease the cogs of data—she heard a knock on the door.

She glanced nervously toward the television. The channel had returned to its normal schedule and was currently taunting game show contestants to press their luck. Sara wasn't big on game shows, but it was one of the few such programs that held her interest. She often watched re-runs while preparing dinner. And even though the screen now showed a half-dozen briefcases beneath the megawatt smiles of beautiful women in sequined gowns, her mind's eye still saw footage of an abandoned van in a wooded area.

It looked much like the view outside her kitchen window.

"Stop it, Sara," she told herself sternly. "Maypole is nearly ten miles away. You've got nothing to worry about."

Despite the warning to herself, Sara made certain the back door was latched before padding into the living room. A woman living alone could never be too careful, even in this sleepy little rural community.

"Hello!" a man's voice called from the other side of the door. "Is anyone home?"

Sara was hesitant to answer. What if the prisoner had somehow made it this far and stood on her front porch? It was foolhardy to open the door to a stranger, especially with an escaped convict on the loose.

"Is anyone there? This is Special Detective Mason Burleson with the Joint East Texas Fugitive Task Force," the man said. His voice had a deep rumble that inspired trust, but Sara wouldn't stake her life on something as fickle as a tone.

"We're going door to door, doing welfare checks," the man with the pleasant voice continued. "I see a car in the driveway. Is anyone home?"

Sara had lived alone in the city long enough to know that single women were vulnerable. For that reason, she had developed a piece of software known as SJ's Big Dog. With the flick of a button, she could activate the sound of two large dogs inside the home. It sounded as if they came running from a distant room, barking ferociously as they approached the potential intruder. She kept several devices around the house, just for this purpose. Next to most of them was a pistol.

"Hold on!" she called above the sounds of her protective 'guard dogs.' Angling her voice away from the door, she said, "Hush, Bruno. Down, Hondo. Heel." With the door still closed, she asked the man on the other side, "May I help you?"

"Just making certain you're okay, ma'am. Can you open the door just enough that I can show you my badge?"

Sensing a trap, Sara shook her head, even though he couldn't see. "Are you alone?" she asked. She wasn't about to open the door and be overpowered by a deceptive criminal.

"Yes, ma'am, I am."

"Come back with your partner. In uniform."

She was infuriated when he sounded amused. "A body for each dog to chew on?" he asked.

"Something like that," she snapped.

"I'll be back shortly, ma'am. Don't open the door to anyone you don't know."

A pregnant pause spoke more than her prim and proper, "Precisely."

Letting the dogs bark until the sound of his vehicle retreated, Sara replaced the device to its proper place. She shook her head all the way back to the kitchen but with less confidence than she pretended. If the detective was for real, did that mean the convict was closer than the newscaster suggested? Was she in danger?

Her hands took on a slight tremble as she stirred her simmering pot of stew. She sampled the broth again, but suddenly, it tasted unappetizing.

Sara abruptly sat at the kitchen table, only to rise a few moments later. This was ridiculous! She had lived by herself in cities ripe with crime and evil deeds. Why should one escapee cause her such strife?

"Because you uprooted your life and moved here to the country to get away from all that," she reminded herself. "The last time your car was broken into, you said enough was enough. This isn't supposed to happen here. You came to the country for some peace and quiet. Who does this Thomas Bernard think he is, invading your sense of security?"

Convinced by her own argument, Sara returned to the oven and slid her pan of cornbread inside. "I can't let him win. No matter what the detective said, the convict is miles away from here. He just dropped by as a precaution. I shouldn't have been so rude. Of course, he was legit. He was simply doing his job."

Sara set a timer on her smartwatch for the cornbread and wandered into her office, where she already had an array of computers and monitors lined up on a long folding table that wrapped around to her desk. She would officially start checking the software tomorrow, running tests and trial runs to work out all the bugs. She planned to get an early start in the morning, so she had done all the prep work today.

She double checked plugs and outlets, as well as cable connections from the computers to the monitors. She arranged her folders, pens, and notebooks and adjusted the floor lamp so that its spindly arms were angled just right. Satisfied that everything was in place for tomorrow, she was about to leave the room. Just before turning out the light, she decided to check the window lock. Despite the pep talk earlier, she couldn't take any chances. She made the rounds through the rambling old farmhouse, finding all of them secure.

Sara had fallen in love with the house the first time she saw it. Even before the realtor showed her inside, she knew this was the house she would buy. The house was old but solid, with a coat of fresh white paint and a newly shingled roof. Huge rose bushes, one on either side of the steps, were neatly pruned and abloom with their autumn offerings. It was nothing like any place Sara had ever lived, but it was everything she wanted.

The inside was every bit as enchanting as the exterior. The rooms were large and airy, most of them flowing into one another, as was customary for the period. Foregoing a formal entry, a long front porch with gingerbread trim and a quaint screen door opened directly into the living room, which opened into the dining room, and then into the kitchen. On either side of the central rooms were two bedrooms, separated by a bath; Sara used one of the front bedrooms as her office. Another small bath opened off the laundry room and exited to the carport at the side of the house.

She loved that the floors were bare wood, the walls original plank, and the ceilings tall. Built before central air was invented, the windows were aligned for optimum air flow, aided in part by transoms above the interior doors. Sara also loved the fact that when the HVAC system was eventually installed, it was done so unobtrusively, keeping the authenticity of the house intact.

Having grown up in a military family, Sara remembered few of the houses she had lived in. Once she was grown and out on her own—and even during her ill-fated marriage—she had lived in duplexes and apartments. All of her previous homes had been generic spaces with little personality. Even the one posh condo where she and her ex lived had been cold and impersonal, meant to impress more than it was to comfort.

When she made the decision to move from the city, she knew she wanted to go somewhere with a story. A simple farmhouse on twelve acres of land with a pecan orchard and mature pear trees obviously had a history. And history came with a story.

Sara didn't know the full story behind the farmhouse, but she wasn't worried. She had plenty of time to learn. For now, it was enough to know that locals referred to it as the Old Miller place, and Cora Miller, the last of the bloodline, had died a natural death here. Real estate laws required that the agent reveal the fact to her, as if the locals wouldn't fill her in the first time they met. Most of the comments had been along the lines of, "Poor Cora. Lived her entire life in that house. Born and died, right there within those walls." Some had been more dramatic. "You do know that Cora died there, right? Took her last breath of life, right there in that house."

News of a death didn't bother Sara. Not if the person had lived a long, happy life, which apparently Cora had done. In an odd way, it made the house that much more appealing. For Cora—and perhaps others before her—the farmhouse was a forever home. With any luck, it would be a forever home for Sara, too. She was totally in love with it.

Until now, Sara had adored all the windows and the open, flowing design. But as evening approached, she suddenly felt exposed. After checking the windows, she closed all the blinds, shut off unused rooms, and returned to the kitchen.

The delicious aromas of hot from the oven cornbread and hearty beef stew rallied her spirits and restored her appetite. Just as she sat to eat, she heard someone knock at the door.

Hurrying to the door, Sara reached for her SJ's Big Dog. Before she could engage the button, she heard someone call her name.

"Ms. Jennings? This is Special Detective Mason Burleson again. I'm here with DPS Trooper J'Marcus Gray. If you'll look out the window on your left, you can see our badges."

Slightly less skeptical than before, Sara's voice was still sharp. "How do you know my name?"

"I'm a detective, ma'am." Again, he sounded amused.

Cautiously, Sara parted the blinds to peer through the glass. The silver badges on the other side looked official enough. To be certain, she memorized the numbers before making a request.

"Turn them face down and tell me your badge numbers. Please." She added the last as an afterthought.

The two men dutifully obliged, quoting the numbers without pause.

The black and white patrol car in the driveway gave her confidence to open the door. She pulled it toward her as far as the deadbolt's chain would allow. Formality lingered in her words. "May I help you?"

The detective with the pleasant voice replied first. "As I said earlier, we're doing welfare checks in the area, ma'am. In case you haven't heard, a prisoner escaped this afternoon and was last seen near Maypole. We aren't sure which way he went after that, so we're going house to house, alerting residents and urging everyone to be vigilant."

"I saw the news alert but thank you for the warning."

The second officer spoke, holding a photocopied paper up to the slit between them. "This is the man we're looking for. Have you seen him?"

"No."

"You didn't even look." Detective Burleson's voice no longer sounded amused. It sounded accusing.

Sara's shrug was pragmatic. "No need. I live well off the road, on private property. I've been in the house all afternoon. No one has been here since the UPS driver, about ten o'clock this morning."

"Is there anyone else in the house?" Trooper Gray asked. "Maybe they've seen him."

"I can assure you; he hasn't been here."

The humor was back in the detective's tone. "So, your dogs haven't been gnawing on any stray bones, I take it?" He shifted just enough that Sara got a glimpse of his tall, solid form.

*Too bad I couldn't see him earlier*, she thought with irritation. *I would have known he wasn't the escaped inmate and saved him a second trip. This man is tall and broad chested, and too young to be the convict.*

And too relaxed. She could see the side of his mouth, which quirked upward in a smile.

"They do seem to be awfully quiet," she agreed. "Maybe they're sleeping off a feast."

The DPS trooper shot a confused look between his co-worker and the woman hidden behind the door.

"She asked me to bring backup with me," Detective Burleson explained. "She thought her two dogs might need a snack."

"Big dogs?" The uniformed officer all but jumped, darting his eyes around the porch in alarm.

His partner slapped a hand onto his shoulder. "Relax, Gray. The dogs exist only on demand."

J'Marcus Gray was now more confused than ever. "Huh? The devil you say?"

"The dogs aren't real. They're a recording."

Sara narrowed her eyes, pinning her green stare upon the detective. "Why would you say that?"

"Because I just bought the same device for my mother and my aunt. BJ's Big Dog, I think it was called. It's a handy little device to have, especially for women living alone."

She couldn't help but be flattered by the officer's opinion of her product, even if he got the name wrong. "Thank you. And that's SJ's Big Dog, by the way. Not BJ's."

"At any rate, ma'am," Trooper Gray said, flapping the paper again, "if you do see this man, do *not* open your door."

His co-worker chuckled. "Why do you think I dragged you out here? She wouldn't even open the door for me! She thought I wasn't who I claimed to be."

The trooper tipped his hat. "Smart thinking, ma'am. You can never be too careful."

"That's exactly what I thought," Sara replied. "Do you mind if I get a closer look at that picture?" She tried snaking her hand through the narrow opening.

"It would be easier if you just opened the door," the detective pointed out.

"It would. But your partner said it best." She arched her brow, the prim gesture barely visible through the slit. "You can never be too careful."

The trooper pushed the paper through the opening so that Sara could pull it inside. She studied the photocopy, memorizing the man's features. There was a small, jagged scar across his chin, and his nose was crooked, as if it had been broken more than once. His dark hair was clipped close to his head, and he appeared to be part Hispanic.

When she took longer than expected, the trooper asked again, "Have you seen him?"

"No. Just committing his face to memory, in case I do." She slid the paper back toward them.

"This man is possibly armed and is definitely dangerous. If you see him, do not cross him," Detective Burleson said sternly. "Call 9-1-1 immediately if you see or hear anything suspicious. If he approaches the house, stay away from doors and windows. Go to an interior room, if possible."

"The same way as with a tornado?"

"Ms. Jennings, I can assure you this is no joking matter. Thomas Bernard is a very dangerous man. There's no reason to believe he is here in the immediate area, but there's also no reason not to take this situation seriously. We don't know which way he's going, so we have to assume it could be anywhere, including here. Please don't make light of the danger."

Sara's eyes went cold. "Believe me, Detective," she said in a pinched tone. "I never make light of danger."

# Chapter 2

## Sara

Sara ate her meal at the kitchen table.

The scarred wooden piece had come with the house, as had much of the furniture. Most were vintage mix and match, with the exception of one full bedroom set. The four-poster bed with its matching nightstands, chest of drawers, and dressing table were a different style and quality than the rest. Sara replaced the stained and lumpy mattress, but with its original pastel green and pink quilt, the back room opposite her own was pretty enough to deem the guest room.

Should anyone ever visit.

The much-anticipated stew and cornbread didn't taste nearly as comforting as she had imagined. Despite being delicious, the food didn't soothe away her cares as it normally did. She wanted to blame the disappointing meal on the fugitive or, better yet, on the detective, but she knew neither were at fault. Her discontent went much further back than just today.

Before going to bed, she watched the local news for an update. The escaped convict was still at large, and law enforcement urged all residents to be on alert, particularly those within the counties bordering Maypole. They speculated that the fugitive was long gone from the area where he was last seen. If he were still on foot, they believed he couldn't have gone far.

The news showed video footage of law enforcement agencies swarming around Maypole and the rural area outside of town where the van was discovered. Sara squinted at the screen, thinking she recognized the field where they gathered. She was irritated to notice one particular man among the crowd of uniforms and officials. If she weren't mistaken, that was Special Detective Burleson. Leave it to the detective to be right in the thick of things.

"Well, obviously, they have this thing handled," she muttered. "Only a fool would hang around with that many badges in town."

When the anchorwoman switched to national politics, Sara turned off the television. She had stayed up later than intended to watch the news, despite the early day she had ahead. Already dressed for bed, all she had to do was turn out the lights, place her pistol beside her on the bed, and settle in for the night.

Badges in town or not, she was smart enough to know she needed to be armed. That was one hard-learned lesson Sara never took for granted, especially with danger afoot.

She knew all her doors and windows were locked. She knew she had her Sig Sauer P365 at her side. She knew there were dozens of law officers patrolling the area. She knew she was safer here than she had ever been in the city.

Even with all that, she still didn't sleep well.

It wasn't because of the escaped convict.

It was because of a man named Shawn.

She had the nightmare again that night.

Not all the dreams were the same; they came with different variations, different levels of terror, different layers. Different memories that surfaced.

Try as she might, she could never suppress all the memories. And when they built up and eventually leaked out, they paved the way for another nightmare.

It began the way it always did, with a loud roll of thunder and bright, zig-zag flashes of lightning. Black clouds swirled thick as smoke, tangling Sara within their wispy web. She tried batting at the imagined haze, her hands leaden with sleep. She was desperate to push through the dark billows, even though she knew terror awaited on the other side.

With another flash of light, the clouds were gone, and she came face to face with the man of her nightmares.

Tonight, to no real surprise, Shawn was angry with her. So angry that the veins on the sides of his neck popped out, throbbing with intensity. He was yelling at her, his voice drowned out by the sound of thunder and rain, but she didn't need to hear the words to know what he said. He was blaming her again. Blaming her for everything that had gone wrong in his life. Blaming her for his own shortcomings. Blaming her for ever being born.

In her nightmare, his eyes glowed red with rage. There was a demon inside him, fighting to be free. Fighting to end the life of the person Shawn hated—and loved—most in the world. The demon inside him wanted Sara dead.

Sara fought back, trying to fend off the advances of a man five times stronger than she. She pushed and shoved, twisting her body to ward off a blow, diving to one side as he lunged toward her.

She almost made it. She was almost free, but her foot hung on something. She kicked and squirmed, trying desperately to pull herself free from his grasp. She cried out for help, hearing the tiny sound of her inept whimper and knowing it wasn't enough. Knowing tonight would be the night Shawn succeeded.

> Knowing tonight would be the night she died.
>
> Then, somehow, she pulled herself free, and she was falling...

Sara awoke with a startled yelp. She hung half off the bed, her foot tangled in the bedsheets. It took a full moment for her to realize that it had all been a dream, and the only danger she was in was the danger she had created.

She righted herself in bed and gulped in much-needed air. With her lungs full again, she practiced breathing exercises.

A slow, deep breath in through the nose.

A quick push out through the mouth.

Repeat.

Repeat again and again, and then again.

Repeat until her thundering heart slowed and her temples stopped throbbing.

Repeat until she could assure herself she was home, alone, and in her own bed.

Sara had anxiety meds she could take, but she needed to be clear and alert starting her project. It was the same reason she didn't get up and wander into the office as she normally did when she couldn't sleep, puttering about on her computer until sleep overcame her again. She needed to be fresh for her early start.

Resigning herself to staying in bed, Sara switched to a routine of slow, shallow breaths, mimicking a sleep pattern. She willed her mind not to think of her nightmare. Not to think of Shawn. Not to think of programming sequences and keystrokes.

In her mind's eyes, she pictured a peaceful wooded area with a stream winding through it. She imagined the leaves as they silently fell from the trees and into the water, where they began a lazy journey down the trickling creek.

Just before succumbing to sleep, another taboo subject flitted briefly through her mind, of an escaped convict just miles from her house.

The alarm clock jarred Sara awake. She groaned and hit snooze, hoping ten more minutes would make up for the two hours she had missed during the night.

They didn't.

Her movements were sluggish as she reluctantly climbed from the bed and dressed in light sweatpants and a comfortable tee. That was one major perk of working from home. No need for makeup or binding waistlines. Not when she wouldn't see a soul today. And not when Sara was long past primping in the mirror for her own vanity.

In the kitchen, she brewed her first cup of coffee; Lord knew it wouldn't be the last. That was why she kept the Keurig in the kitchen and not in her office.

On days she was engrossed in a project, coffee and bathroom breaks were the only exercise she had.

With a noisy yawn, she fixed a bowl of cereal and spoke aloud to herself, "I wonder where and when they caught the convict. Maybe I can catch the local news before the network shows start."

She found the remote and turned on the television. As she poured milk and sat down to eat, the program was in the middle of a segment about upcoming entertainment for the weekend. Being a rural area with no major towns within its boundaries, Apple County didn't have a channel to call their own. Residents watched the next best thing, which was a channel based out of Tyler.

When the meteorologist appeared on screen, Sara wrinkled her nose. Apparently, she had missed news of the convict.

She vaguely heard the weatherman talk about warm days, cool nights, and a front that could potentially bring thunderstorms and rains by early next week. Before turning the program back to the morning anchor, he promised to keep a close eye on the forecast models for viewers.

"That wraps it up for today's Eye Openers," the anchor said in a cheery voice, "but remember to stay tuned for a special broadcast, live from Apple County. News Five Reporter Damien Edwards is on the scene of what has become a broadened manhunt for prison escapee Thomas Ramon Bernard. Several law enforcement agencies, including officials from TDCJ, Apple County, DPS, and the U.S. Marshal Service are combing the area for Bernard, who escaped from the Roscoe Unit yesterday afternoon. As of yet, Bernard has not been apprehended. That live broadcast should be coming up on the eight o-clock hour, so stayed tuned right here to Channel Five for the latest update." She went on to remind viewers of their online app and how to stay informed of breaking news, weather, and sports.

Sara frowned, talking to herself again. "They haven't caught him yet? That's not very assuring."

Finished with her cereal, Sara took her bowl to the sink and brewed a second cup of coffee. She decided to watch the live broadcast on the larger television in the living room. At least that put her one room closer to her office.

The live news conference was already underway, allowing her to miss the tedious introductions and the plug for KRXX. The handy caption at the bottom of the screen told her the man speaking was Peter Gates, official spokesperson for the Texas Department of Criminal Justice.

"At approximately 4:45 p.m. yesterday afternoon, Thomas Ramon Bernard escaped from the TDCJ Roscoe Unit. The investigation is in its early stages, and there is still much to be learned, but it is believed that Bernard sneaked aboard a delivery van that had business at the prison. Once the van exited the prison gates and was several miles away, Bernard overcame the driver, pushed him from the moving van, and hijacked the vehicle. The driver, who was found unconscious near the town of Carmichael, sustained non-life-threatening injuries and is currently recovering in a nearby hospital.

"After commandeering the van, Bernard continued on a northwestern trek and entered Apple County. About five miles from the county line, an Apple County sheriff's deputy recognized the van described in the BOLO report and followed in pursuit. Bernard immediately sped up, and it soon escalated into a high-speed chase. The chase careened through the town of Apple and continued westward on State Highway 38, which runs directly behind us. About four miles out of town, Bernard swerved into the westbound lane, narrowly missing an oncoming vehicle, and made a sharp turn onto County Road 147. Less than two hundred yards down the road, the van crashed into a nearby tree. By the time the deputy could safely turn onto the gravel road and determine that Bernard wasn't in the wrecked vehicle, the inmate had already vanished. It is believed Bernard jumped from the van and escaped on foot before the crash took place.

"Roads were shut down shortly after the incident and will remain that way for the foreseeable future. As you can see," he said, motioning to the highway behind him, "the Texas Department of Transportation has shut down all traffic on State Highway 38 between Maypole and Wayside. Barricades and troopers are forcing travelers to find alternate roadways to reach their destinations. This is a heavily traveled road and one of the main thoroughfares in Apple County. Here behind us, you can see eighteen wheelers, service trucks, and personal vehicles being diverted around the roadblocks. DPS is asking all drivers to avoid the area and allow law enforcement to do their jobs.

"Despite early beliefs, there is no indication that Bernard has left the immediate area. Eyewitnesses report seeing movement in the woods near their home and finding footprints leading southwest, presumably left by Bernard as he ran from the crashed van. Remember, this is a very rural area, comprised mostly of pastureland and heavily wooded thickets. Bernard has been out now for almost sixteen hours and is probably seeking food and water. If you live west of Apple or within a three-to-four-mile radius of County Road 147, you are urged to use extreme caution. Keep your doors locked. Do not, I repeat, do NOT open your door to unknown persons. Use caution when outside. Law enforcement is going door to door, alerting residents, and doing searches of empty properties. At this time, residents are not being evacuated from their homes, but if you have somewhere else to stay, we strongly encourage you to do so.

"Bernard is currently serving time for multiple convictions, including a life sentence for the capital murder of a San Saba County woman. It is unclear if he is armed, but he is known to be a very dangerous individual. Do not confront this man. If you see or hear anything suspicious, you are to contact the local sheriff's office or 9-1-1 immediately. Again, do NOT confront this man. If you have elderly neighbors or know of someone who lives alone or seldom follows social media or television news, please give them a call to check on them. Please, do not approach an empty house, as Bernard could have taken refuge there. Alert the sheriff and let them search the property."

Sara's gut tightened. She assumed the escapee had been promptly apprehended.

If she had been on social media—which she avoided like a plague when working on a big project—she would have known he was still at large. She would have also known he was closer to her than she first believed. At most, County Road 147 was only five miles away. Much too close for comfort.

Spokesman Gates continued parceling out information. As he held up a mugshot, he gave a physical description of the escaped inmate.

"Bernard is a five-foot, seven-inch white Hispanic male with dark hair and a slender build. He weighs approximately one hundred and fifty-five pounds. He was last seen wearing prison-issued white pants and shirt. There is a scar on his chin and multiple scars across his entire body, at least two of them from gunshot wounds. Some of his wounds were self-inflicted. He has numerous tattoos on his back, torso, neck, and arms. If you see anyone matching this description, do not approach them, offer them a ride, or do anything to engage with them. Call the sheriff's office or the hotline number listed on your screen. Avoid making contact with Bernard at all costs. Stay alert, stay informed, and stay vigilant until this man is back in custody again."

As Gates took questions from the gaggle of reporters surrounding him, Sara scanned the television screen. In the background, she recognized the self-serve car wash where the impromptu press conference took place. It stood at the western edge of Maypole, the last business within the city limits when coming her direction. The state highway was blocked not far from there, with troopers and first responders from various units stopping traffic and advising them of alternate routes. A side street was in heavy use as one after another vehicle was forced to detour. Seeing the hustle and bustle in the normally sleepy town made the situation feel more real.

"Stop it, Sara," she spoke sharply to herself. "You have work to do. You can't be distracted by things you have no control over. They'll catch this man in no time and have him back behind bars." She snorted in disgust. "And where will you be? Behind schedule, that's where!"

With an emphatic huff, Sara turned off the television and marched into her office. She had a long day ahead and was already late starting.

# Chapter 3

## Bernard

Morning sun filtered through the trees, poking through the overhead canopy of withering leaves to hit Thomas Bernard in the eye.

He jerked awake. For three blinks of the eye, he forgot where he was. Wondered why the mattress on his jail cell bed was damp and unforgiving. Never comfortable, this morning it felt like it was stuffed with twigs and spindly pine needles. Smelled that way, too. Damp and earthy, while pleasantly fresh at the same time. It made no sense.

Then a bird tweeted out its morning song, and it all came back to him in a torrid rush.

The compromised guard, already sluggish from his drugged midday coffee.

The way he easily slipped from his constraints and placed them on the guard.

The maze of the prison compound, weaving his way quickly but strategically between security cameras and automatically locking gates.

Pushing his way into the kitchen, past the surprised faces of fellow inmates lucky enough to pull KP duty.

Deftly switching the drum of used kitchen grease for an empty one. Empty until he crawled inside, ignoring the stench of old grease from previous use and praying no one thought to check the barrel's bulky weight.

Being hefted roughly into the van and slammed up against the other steel drums, the clank and bang so loud it reverberated in his ears.

Cutting curbs too close and hitting what seemed like every pothole and every bit of broken pavement on the roadways.

Judging the time, allowing for ample distance between him and Roscoe.

Listening for the wail of sirens chasing after him.

Feeling the euphoria of blessed peace, save for the constant clank of the barrels and the steady hum of the road beneath him.

Working his way out of the barrel and stealthily advancing upon the unsuspecting driver.

Punching the driver in the back as hard as he could, taking his breath and his van.

Pushing the driver aside and out of the van, never looking back.

Driving as fast as he dared, afraid of calling attention to the stolen vehicle.

Cruising across county lines, thinking he might have a real chance of sneaking past the sleepy little rural community and breaking out into the wide-open space of Texas.

Seeing the Apple County deputy car appear behind him, steadily gaining on his progress. Stepping onto the accelerator, only to find the deputy keeping pace.

Trying to outrun the officer, swerving around or into anything in his path.

Seeing an opportunity to lose the law, if only for a moment. Doing almost a ninety-degree turn, right in the path of an oncoming car. Bumping onto a rough dirt road, almost losing control of the van as gravity made a play for control.

Knowing that his only chance was on foot.

Taking his foot off the pedal, grabbing the sack lunch the driver had thoughtfully left behind, and bailing out of the van, even as it continued to roll at a perilous speed.

Hitting the dirt road hard enough to knock his breath from his lungs. Rolling and skidding against the rocks, the gravel scraping his legs and bruising his ribs.

Coming to his feet and taking off at a dead run, even though his lungs burned, his side was on fire, and his legs protested with every jarring step.

Thrashing through trees and brush and thorns, pushing deep into the wooded area known to harbor wild animals. Catching the unmistakable smell of a wild boar and hoping he didn't invade the vicious animal's space.

Stopping to catch his breath, hearing the wail of multiple sirens, the screech of tires as they careened to a sudden stop, the sound of voices growing nearer.

Hunching his shoulders and drawing his knees up to his chin, making himself as small and inconspicuous as possible. Holding his breath as booted feet rushed mere yards from where he hid.

Waiting long, arduous hours until those same feet came back, this time more slowly. Hearing the sudden quiet of the afternoon as traffic on the highway stopped, most likely diverted, magnifying the sounds of the searches as they came perilously close.

Catching a glimpse of the searchers through the tangle of vines and limbs and debris, thankful that his now dirty whites blended well with the pale bark of the yaupons. Sensing, as much as seeing, a few of those feet dawdle, stabbing the perimeters of the thicket with long sticks and the barrels of their rifles. Inwardly laughing at their pathetic show of 'searching.'

Tuning his ears for the sounds of evening as it approached. Distinguishing the bawl of a cow from the bawl of a police radio, the croak of tree frogs from the croak of fire engine horns, the hum of voices from the hum of idling motors. Hearing the twinkle and tumble of a running stream, and the sound of possible freedom.

Waiting until darkness fell, and silence surrounded him before venturing slowly, ever so slowly, from his hiding place. Letting his eyes adjust to the darkness and his ears tune to the muted sounds of activity back at the crash site. Stripping off his white shirt and bunching it around the sack lunch he still carried. Making his run across an open field, hoping the moon was too weak to track the dull glow of his prison-issue pants. Expecting to hear shouts of 'I see him!' and 'There he goes,' only to hear the sound of his own breathing and the way his feet tore at the grasses he trampled.

Making it to the creek, feeling the initial shock of cold water, but knowing it was his best hope for escape. Hiding beneath the dark shadows of overhanging trees as he pulled his shirt back on. Digging, at last, into the paper sack to find a soggy tuna sandwich, a dill pickle wrapped in plastic wrap, and a stick of jerky. Standing in the water eating everything but the jerky and tucking it into his waistband for later.

Wading downstream, stopping every few minutes to listen, deciding whether or not it was safe enough to continue. Shivering from the cold and the adrenaline and the anticipation of making it out alive.

Coming to a dark tunnel of trees that choked out what little moonlight tinged the sky. Knowing the night was too dark to navigate, and therefore too dangerous to traverse. Knowing he couldn't go much longer without sleep, not if he wanted to keep his wits about him and outsmart officials for another day.

Climbing up the creek bank only to slide back into the water, twice, before managing to claw his way up and out, and into the thicket of trees crowding around the creek. Finding a cleared spot just large enough to use as a bed.

Succumbing to the sweet call of sleep, before the sunlight found his eyes and the birds tweeted out their morning greeting.

He remembered it all now and just in time.

In the distance, he heard the baying of track hounds.

# Chapter 4

## Sara

By noon, Sara was overdue for a break. Her eyes were dry from moving back and forth between multiple screens. Her shoulders were tense from being stooped over for so long. Her back and legs needed stretching.

Normally at this point, Sara would take a walk down to the pecan orchard. There was nothing like getting outdoors for some fresh air and exercise. The walk was easy, and the scenery was breathtaking, especially when she reached the grove of massive, decades-old pecan trees. The oldest of the old were so large she couldn't reach her arms around them for a proper hug.

A walk down to the grove was the best stress-relief tool she had in her arsenal, but today, Sara had second thoughts about going outdoors.

She knew the escaped convict was several miles away from here. Logic told her she was safe.

Experience told her that she could never be too cautious.

In lieu of a walk outside, Sara did a few stretches and made a high-stepping lap through the house.

She ended her loop in the kitchen, where she warmed up a bowl of leftover stew.

Against her better judgment, she logged onto her social media account while she sat to eat. Pictures and stories of the escaped convict immediately popped up. People were sharing articles and posts from a variety of sources, some of which gave conflicting accounts. Most were reasserting known 'facts,' while others offered speculation. Locals mentioned their dogs barking all night, strange sounds coming from outside, or sightings of something white through the trees. Several people shared video of the press conference that morning, mentioning that the next one would be at one o'clock.

Sara turned off her phone and turned on the television. The update hadn't started yet, but the feed was live. It showed a steady line of vehicles rumbling past in the background, only to be thwarted by the roadblock. One by one, the cars and trucks dutifully turned onto the side street, but Sara could imagine the grumbles and curses coming from the drivers. No one liked a detour, and the only way to get from Maypole to Wayside was to travel a spider web of intersecting dirt roads or to take an alternate route that added a good twenty or so miles to their destination.

She saw fire trucks from at least two of the nearby departments, numerous patrol cars, and trucks boasting various insignias on their doors, and a swarm of uniformed men and women in the background. After a minute or so, Peter Gates came into view. He took the microphone to introduce himself and to acknowledge the tireless, hard-working people behind the scenes. He named off a long list of agencies and departments helping in the search before getting to the meat of the update.

The list of agencies involved was longer than the paltry list of facts learned. As of that hour, the escapee was still at large. There had been no sightings and no evidence of his whereabouts, but officials believed he was still in the area. With little new information to share, he repeated facts from the earlier update. When reporters pressed for more specific intel, he repeated those same facts again.

"That was a poor waste of ten minutes," Sara muttered, turning off the television.

After a bathroom break and a refill on iced water, she returned to her office. With any luck, she could complete her first trial run to see where the glitches were. There were *always* glitches the first go around, a fact she had accepted long ago. The key was to work them out so that the second round went more smoothly. If she were truly lucky, the third round might be the charm.

As five o'clock neared, Sara's eyes strayed toward the living room. The local news came on at five, and they probably had an update to share. It wasn't that she was nervous about the inmate—not exactly—but she had to admit, if only to herself, it was rather concerning. It had been over twenty-four hours, and he was still at large. Assuming, of course, that he hadn't been caught in the last few hours.

Maybe, she told herself, the reporter would be the bearer of good news. It was worth a shot to hear what they had to say.

She didn't turn off her computers, not ready to call it a day. She was running a diagnostic program now to find any obvious problems in her system. As suspected, the first trial run hadn't gone so well. At one point, the entire program had frozen.

She settled into a chair in the living room, more than ready for some good news. As it turned out, the update wouldn't come until six, so Sara returned to her office. The diagnostic program was more than three-fourths through, meaning she still had time to work out some of the kinks before bedtime.

Sara was making notes on what to try next and what might have gone wrong the first time when she heard a knock at the door. More startled than she was afraid, it took her brain a moment to compute the fact that someone had come up her lane, and she hadn't even heard them.

So much for being alert and on guard!

She hit the SJ's Big Dog button and headed for the front door. The closer she came, the faster her heart ticked. Did she have anything to fear? She wasn't expecting a delivery today and given the fact that the highway was shut down, she doubted it was someone delivering a box. Anyone concerned about her was advised by officials to call, not personally check in on her.

She was reaching for her gun when her visitor rapped on the door again, this time calling out to her. "Miss Jennings? This is Special Detective Burleson and DPS Trooper Gray. We were here yesterday. Do you remember us, ma'am?"

Sara gave a disgruntled huff. "Of course, I remember you," she replied testily. She couldn't say why, but there was something about the detective that got under her skin. He seemed to bring out the worst in her.

"If you'll look out your window," he offered, "I'll show you our badges."

Her tone was frosty. "That won't be necessary. I recognize your voice." To herself, she fumed, *And I recognize that hint of amusement in it, too!*

"We just came by to check on you, Miss Jennings. If you'll call off Bruno there, we'd like to speak with you."

"Just a minute."

Refusing to confess to the ruse, she pretended to shoo the dogs away. She even went so far as to open and close a closet door, presumably to shut the dogs in another room. On the way back to her front door, she ran a hand over her dark hair and straightened her tee.

"Are you still there?" she asked as she reached the door.

"Yes, ma'am," the detective assured her.

Cautiously, Sara opened the door the same width as she had yesterday.

"Not to cause you distress, ma'am," Detective Burleson said in a pleasant enough tone, "but you do realize that chain is essentially useless. If a person is strong enough, or determined enough, he can bust that all to pieces and barge right on inside."

Unruffled by his comment, Sara replied smoothly, "But it would take him—or her—an extra moment. And that extra moment might give Bruno and Hondo time to cover me while I reach for my Glock."

His pleasant tone turned stern. "Never pull a gun on someone unless you're prepared to use it."

"I'm no novice, Detective. I've taken my handgun certification course as well as additional safety classes. I'm well aware of my responsibilities as a gun owner."

"That's always refreshing to hear."

The hint of animosity hovering between them confused Trooper Gray, just as it had yesterday. Attempting to smooth any ruffled feathers, he spoke up. "If you don't mind me saying so, Miss Jennings, it would make things a whole lot more pleasant if you could just open that door up a bit. It's hard to have a conversation through a one-inch gap."

After a slight hesitation, Sara pushed the door closed, slid the chain back, and reopened the door.

About five inches.

"That's better," Detective Burleson said, the humor back in his voice, "but all we can see is your shoulder. I prefer looking people eye to eye during a conversation."

"So do I," Trooper Gray agreed.

The trooper's wide smile was the first thing Sara saw when she opened the door at least a foot and a half wide. He was taller and ganglier than she thought after yesterday's brief glimpse of him. Younger, too. She doubted he was much more than twenty-five. He was dressed in a somewhat wrinkled state-issued uniform and looked like he had been up all night.

Half her body was still wedged behind the door like some last show of defense, but his rumpled state got to her. With a rush of empathy for the officers and their sacrifice of a good night's sleep, she opened the door wider.

The other officer, the detective with the smooth, rumbling voice, was as tall and broad as she remembered. Now that she could see more than a slice of him, she realized he was much more muscled and more mature than his counterpart. He wasn't heavy; solid seemed to be a more fitting word. He looked a few years older than she was, but Sara guessed he wasn't quite forty yet. His eyes were surprisingly dark, considering his hair was as much a rusty red as it was blond. If not for his weathered tan, she imagined his skin would be light and slightly freckled.

She stubbornly refused to worry over her dowdy appearance, even when the detective's eyes ever so subtly flicked over her. She knew she hardly looked her best. She also suspected he didn't look *his* best, which meant he was even more attractive without a half-day's growth of stubble, slightly bloodshot eyes, and a white, pearl-snap western shirt that had lost most of its starch and some of its brightness. She saw a smudge of something greasy—a dropped hamburger or perhaps pizza—on one shirt pocket.

"That's much better," the detective declared. "Allow us to formally introduce ourselves, ma'am." He touched the brim of his black felt cowboy hat as he ducked his head in a nod. "I'm Special Detective Mason Burleson, and this is my colleague, DPS Trooper J'Marcus Gray."

"I remember," she said, holding his eyes with her own. Even after yesterday's testy exchange, she didn't want him thinking she opened her door to just anyone claiming to be an officer. Not with a convict still on the loose.

Her eyes wandered back to the greasy stain, and something in her softened even more. She took a deep breath and offered the men a tentative smile.

"Sara Jennings," she needlessly introduced herself.

Trooper Gray grinned, tipping his hat her way. "Pleasure, ma'am."

"Likewise," the detective reiterated. The formality of his acknowledgment dissolved into a devilish smile. "It's nice to put a face to the one eyeball."

"I'm sure you're pleased to see that I have two," Sara replied smartly. She chose to look at Trooper Gray when she asked, "Do you have an update for me?"

"Unfortunately, no. We're just checking in with you, ma'am. Making certain you're okay out here in the woods, and that you haven't had contact with the escaped convict."

"I'm fine, and no. No contact."

Detective Burleson asked, "You haven't seen or heard anything suspicious? Last night or today?"

"No. Admittedly, I've been working today, so I haven't been listening closely, but nothing sounded unusual to me."

"Do you work outside the home?" He looked slightly concerned.

"No, my office is here," Sara confirmed. "And it's a good thing," she added. "I hear that the highway is closed. How are people supposed to get to work if they can't get through? And what if I need to go into town?"

"We're allowing residents through for necessary business," he assured her. "You'll need to show proof of residence and may be subjected to a brief search of the vehicle, but at this time, residents still have access to and from their homes for legitimate purposes."

"A search? Why on earth would you search our vehicles? Surely you don't think someone would smuggle him out and set him free!"

"Not intentionally," he agreed. "The search is for the residents' own safety. Bernard could be hiding in the back of a personal vehicle, the same way he hid in the delivery van to sneak out of prison. For all we know, he could hold a driver at gunpoint to make his escape. Our main concern is keeping everyone safe and out of harm's way."

"I suppose that's some consolation, considering he's still at large."

"There's a lot of ground to cover," the detective reminded her. "We're working around the clock to search every square inch."

"Even when it means coming back to the same places," Trooper Gray pointed out. "Like the detective said, our main concern is to keep residents safe."

"I'm sure I speak for everyone in the area when I say thank you for your dedication." The reluctant words were warmer than her tone.

A smile hovered around Detective Burleson's mouth. "I don't know about that. My ears are still smarting from the dressing down we got from one of your neighbors. Apparently, we're interfering with his social life by keeping him off the roads and out of trouble."

Sara's mouth pinched. "I suppose socializing doesn't fall under necessary business?"

"No, ma'am. Not with a dangerous criminal on the loose. Shooting the breeze down at the café doesn't fall under legitimate purposes. We're asking all residents to limit their trips into town and not waste the time and attention of our officers by doing unnecessary checks. Legitimate reasons include going to the grocery store, post office, bank, a doctor's appointment, that sort of thing. *Not* playing a game of bingo at the VFW hall."

"So, basically, we're captive in our home except in dire circumstances."

"We're simply trying to keep people at home and safe," Detective Burleson insisted.

Sara didn't know why she reacted the way she did, but she heard herself snap, "Maybe you should be out trying to catch him, then."

The detective looked suddenly weary. "We're trying, ma'am. We're trying."

"I—I'm sorry," Sara apologized contritely. "I shouldn't have said that. I know officials are doing everything they can to find this man and take him back into custody."

"Everyone's on edge, ma'am. We understand and share your frustration." His reply was more than generous, considering her outburst.

"Would you officers like a glass of tea?" she asked unexpectedly.

The moment the words were out, Sara wanted to recall them. She didn't know where that offer came from, any more than she knew where her rude reply had come from.

"That's kind of you, ma'am," the detective said, "but we need to finish our rounds."

Trooper Gray nodded his agreement. "Maybe next time."

"I hope there's *not* a next time!" After snapping out the words, she paused to awkwardly amend, "I meant... I hope he's caught soon."

"We all do, Miss Jennings."

Breaking into the awkward exchange, Detective Burleson was all business again. "You'll call the sheriff's office if you see or hear anything suspicious." It wasn't exactly a question, not with that look in his eyes.

"Yes. Of course."

"And you'll keep your doors and windows locked."

She knew he was only doing his job, but Sara resented being treated like a child. "And my dogs heeled," she said with an artificial smile.

The detective frowned. "Have you ever considered getting a real dog, Miss Jennings? No offense, but a woman living alone, out here in a secluded area... It might be something to consider in the future, don't you think?"

"I'm doing just fine out here on my own, Detective Burleson," Sara replied coolly. She never told him she lived alone. "But thank you for your concern."

"Just doing my job, ma'am." He touched the brim of his hat. "We'll let you get back to work now, but please remember what we said. Don't open the door to anyone you don't know or trust. Watch and listen for anything that doesn't seem normal. Call if you have any concerns or any problems. Someone will be here as soon as possible."

Sara knew that was one of the few downsides of living out here in the country. 'As soon as possible' wasn't the same speedy response seen in large towns and cities. Under normal circumstances, and without all the extra badges in town, 'as soon as possible' might be as long as thirty minutes. Apple County covered a large area, most of it rural, and didn't have the number of law enforcement it needed for its size.

"I won't forget," she promised the officers.

As they bid her goodbye and turned to leave, she stopped them with an afterthought. "Will you stop by regularly with updates? How will we know what's going on and if the roads are opened?"

"If the escapee isn't in custody by morning, there will be a general alert coming from the county, advising of road closures and possible evacuations," Detective Burleson told her.

She immediately thought of her big project and what a delay might cost her. "Evacuations? I'm not leaving my house!" Sara stated emphatically.

Trooper Gray made a hasty motion with his hands. “Don’t worry, ma’am,” he assured her. “You’re on the outer edge of the main perimeter. We believe Bernard is still in the general area where he crashed the van, which is a good four or five miles from here. At this time, we don’t believe you have cause for worry.”

“At this time,” Sara echoed, her tone skeptical.

Detective Burleson broke in with his deep, trust-inspiring voice. “If we have reason to believe he moves in this direction, I promise someone will be out to give you an update.”

His promise made her feel marginally better.

But Sara, more than anyone, knew how flimsy promises proved to be.

# Chapter 5

## Sara

Sara stayed up late to work on her project.

It also served to exhaust her. With any luck, she would sleep soundly enough to keep the nightmares at bay.

Despite their assurances, speaking with the police officers did little to create confidence. If anything, it had the opposite effect. Their presence made the danger that much more real.

Hearing the live update at six made things even worse. It had been over twenty-four hours, and the convicted killer was still at large. Officials shared no evidence to support their claims, but TDCJ insisted he was still in the immediate area of County Road 147. They asked all residents to remain vigilant and be on guard, on the slim chance Bernard had slipped past them.

Sara wasn't afraid of Thomas Bernard. Sure, she felt a bit uneasy, just knowing that something like this could happen in their peaceful little town. She didn't know anyone who lived on County Road 147—she knew very few people in the area, to be honest—but she was acquainted with someone who lived not far from there. She was worried on their behalf, and for anyone who fell within the inmate's path. She had no doubt that if Bernard *had* managed to slip past the search parties, he wouldn't still be in the area. Any criminal worth his salt would have stolen a vehicle and hightailed it out of Apple County.

No, it wasn't the escaped inmate that scared her. It was the memories stirred up by the recent upheaval in their community. It was the reminder of a dark period in her life, when she lived with this same sense of apprehension, twenty-four seven. A time when stress and tension had been her constant companion. A time when her entire world was in turmoil. A time of waiting for the thunderclouds to build, knowing that the brewing storm was inevitable.

Knowing that the storm would be something akin to a hurricane, with the power to destroy her life.

Sara didn't have time for the memories. She didn't have time for looking over her shoulder, worrying that Shawn might find her. She didn't have time for regrets or time for worries. And she certainly didn't have time for nightmares.

She worked into the wee hours of the morning, until she was on the brink of crashing. She fell into bed wearing the same clothes she had worn all day and let the black abyss of exhaustion take her away.

Sara didn't wake until morning. Her head was already pounding when she looked at her watch. Nine o'clock! She flung back the covers and jumped from the bed.

It came as a surprise that she didn't have a headache. Only then did she realize that the pounding wasn't in her head. It was on her front door.

Not bothering with shoes, she hurried into the living room, where the pounding persisted.

"Hello!" a man's voice called from the other side of the door. "Is anyone home?"

Sara didn't recognize the voice. Blinking away the cobwebs of sleep, she was awake enough to remember there was a convict on the loose. She peeked carefully out the window.

A black and white patrol car sat in her driveway.

"Is anyone in there?" the man repeated. "This is DPS Trooper Bart Pettaway. Please answer if you're in there. Detective Burleson sent me with an update."

"I—I'm here," Sara said, her voice rusty with sleep.

"He told me to show you my badge. If you'll look out the window, you can see it."

Cautiously, she answered, "I see it."

"Can you open the door? He said to leave the chain in place, so Bruno doesn't get out."

Sara couldn't help but smile. The detective was sending her a secret message, letting her know the man outside could be trusted. The smile wilted when she realized she had forgotten to use the Bruno guise this morning.

Unlocking the door, Sara cracked the door just enough to peer outside. "Yes?" she asked the officer standing on her porch.

"Special Detective Mason Burleson asked me to deliver a message to you. He said he and Trooper Gray promised to keep you updated with any changes in status about the escaped convict."

"Yes, that's right. Has he been caught?"

"I'm afraid not, ma'am. That's why I'm here. The detective couldn't come himself, so he asked that I deliver the message for him. We don't want to alarm you, ma'am, but there was a sighting this morning of a man believed to be Bernard. He was less than two miles from here, headed in this general direction. The detective wanted you to be aware of this new development and wants you to be extra vigilant until Bernard is captured."

"Less than two miles away?" Sara asked. For the first time, a ripple of true fear washed over her. "But the TV said..."

"It's a new development, ma'am. Two miles is still quite a way off, and there are officers staged between here and there, but Detective Burleson wanted you to be aware of the increased danger, no matter how slight."

"Tell him I appreciate that."

"He also wanted me to give you his card. He said if you see or hear anything, call 9-1-1 first, and then his number. He'll do his best to personally respond."

"Oh." Sara was surprised by the unexpected gesture. "Oh, okay. That's very kind of him."

"Special Detective Burleson is one of the best, ma'am. He always puts the public's safety first. He's dependable and honest to a fault."

"Good to know," Sara murmured. She took the card offered through the narrow slit.

"Are you doing okay out here, ma'am? Is there anything we can do for you?"

"Uhm, no. I'm good. Just catch this man."

"We're doing our best, Miss Jennings," the patrolman told her. "Remember to keep your doors and windows locked and never open the door to strangers."

"Now you sound like the detective!"

Trooper Pettaway confided with a smile, "He instructed me to say that. But even if he hadn't," he was quick to add, "I would anyway. You can't be too careful, not with a man like Thomas Bernard."

"I'll keep that in mind. Thank you, Officer."

"My pleasure, ma'am." He tipped his hat as she closed the door.

Sara headed to the kitchen for coffee. The clock may have said nine, but it was still too early in the morning to hear that a killer inched closer to her home. Hearing the news without coffee in her system was ten times worse.

Sara knew the morning news shows were over, so she did the next best thing. Already behind schedule for the day, she found her phone and pulled up social media.

She was shocked to see that several national news outlets had picked up on the story and were reporting it. Almost every post she saw mentioned the escaped prisoner, the closure of Highway 38, and the potential danger the career criminal posed to Apple County residents.

If the posts were true, Thomas Ramon Bernard had a long history of run-ins with the law. He served his first jail sentence at the age of eighteen for aggravated assault and intent to cause bodily harm. After that, there was a long string of arrests for robbery, grand theft, evading arrest, substance abuse, and the illegal habitat of a building. In his late twenties and early thirties, he moved on to bigger crimes. Armed burglary, forgery, attempted manslaughter, and arson all landed him behind bars. He was currently incarcerated after brutally killing a San Saba County woman, taking another person hostage, and attempting to carry out a plot to murder a third. He was suspected in the murder of two other individuals, but there wasn't enough evidence to pin him with the crime. Until his breakout two days ago, he was serving a life sentence with no chance of parole.

In other words, people pointed out, he had nothing to lose by trying to escape.

That made him even more dangerous.

"Okay, Sara," she scolded herself, making her second cup of coffee, "you've wasted enough time this morning. And you need a shower. Hop in, hop out, have a bite to eat, and get to work."

Less than thirty minutes later, she was in her office doing another trial run. She worked through lunch and missed the midday newscast. She only stopped when the program crashed again.

"Arrgg!" she bemoaned, running her hands through her dark hair, rendering it a tangled mess. "What am I doing wrong? This is ridiculous!"

She needed a break. Working the kinks from her hunched shoulders and stretching her stiffened legs, Sara creaked a bit when she stood. "Come on, girl, you're not that old!" she told herself. Nonetheless, she limped her way into the bathroom.

The entire time, her mind went over different scenarios of what could have gone wrong with her program.

"Okay, this isn't working. You need to take a break, get your mind off the project, and attack it again with fresh eyes." She splashed water on her face and patted it dry with a hand towel. "You can't go down to the orchard, but you can bake something. Cookies? A cake?" She contemplated the two as she turned out the light and headed to the kitchen. "Hmm. Not sure what I feel like."

She finally decided on cookies. They would last for days in a tightly sealed container, giving her something to munch on while working. And she knew just what recipe to use.

Like much of the furniture, the recipe came with the house. Cora Miller's personal effects had been cleared out, save for one box in the attic and a few odds and ends in a random closet. Three cookbooks were tucked away in a kitchen cupboard, either forgotten or left in welcome for the new occupant. All had hand-written instructions. The newest one was a mix of blank pages plus pockets for additions, such as random clippings from the back of flour sacks and magazines, and recipe cards written by a different hand. Sara imagined those had been swapped at church socials, wedding showers, and the like. The two older cookbooks had no preprinted recipes, only blank pages meant to be filled.

The hand-written recipes were her favorite. It took awhile to adapt some of the measurements—a mound of flour, a smidgeon of salt, a handful of nuts, a stirring of sweet cream—but by experimenting, she came up with her own equivalents. She stored the adaptations in her mind, reluctant to alter the original recipes. There was such eloquent beauty in the old-fashioned handwriting. The older the recipes, the more adorned the cursive, with graceful loops and little curlicues. Sara hoped that when the time came to leave her little home, some day in the faraway future, she could leave the same gift for the new owners. It would be a little piece of the past for their new future here, the same as it was for her.

Today, she would make the hearty oatmeal cookies with chocolate chunks and pecans. It gave her special pleasure to know the nuts came from her own orchard. The cookies themselves had no name, but there was a small heart around an 'R' on the top right corner of the page. Sara assumed they were a favorite of someone whose name began with the letter.

As she gathered her ingredients, she purposefully cleared her mind and concentrated on one thing. Baking.

She imagined the hands that had prepared this same recipe in the past. It came from the oldest cookbook, but the heart and the R were written differently. The ink wasn't as faded, leading her to assume it was added in later years. She knew only of Cora, but as it was the Miller family homestead, there were women who came before her. Cora's mother, and perhaps a grandmother.

According to the real estate agent, the house was built in 1901. For over a hundred and twenty years, some woman had stood in this very spot, preparing this same recipe, or one like it. These days, the work area in the middle of the room was called an island. But in 1901, it was known as a dough table. It even had drawers on one side and a tin-lined barrel belly to hold flour.

Even though she currently wore a pair of sleep pants and a tee that had already seen better days, Sara felt duty-bound to loop an apron around her neck. It was her brand of homage to all the women who came before her. She wondered how many biscuits and breads had been kneaded here, how many pie crusts and dumplings had been rolled out.

In 1901, and for several decades after that, thrifty homemakers didn't buy their bread in stores or their biscuits in tubes. They made them all from scratch, the same way they made cakes and pies, vegetables and main courses. Canned and frozen offerings didn't compare with their homegrown, hand-crafted varieties.

Sara wondered again about Cora, the last Miller to live in this house. To her understanding, she was the only girl out of seven children, and had never married. When her mother died at a young age, Cora took over as the woman of the house. She cooked and cleaned for her father and helped raise her two younger brothers. As the years passed and her brothers moved away and their father died, Cora stayed behind to tend the orchards and the family home. When she died in her sleep at the age of seventy-nine, she was still active and tended the orchards. Her only hired help were seasonal workers.

*Had she ever been lonely out here?* Sara wondered. Someone told her that Cora was once engaged, but that her fiancé called off the wedding just one week before the big day. No one was quite sure of the particulars, but everyone agreed that Cora didn't seem too heartbroken over the fact. She went on a trip not long after that, sending back postcards and pictures of a well-deserved vacation in Galveston. It was the only time anyone could remember Cora ever leaving the farm for any length of time.

The telephone rang, jarring Sara from her musings. She answered as she slid the first cookie sheet into the oven.

Hearing no one on the other end, a cold shiver of dread spiraled down her spine. Had Shawn found her again? With a trembling hand, she ended the call.

The phone rang a second time.

She let it go to the fourth ring, but the lure was too strong. *Not* knowing was as bad as knowing.

Sara answered the phone.

Relief flooded through her when she heard the recorded message from Apple County Emergency Management. It told her little more than she already knew. There was an escaped convict in the area, residents should remain on high alert, and were advised to find alternate routes other than Highway 38.

To Sara, what the call *didn't* say was more important. Shawn's voice wasn't on the other end of the line, and that was what really mattered.

Taking deep, calming breaths, Sara finished baking the cookies. She washed and put away her baking paraphernalia while the last batch cooled. Layering wax paper between stacks, she concentrated on placing the cooled product in a sealable container.

With the refrigerator's loud purr in her ear, Sara didn't hear the vehicle pull into her driveway. When she did hear the unmistakable rap of knuckles against her front door, she jerked in surprise and dropped the entire roll of waxed paper. It fell onto the floor and rolled, unwinding as it followed the slope in the floor.

With new worry of the inmate moving in her direction, and with the constant worry of Shawn finding her, Sara felt vulnerable. She normally kept a Springfield Hellcat 9mm in the kitchen, but she had left it in the laundry room while hanging up clothes. Now she was here, the gun was there, and someone was at her door.

Flustered, she grabbed the only weapon she could find as she slipped through the living room. In her hand was a heavy rolling pin.

Another persistent knock, and then a familiar voice. "Miss Jennings? It's Special Detective Mason Burleson."

Sara was so relieved that she opened the door without conscious thought. No demand to see his badge. No demand to know his partner was present. No Bruno and Hondo. She just opened the door, slightly out of breath.

"Is everything okay, Miss Jennings?" he asked. He darted his eyes behind her, peering into the depths of the house.

"Yes, yes," she assured him, brushing his solicitude aside.

"Are you certain? You didn't ask for verification." Amusement overtook concern, as his brown eyes took on a familiar twinkle.

With a nonchalant shrug, she said, "Bruno knew it was you."

The amusement dimmed. "I hope he's as good at sniffing out Thomas Bernard as he is me."

Sara latched on to mention of the name. "Is there any news?"

"No good news, that's for sure."

"Is it true he's moving closer in this direction?"

"It seems so. The dogs tracked his scent to Orchard Creek but lost it after that. We assume he's traveling up the creek, keeping his tracks and his scent covered. A disturbance of brush suggests he came west, toward this area, but that's still unconfirmed."

Sara sucked in a quick breath. "Orchard Creek runs behind the house. Along my pecan orchard, in fact."

"Unofficially, I came to tell you there will be helicopters out here in the morning, doing surveillance of the area. I didn't want you to be unnecessarily alarmed."

Unbidden, words leaked out of Sara's mouth. "Unofficially, can I offer you that glass of tea? I just made a fresh batch of cookies."

Sara knew he was tempted. He practically salivated at the mention of food. She wondered when he had eaten last.

"I really shouldn't..." he said, clearly torn. He glanced down at the apron she wore, and the rolling pin still clutched in her hand. A small smile hovered around his mouth when he saw the same smear of flour and butter in the tendrils of her hair. "Now if it were coffee and cookies..."

"Coffee it is."

He waited for her to invite him inside, but the invitation never came.

"Wait here," she said. "I'll be right back. How do you like your coffee?"

"Strong and black."

She nodded, closed the door, and disappeared the way she had come. Ditching the apron, she made two cups of coffee, grabbed a handful of napkins, and the cookie container, and hurried back outside.

The officer sat on the porch swing, scanning the woods around her house. When he would have stood as she approached, she shook her head for him to stay.

Sara handed him both coffee cups before taking a seat beside him. She wished the swing were wider than it was, or that there was somewhere else to sit. Even though it was a three-person swing, it put her too close to the man. Closer than she had been to any male in well over three years, which created an anxiety all its own.

"These look great." Detective Burleson nodded to the cookies as he traded her coffee cup for the see-through container.

"It's an old recipe," was all she said.

"Usually the best kind." His hand hovered over the lid. "May I?"

"Of course."

He held the opened container under his nose for a reverent sniff. "If these taste half as good as they smell, I'll be in hog heaven."

He pulled three cookies out and ate the first one in two bites. After gobbling down the second cookie, he paused long enough to say, "These are delicious. Possibly the best cookies I've ever eaten."

Sara laughed. Actually laughed. The sound was foreign to her own ears as she said, "Or possibly you're starving. When was the last time you ate?"

He thought about his answer as he downed a third cookie and chased it with a gulp of hot coffee. "Breakfast?" he guessed. "About three o'clock this morning."

"Have another cookie."

"I plan to." He flashed that devilish smile again, making her more conscious of the narrow distance between them. She had been taken in by a devilish smile before, and it hadn't ended well.

Sometimes, she wondered if it would ever end.

"I—I can make you a sandwich if you like," she offered, feeling his sacrifice demanded some sort of offering.

"Thanks, but we have a meeting scheduled at the station. One of the restaurants has volunteered to serve barbecue."

"That's nice." Sara retrieved a cookie for herself and nibbled on it as she sipped her coffee. "This is the first time I've been outside in three days," she confessed.

"I know it's tough, but it pays to be cautious."

"Believe me, I know all about that."

Hearing the sharp edge in her voice, he gave her a curious look but didn't question her. Not about that. "How long have you lived out here?" he asked instead.

"I moved here fourteen months ago."

"Family place?" he asked, looking around in appreciation.

"No, I bought it. The previous owner died a year or so before that."

"It's a great property. I wouldn't mind finding something like this for myself."

"Do you live around here?" She'd never seen him in town before but, then again, she didn't get out all that often.

"I'm renting a place for now," he said.

"Because of the escapee?" she asked, surprised.

"No, because I travel a lot. I work with the Joint East Texas Fugitive Task Force. It's headed up by the U.S. Marshal Service and is comprised of numerous partner agencies." Mason shrugged. "I travel where I'm needed."

While he took a long draw of coffee, Sara rolled her head around to dispel the tension gathered in knots around her shoulders.

"I know this is tough on residents," the detective repeated. "We're doing our best to get the fugitive back in custody."

"It's not just that. I've been working on a computer program for two days, and it's not cooperating."

"Have you called the tech line?" he suggested.

He didn't understand the wry smile she offered. "I am the tech line." Sara looked back toward the woods, wishing she could walk down to the orchard, or even just around the yard.

It was funny, how she already took such luxuries for granted. The freedom and openness were the things she loved most about her new home, finding it a refreshing change from the city's limitations. She gloried in the ability to roam about whenever she wanted. She had already forgotten what a luxury it was, until it was stolen from her these past two and a half days.

"Thank you for sending Trooper Pettaway this morning," she said, remembering the kind gesture.

"A promise is a promise."

Sara was so accustomed to broken promises, the idea of having one kept was quite a novelty.

"As much as I have enjoyed the break, I really do need to go," Detective Burleson said. Yet he made no move to stand.

"I understand. You probably have other homes to visit before your meeting."

"Are you certain you're comfortable staying out here? You might feel more secure with friends, or at the motel in town."

"I'm good out here." She didn't bother admitting that in the year plus she had been here, she hadn't made any friends close enough with whom she could stay. Most fell more into the 'acquaintances' category.

"Did Emergency Management send out a call this morning?"

"More like thirty minutes ago."

He frowned when he heard this but remained silent.

"I missed the noon update. If you hadn't sent the trooper out, I would have no clue he had moved this way."

"It's still not for certain," he reminded her. "That's the reason for the choppers tomorrow. You may also see more activity and hear the dogs running. Don't be alarmed. It's all part of the strategy to locate him and push him out."

"I hope it works."

"So do we, ma'am." His smile was weary as he finally pushed himself to his feet. "You may want to go back inside, just to be safe."

"I would love to go for a walk again," she admitted on a sigh. "I guess that will have to wait until after tomorrow. Thanks for sitting out here with me today."

"My pleasure, ma'am." He dipped his head and touched the brim of his hat with his fingers. "Thank you for the delicious cookies."

"Here. Have the rest." She thrust the container into his hands on impulse.

"Thanks, but you don't have to do that."

"And you didn't have to send the trooper this morning or come out here this afternoon. Take them. I insist."

Their fingers bumped as they pushed/pulled on the container. It almost slipped from both their hands as Sara jerked hers hastily away.

"I'll take them on one condition," he relented.

"And what is that?"

A slow smile spread across his face. "That you don't ask me to share with the others."

# Chapter 6

## Mason

"Here's what we know so far."

Director George Lehman of the Texas Department of Criminal Justice – Office of the Inspector General addressed a dozen officers at the Apple County Sheriff's office. He was flanked on either side by the senior warden and OIG's top brass from the Roscoe Unit. Leaders of various support teams clustered around a long table, studying white boards and oversized maps while devouring barbecue sandwiches and hot coffee.

For some, it was the first hot meal they had had in two days.

The long pointing stick made a sharp *click* against the board as Lehman barked out the details.

"Thomas Ramon Bernard. Five foot, seven inches of wiry strength. One-hundred and fifty-five pounds of mean. Don't be fooled by his slender build. He's mean and ornery, and he fights dirty. He's a career criminal who's spent most of his forty-seven years behind bars. Make no mistake, Bernard is cunning, vindictive, and smart. That makes him one very dangerous man.

"Until two days ago, he was incarcerated in the Roscoe Unit, serving life for capital murder. That sentence was followed by a second life sentence for kidnapping and intent to carry out a hit. Because of his violent nature and his affiliation with various gangs, he has been moved numerous times among G5 facilities.

"Bernard has a long rap sheet. It's never been proved, but there's substantial evidence tying him to the Casman Cartel. We suspect the cartel hired him more than once to dispose of their rivals. There is belief that he was responsible for two or more murders of underworld actors, but there hasn't been enough evidence to convict him. Yet. The woman Bernard was convicted of killing had ties to one of the murder victims, increasing the likelihood that he was involved in their deaths. Currently, he is associated with an organized prison gang that calls themselves The Seven, though word has it that he's fallen out of their favor. All of this reinforces the assertion that Bernard is a highly dangerous individual."

Lehman moved to the next board, his pointer tapping against key facts.

"At approximately 4:45 on Thursday, Bernard managed to disable a guard and make his way to the prison kitchen. Details are still sketchy at this time, but prison officials say he may have hidden inside a fifty-five-gallon drum that was taken out. The OIG is conducting a full investigation, but it's unlikely that he managed his escape without someone on the inside. At best, it was other prisoners working kitchen detail. At worse, it was someone employed at the prison.

"Bernard waited until they were well away from the prison before taking the driver by surprise and commandeering the van. Eyewitnesses report seeing the van swerving all over the road before something tumbled out and rolled down a slight incline. That something proved to be the driver, who sustained minor injuries including a broken arm and a dislocated collarbone. Within twenty minutes of the hijacking, a BOLO went out with details of the van and the suspect.

"By the time Bernard entered Apple County, officials were on high alert. Apple County Deputy Carlene Duranja recognized the vehicle and followed in pursuit. She called for backup, but all officers were detained with other incidents. In the course of the high-speed pursuit through the community of Sunrise and the town of Maypole, one vehicle was side-swiped, and another was clipped in the rear and spun into oncoming traffic. This resulted in a minor accident with no injuries. Three and three-quarter miles out of Maypole, Bernard eluded the deputy by making a sharp turn onto County Road 147."

The director tapped one of the maps on display at the front of the room, calling attention to the location.

"Deputy Duranja did the only thing possible to avoid a collision with oncoming traffic. By the time she successfully turned around to continue pursuit, Bernard had disappeared on foot into the woods. Evidence at the scene of the crashed van indicates that he jumped while it was in motion, some twenty feet or so before the crash site. The woods there were thick and provided enough cover for Bernard to flee from the immediate area of the county road.

"TDCJ immediately dispatched several search units as well as tracking dogs to the site. The Apple County Sheriff's office and three officers from the adjacent county aided in the search but were unable to locate Bernard's whereabouts."

Lehman turned a hard glare to the officers around the room, all but accusing them of the atrocious failure. "As of this moment, it has been forty-eight hours and forty-four minutes since Bernard escaped from confinement. He has been in the wind for over two days now, *in this county*. He is on foot, with little to no food, wearing prison-issued white clothing, and presumably has no official weapon on him. Nonetheless, this man is cunning, and he has managed to allude all efforts to locate him. My question is *how*. How can a prisoner execute such a blatant and daring escape? How can he drive five miles down State Highway 38 before being spotted and pursued?" Lehman's voice rose with each question. "How can a man wearing bright white clothing disappear and blend into the woods? How can he maintain his energy without food to sustain him? How can he not be traced by dogs specifically trained to run tracks?

"How can this man"—Lehman stabbed the photo of Thomas Bernard with the end of his stick—"a dangerous menace to society, still be roaming free?" He made a wide circle around the highlighted area of County Road 147. "*How*, I ask you?" he continued on a roar. "How?"

No one answered.

Some shifted beneath the director's steely gaze. Others cleared their throats and studied the boards with renewed purpose. Lehman darted his accusing glare around the room, waiting for someone to provide answers.

Special Detective Mason Burleson was the first to speak. "I can't speak to what happened before Bernard exited the van, sir," he said in a respectful voice, "but I do know that the woods surrounding County Road 147 are dense with underbrush, saplings, and yaupon. Feral hogs and other wildlife live in those woods, rooting their way inside the tangle to create trails and pockets where Bernard could be hiding. Many of the officers here have been hunting in these or similar woods, sir, and can attest to the fact. The underbrush is more difficult to penetrate than many people realize. As for the dogs catching his scent, Orchard Creek runs alongside 147 before cutting west and running closer to County Road 149. If Bernard keeps to the creek, his scent would be difficult for the dogs to find."

"You believe the woods are so thick that his white clothing can't be detected?"

Detective Burleson didn't flinch beneath the OIG director's hard stare. "I believe that any man as smart and cunning as Thomas Bernard," he replied, "would know to smear his white clothes with mud from the creek banks. A good roll in the dirt and fallen leaves would provide additional camouflage. As for sustaining his energy, it's fall, sir. There are plenty of nuts, berries, and plants that grow wild in this area. If residents have them, fall gardens are close to harvest. There're several orchards around here that produce pecans, apples, pears, and other fall fruits. Bernard could find enough to eat to hold him for several days without causing weakness."

Someone else gathered enough courage to add his input. "If Bernard did escape through the prison kitchen, he could have grabbed some sort of food on his way through," the officer suggested.

Lehman considered the possibility. "All right," he relented. "Let's say all of this is possible, and Bernard can maintain enough energy to stay on the move. Where is he headed? What is his next move? Where can we stop him?"

"We have roadblocks on the fourteen-mile stretch of highway between Maypole and Wayside," a state trooper volunteered. "Officers, volunteers, and TDCJ personnel are stationed every one-hundred feet, in case Bernard exits the woods or attempts to cross the highway."

"We also have people patrolling all county roads in the immediate vicinity, particularly roads 147 and 149," an Apple County deputy added.

"And *still*," Lehman said, the accusation back in his voice, "evidence shows that Bernard has managed to work his way west. He was spotted on a hunter's game cam in a field adjacent to County Road 149. The camera is one of those fancy models that sends a message to the owner whenever it's activated. The hunter reported what appeared to be a man, believed to be Bernard, moving along the wood line in a westward direction. Experts are analyzing the video now."

Another officer raised his hand to ask a question. "What day and time did the sighting take place, sir?"

"It was time-stamped at sixteen minutes after eight *this* morning. That means Bernard is daring enough to move about in daylight hours, not just at night. With this new shift in direction, it is necessary to conduct a helicopter search tomorrow morning before dawn. Our focus will be on Orchard Creek, the immediate areas around County Road 149, and this triangle here between the creek, the road, and the railroad line that runs at the south side of this property, approximately four miles away. We are referring to this area as the Danger Zone." He referenced the map again with his long pointer. "We will have officers on horseback sweeping along this line, pushing Bernard toward the creek and the area we'll be covering from the air. Each of you has been assigned a particular area to patrol or a task to perform. You will be responsible for your team and the job that they do in protecting this community and bringing Bernard to justice."

Detective Burleson again raised his hand. "Have the people living within and around the Danger Zone been adequately warned?"

"The Apple County Emergency Department sent out a general alert this morning. This escape has been widely publicized and reported over local, national, and social outlets. I'm confident that residents are well aware of the danger. We don't have the manpower to babysit these people. We need all hands on deck, searching for this SOB. Make no mistake, Bernard is dangerous and getting desperate. Capturing him is paramount. With him in custody again, there will be no danger to warn against."

"I'd like to volunteer my own personal time, sir," the detective said in a firm, steady voice. "DPS Trooper J'Marcus Gray and I made initial sweeps of that area, alerting residents and making inquiries. The adjacent area is even more sparsely populated, and we found a few residents who were unaware of the escape. Some of these are elderly and have little or no access to the media. If Bernard should cross the highway, these people will be in imminent danger."

Detective Lehman gave him an icy stare. "Then let's make certain he doesn't cross the highway." Clearing his throat, he dismissed the detective's request as he addressed the room in general. "You have your assignments. Go out there and catch this man."

He quickly left the room, allowing no further opposition.

An officer with the Roscoe Unit OIG chuckled as he slapped Detective Burleson on the back. "Whoo-wee! You like pressing your luck, don't you, Burleson? You got a death wish or something? If looks could kill, you'd be a dead man right now. Lehman's glare would have stabbed straight through your heart."

"I took an oath to serve and protect," Mason insisted. "It doesn't sit well with me, abandoning that promise."

"You aren't abandoning it," Officer Ingalls reminded him. "Every one of us is doing his or her best to find Bernard and bring him in. That's protecting the community."

"I still say residents should be updated on what's happening in the investigation and notified of the area Bernard's believed to be in. These residents can't afford to let their guard down by assuming

Bernard is miles away, when he's actually much closer."

"How many houses are we talking about?"

"Less than a dozen. I visited three of the houses on the north side of the highway this afternoon, alerting them of the helicopter search in the morning. I don't see the point in scaring them half out of their wits by not giving them a head's up."

"Are these old folks who can't protect themselves?" Ingalls asked. "Maybe they should consider relocating for the time being."

Burleson's reply was a half-laugh, half-snort. "Good luck," he mumbled. "Mamie Hutchins didn't take kindly to my suggestion of just that. Eighty-five if she's a day and weighing *maybe* 110, she threatened to tan my hide and run me off with a 12 gauge if I tried forcing her to leave."

A DPS officer joined them. "What about that pretty little lady you sent me out to warn this morning?" Trooper Pettaway asked. "Think she'd leave?"

"I doubt it. She seems to have dug her heels in, too," Burleson replied.

"Wait a minute, wait a minute," Ingalls said, a grin appearing on his face. "*What* pretty little lady?" He turned to his friend. "Burleson, you have you a girl here?"

"Hardly." The detective's voice was short. "I met her the day before yesterday, when I took it upon myself to check with people in the outlying areas. If you ask me, she and her neighbor, Bill Hewitt, are in a vulnerable location. They both live down long, private lanes. One way in, one way out. Their homes are in clearings surrounded by heavy woods. Both live alone. Neither appears to have many visitors. They're on the opposite side of the highway, but if Bernard manages to get across, their houses would be a likely place for him to hide."

"We're watching the highway. I don't think he'll make his way across," Pettaway predicted.

"I sure hope not." Burleson frowned. "Because if he should manage to get across, he could make his way to Wayside, and eventually to the interstate. And at that point, he would definitely be in the wind."

# Chapter 7

## Sara

The fresh air and the muted sunshine had done Sara a world of good. After being cooped up in the house since Thursday, the simple act of stepping over the doorsill and onto the porch had been a treat within itself.

She came back inside, inspired by the feel of the autumn breeze against her skin. Struck with a new approach to her program glitch, she decided the cookie would suffice as her lunch. Possibly dinner. If this new idea worked...

It did! Or, it seemed to, which was good enough for tonight. Sara tapped happily away on her keyboards, reassigning keystrokes, and setting up new parameters. She juggled her focus across all five computer screens, moving from this keyboard to that, tweaking the tiniest of details and revamping the largest.

She timed yet another diagnostic test to coincide with the local ten o' clock news.

Warming up the last of the stew and cornbread, Sara carried it with her into the living room. While the computer program went through its sequences and the last scenes of the prime-time drama wrapped up, she noisily slurped her dinner. She hadn't realized until now how hungry she was.

The news anchor's lead story dampened her appetite. Thomas Bernard was still at large, but details of his sordid past were slowly coming forth. Many of his crimes were fueled by revenge. His first jail sentence was for the aggravated assault of his stepfather. He harassed and robbed two of his former teachers. He set fire to a rival's home. Even worse, Bernard had ties to organized crime. There was now a $25,000 reward for information leading to the capture of a very dangerous and cunning criminal.

For her own peace of mind, Sara rechecked all her doors and windows, even though she knew they were locked. After a moment's hesitation—this was her home, for goodness sakes, and she shouldn't be bullied like this—she nonetheless barricaded the back door leading to the carport. It wasn't like she was using her car anyway. Not with the road blocked, the inmate still at large, and her big project still not finished. Sooner or later, she would need to visit the grocery store, but she would put it off as long as possible.

The laundry room and attached half bath weren't original to the house. The style of their scarred linoleum and iron-wash basins had a fortyish vibe, suggesting someone before Cora had them added. Neither room was fancy, but both were functional.

The laundry room had all the basics—washer, dryer, sink, even a deep freezer. None could be moved. Things like the step stool, brooms, mops, or vacuum cleaner wouldn't secure the door or keep someone from pushing it in. The only thing helpful, if Sara could move it, was a large old box that once held firewood. She had used what little wood was left inside for her firepit.

Judging by the worn red paint, rusted nail holes, and rough textured planks, Sara suspected the boards had come off an old barn. Eying the box with trepidation, she addressed it aloud.

"I hereby assign you the temporary but honorable position of *barricade.* Please cooperate while I attempt moving you."

It wasn't easy, but Sara managed to push, shove, pull, and tug, eventually moving the heavy box against the outside door. Her back ached as she straightened upright and surveyed her work.

"There!" she said with weary satisfaction. "If someone manages to push that aside, I don't stand a chance against them, anyway." As she brushed off her hands and clothes, she noticed a folded paper that had fallen behind the box. It was dirty and yellowed with age, but Sara wasn't afraid of dust mites or tiny spiders lurking within its pages. She tapped the paper against the sink's edge, shook out the loosened debris, and carried it with her as she returned to her office.

With the diagnostics done, Sara fixed errors and made more adjustments. By the time she sat back and stretched, it was well past midnight. She picked up the forgotten paper from behind the wood box while waiting for the improvements to install.

It was a newspaper, dated 1966. *The Apple's Core*, a weekly edition that covered news from across the county. Seven days' worth of breaking news, advertisements, and local gossip columns that were the staple of small-town rags, all tucked within six tidy pages. A full week's worth of happenings in the community she now called home.

In the late summer of '66, the biggest stories of the day were the opening of *Hollister Drug Store*, the surprising theft of *Mercer's Dry Goods* in a neighboring town, and a record harvest at some of the local orchards. She read the orchard story first, delighted when she saw the name Miller beneath a photo of several men dressed in overalls and tattered straw hats. The bushel baskets at their feet displayed various crops.

Sara read the accompanying article, eager to learn another piece of her property's past. There was a recap on all the farmers, but she skimmed over the paragraphs until she saw the one of interest. According to the paper, Leroy Miller had been farming the land since he was a young boy, right alongside his father and grandfather. He had taken the helm after their deaths and was grooming his own sons to one day do the same.

There was no mention of a daughter, but it had to be Cora's father. The timeline fit.

So did the omission of women working in the fields, Sara supposed. Even though many women had worked the fields as hard as any man, it wasn't the sort of thing mentioned in public, and certainly not in the newspaper. The 'ladies' section' of the newspaper was the insert sheet, pages three and four, where recipes and home remedies existed alongside wedding announcements and gossip columns.

The front-page article talked about the exceptional crop yields and the boon they provided to the local economy. Business was so good that many of the farmers hired migrant workers to help bring in the harvest. Some had such a bumper crop they could send their goods to the larger markets by rail car.

Wishing there was more about the Millers than one brief paragraph, Sara made a mental note to do some research on her own when her schedule allowed. For now, she had to concentrate on her work.

She perused the rest of the newspaper, recognizing *Hollister Drug Store* in the photograph as the present-day used bookstore. In 1966, the Hollisters had high hopes for a long and prosperous future of serving the community. Sara didn't know how long their business had lasted, but she hoped it had been good for them.

The other top story of the week was a theft that took place at *Mercer's Dry Goods* in Jonestown. Several items of clothing were taken, along with a locket from the jewelry case, pencils and notebooks, and possibly a box of candy. Theft was so rare in their little community that such an event was shocking. Definitely worthy of the front page.

Aside from the brief mention of Leroy Miller, the most interesting part of the paper was the advertising section. Sara was amused by the simplicity of the ads. They may have had curly lettering, but there were no fancy graphics, no empty promises, no flashy colors. Just simple words in a simple, black and white, straightforward approach.

Done with the paper, Sara refolded it and put it aside as she watched the monitors for signs of progress. When the installation finished, she glanced at the time. Almost two in the morning. Too late, she decided, for another test run. She would turn off her computers for tonight and get a start fresh in the morning.

She wasted no time crawling into bed and falling asleep. But instead of a peaceful slumber, she was confronted with dreams that borderlined as nightmares. There was nothing restful about them.

She dreamed she was back in Oakland, in the last apartment where she and Shawn had lived. This wasn't the posh townhouse he insisted they buy when times were good; this was the plain-Jane apartment they rented, now that things were different. And tonight's episode wasn't really a dream. It was just another memory, posing as one.

> Sara came home from work so excited, eager to tell him about the promotion she had gotten at Hughes and Company. She would be moving from the endless line of cubicles into a real office. She would share the semi-private office with three others but, nonetheless, it was an office. Plus, it came with a substantial pay raise.
>
> She made one of their favorite meals that night, a pasta dish served over a bed of fresh spinach leaves. She had picked up two pints of ice cream—strawberry cheesecake for Shawn, rocky road for her—and a small loaf cake to serve with it. There was a bottle of wine chilling on ice.
>
> Shawn was thirty minutes late coming home, the smell of liquor already on his breath. Sara knew better than to confront him over the matter. Instead, she used a nonchalant approach.
>
> "Anything new happening down at Joe's?" she asked as she sprinkled spinach leaves in the bottoms of two shallow pasta bowls.

"Who said I was at Joe's?" He stopped what he was doing to give her a hateful glare. "You checkin' up on me?"

"No, of course not," she hastily assured him. "I know after a hard day of work, you sometimes need to unwind before you come home. Joe's is your favorite bar, so I just thought..." She lifted one shoulder in a casual shrug, hoping to defuse the situation. These days, she never knew what might set him off.

Shawn slammed the refrigerator door shut, beer bottle in hand, and stomped to the small dinette table tucked strategically into one corner.

"I guess you're timing me now," he sulked, "seeing how long it takes for me to leave work and trot up those steps like an obedient little puppy dog." After a long draw of beer, he sat the bottle down with a thud. "What is it you want from me tonight? To take the trash out again? You do it. I'm not your slave."

"I don't want you to do anything, other than to have a nice dinner with me. I even bought the wine you like."

"I'm doing just fine with my beer." Another guzzle, and the bottle was empty. "Bring me another, why don't you?"

"Wouldn't you like to eat first? I'm about to put it on the table." She presented the filled plates as proof, already walking his way.

"I said to bring me a beer."

Sara plastered a smile on her face, refusing to let him see her seethe. "Sure. Let me set these down, and I'll get it for you."

"I want it now."

She deposited the plates before scurrying off to do his bidding. She brought the beer first, then went back for glasses and the bottle of wine.

Shawn hadn't bothered to wait on her before diving into his food. He was already on his third forkful by the time she was seated.

"Something's missing," he criticized. He waved a fork over the pasta. "What'd you do different?"

Another half-shrug. "I dunno. I made it the same way I always do."

"No, something's different."

"I don't think so."

Her denial made him angry. "I. Said. You did. Something. Different."

"I—I may have used a different brand of pasta," she offered. To her, it tasted the same as always. "Or maybe I didn't squeeze enough lemon on it."

"If it had any more, it wouldn't be fit to eat!" he complained.

Sara let the comment slide. She moved to open the wine. "I'm having wine. Would you like some?"

"I have my beer."

She kept the smile in place. "No problem."

"What, you suddenly too good for beer?" he demanded.

Sara hid a weary sigh. It would be another of those nights. One of those nights when she could do nothing right. When everything she did pushed Shawn one step closer to the edge.

And he always dragged her along with him.

"I was saving the beer for you," she improvised. "I know it's your favorite, so I thought I'd just have the wine and let you drink the beer."

His only reply was a grunt.

She tried making small talk, but Shawn was in

no mood for chitchat. He was too busy complaining. The dish was too salty. The noodles were firmer than he liked. The spinach was wilted. Had she remembered to do the laundry?

Not even the cake and ice cream appeased him. Why did she insist on spending his money on two kinds of ice cream? Couldn't she just eat the kind he liked?

Sara decided now wasn't the time to mention her promotion. But then a friend called to congratulate her, and Shawn overheard the conversation.

"Are you keeping secrets from me?" he thundered. "You conniving little twit! You're planning on leaving me, aren't you? You were planning on saving up your money so you could leave me."

"Of course not." She hadn't considered such a blatant show of bravery until he mentioned it. It was definitely worth more thought. Not that she would tell him that. To him, she said, "I was planning on telling you tonight. That's why I fixed a special dinner and had the wine on ice. I thought we could celebrate."

"Celebrate what? That you've got a fancy-shmancy career when my career is down the drain?"

"That's not true, Shawn. You're an excellent basketball coach. The high school is just a stepping board. Think of it as building your resume," she encouraged. "You can coach anywhere you like, even at the college level."

"You think?" he asked. A note of hope slipped into his voice, bumping against the slur of too much alcohol.

"Of course, I do. It's just a matter of time."

"Maybe you're right. Maybe I should start putting out feelers. See what colleges are hiring." He drained another beer bottle, his mood shifting.

"Absolutely," Sara encouraged.

"After that, I can move on to a real coaching career. I'll be back in the pro arena in no time, don't you think?"

She had no way of knowing the disaster that would come of her encouragement.

Like with most dreams, the scenes shifted. An out-of-sequence conversation with a friend from college, in which they both vowed to never let a man dominate them. That conversation gave way to the sound of shouted voices. Arguments blurred into a snarl of anger and pain. Hurled words gave way to hurled objects.

Sara squirmed in bed, as if to dodge a missile. In her dream, a glass bounced off the wall behind her and shattered into a hundred pieces. She covered her ears to the ominous sound of Shawn's anger. Held her hands there until the scenes shifted again, to another out of context memory. A newspaper, telling of a theft in their sleepy little community. A dark cloud drifted through her mind. She saw a crashed van and a man in white clothes running from the scene. Then another man, this one wearing a badge and the shadow of a day-old beard.

And then came the thunder.

# Chapter 8

## Sara

The thunder became a thump. A steady beat of *thwack, thwack, thwack.*

With a start, Sara sat up in bed. Early dawn cast her bedroom in shadows, the lines of furniture fuzzy and indistinct.

"Helicopter," she mumbled. "Not thunder."

In relief, she lay back down, only to sit up once again. "The search!" she remembered, scrambling out of bed.

She hadn't expected it to start so early. She thought they would wait until broad daylight to get a better view of the woods below.

Maybe it wasn't the search. Maybe it was a life flight. It could mean someone needed immediate care.

She caught a glimpse of bright, sweeping lights, just before she turned on her bedroom light. These weren't the steady bleep of an aircraft in flight. These were definitely search lights.

Leaving the room dark, Sara hurried to the living room and peeled back the shade to look outside.

A startled gasp escaped her. Where had all these vehicles come from? How had she not heard them? In the dim light of early morning, she saw the outlines of a dozen or so police vehicles parked along her private lane, plus the bulky shape of an ambulance.

Apprehension crawled over her skin. Did this mean the fugitive was here, practically in her front yard?

The very thought demanded coffee.

Five minutes later, with a cup of fortification in her hand, Sara curled up in her favorite chair and watched the limited activity outside. Other than the sweep of lights, there wasn't much to see. As day broke, even the lights vanished.

The sound coming from the chopper ebbed and waned, suggesting it traveled in a circular pattern. For the first time in days, Sara fully opened the shades. If she weren't safe with law officers literally in her yard, even a closed shade couldn't help her.

A uniformed officer stepped from the wood line, followed by another. Was something happening? Her heart rate ticked up a notch. Dust swirled in her yard. Tree limbs flapped carelessly beneath the chopper's blades, as haphazard as a kite on a windy day. The chopper hovered over her house.

After what seemed an eternity, the helicopter lifted and headed southeast. She ran to the window to watch its retreat. It headed steadily away from her.

Should she be relieved? Worried? Did this mean the officers would leave, as well? For the first time, Sara felt truly vulnerable.

While she debated her situation—good or bad, shades up or down—she saw a familiar figure approach the house. The broad shoulders and easy, confident stride could only mean one person. Special Detective Mason Burleson.

Without conscious thought, Sara opened the door.

"What's going on?" she demanded. "Why is the chopper leaving? Does that mean the area's clear?"

As he opened the screen door onto the porch, his dark gaze swept over her, brief and subtle. It crossed Sara's mind that her feet were bare, her clothes crumpled from yesterday's wear, and she probably had a bad case of bedhead.

Whatever. She was more worried about his answers than she was his appraisal.

"Well?" she demanded.

"And good morning to you, Miss Jennings." That infuriating hint of a smile twitched around his mouth as he touched the brim of his cowboy hat.

She wasn't certain about the *good* part. "Morning," she acknowledged, somewhat grudgingly. She waited for him to climb the steps to her porch before bombarding him with questions. "Did the chopper see anything? Where are they headed now? Why did they come before full daylight?"

"It's all part of our strategy, ma'am," he assured her.

"What is that supposed to mean?"

Instead of answering, he made a suggestion. One that didn't set well with Sara. "Maybe you shouldn't be out here on the porch, ma'am."

"Stop with the ma'am part!" she snapped. "I'm younger than you, for heaven's sake!"

"I meant it as a show of respect, ma'—Miss Jennings." He caught himself before repeating the same mistake.

She huffed her exasperation. "Are you going to tell me what's going on or not?"

"Out here?" He twirled his finger, indicating the open surroundings. "Not."

Sara understood his meaning. If Bernard were nearby, he could overhear their conversation. If he knew their plan, he could stay one step ahead of the law. And if he was close enough to hear that plan, he was close enough to put her in direct danger.

"Come inside." From the sound of them, the hissed words were ripped from her throat.

Waving him over the threshold, she refused to think about how this man invaded her personal space. She refused to acknowledge that he was breaching the privacy of her home, even if by invitation. She wanted answers badly enough to throw her hard-learned caution to the wind.

"So?" she demanded, shutting the door behind him. "What did they see? Where are they headed now? Why didn't they wait until daylight to start the search? Did they have a tip he was in this area?"

The detective answered in random order. "We hoped to pick him up with infrared heat sensors, but with no luck. The bird's headed over toward County Road 147, before coming back this way. With enough sweeps, we hope to push him out in the open."

"And then what?"

"Then we catch him."

"Where?"

"Wherever we see him."

"You can't be everywhere at one time," Sara argued. "What if he exits the woods, and there's no one there to see him?"

"We have hundreds of eyes on the lookout. While the bird is checking out other areas from the air, TDCJ will bring in their dogs to do a ground search here. They'll reverse the order and rotate as necessary."

Unimpressed, she persisted, "You didn't answer my question. Did you get a tip that he was over here? I thought the main area of concern was across the highway, between 147 and 149."

"That's correct," the detective calmly confirmed. "At this time, there's no reason to believe Bernard has changed course, but we'd rather err on the side of caution. We're doing a thorough search of the entire area."

"It's Day Four," she pointed out. "Law enforcement should have done a thorough search days ago!"

His tone remained patient. "We're doing the best we can, ma'—Miss Jennings. Coordinating this many agencies and resources is quite an undertaking. Some of our resources are volunteer, and Bernard is a dangerous criminal. We can't let civilians go in without warning them of the potential danger they face."

"I think everyone's aware of the danger, Detective."

"Maybe. Maybe not. It's like playing soldier. It's a fun game, until it's no longer a game. Hunting down the bad guys is the same. It's exciting, until the bad guys start hunting you back."

He had a point. Sara almost felt guilty for grilling him earlier.

Almost.

"If it's any consolation," Mason Burleson said, "we'll have officers and volunteers stationed here for the rest of the day. It's a long shot that he made it across the highway, but in case we push him this way, we want to be prepared."

"If he's as cunning as everyone says he is, surely he's smart enough to have already left the area."

"Until we have reasonable evidence to the contrary, we're operating on the theory that he's within a very concentrated area."

"But you just said—"

"You're at the very edge of the line," he was quick to assure her. "Like I said, today's search is more about precaution than suspicion."

"I guess that's something," she mumbled. She had abandoned her orchards these last few days. It would be nice to walk down and check them again.

He seemed to read her mind. "That said, you'll need to remain vigilant. And indoors."

Sara's gaze snapped up to his. "Even if my yard is full of officers and volunteers?" she asked in an incredulous tone.

"They'll be busy watching the woods."

"I could help." Judging by the dark expression on his face, he was about to quickly disagree. She was quicker. "I wouldn't get in the way."

Detective Burleson's mouth pressed into a firm line. "We strongly urge residents to stay inside their homes."

"You can't hold me prisoner here! I need to check my orchards. The last of the pears are ready for picking. The pecans are getting close to harvest. I can't just neglect them!"

A look of uncertainty crossed what she refused to acknowledge as a handsome face.

Sensing weakness, she pressed, "You're saying I can't check my crops?"

His resolve hardened. "Not without backup. We have no reason to think Bernard came this far, but it can't be ruled out. It's too dangerous to wander through fields and orchards on your own."

Sara crossed her arms in a gesture of stubbornness. "Then send me backup. I need to check my orchards. It's my livelihood," she threw in, although it wasn't exactly true. The bulk of her income came from her software business.

The detective ran a hand along his recently trimmed whiskers. "I'll see if I can arrange it. Would this afternoon work?"

It was more than she had hoped for. "Of course!"

"I can't make any promises, but since we're in the area and on patrol, I don't see why we couldn't wander down to your orchards and take a better look around."

She didn't even try to contain her enthusiasm. "That would be awesome!"

"Don't get overly excited, Miss Jennings," he cautioned. "It depends on what our search turns up."

She bestowed him with her best smile. "If it turns up Bernard, then you're off the hook, right?"

"Uhm, right." Accustomed to her scowl, he seemed confused to see her smile. Clearing his throat, the detective straightened to his full height of six-plus feet and adjusted his belt. Sara couldn't help but notice he had replaced his dress belt with a service belt, complete with gun, baton, taser, and other necessary items. "Right," he repeated.

Not one to gloat over victory, even such a small one, Sara made a daring but sincere promise. "If there's any pears, I may even make a cobbler."

"You do realize, Miss Jennings," he said, that infuriating smile hovering around his mouth once again, "that such a promise could be construed as a bribe."

"No bribe. Just a show of appreciation."

"Again, I make no promises, but I'll see what I can do."

"That's all I can ask." She moved to open the door for him. "Well, that," she conceded, "and finding Thomas Bernard and putting him back behind bars where he belongs."

"Amen, Miss Jennings. Amen." With a dip of his hat, Mason Burleson stepped through the doorway and out into the fresh air. He turned back to add a final word of caution. "Until you hear from me or one of my fellow officers, please take my advice and stay indoors. If you do sit on your porch, make sure there are at least two officers within sight."

"And the orchards?"

"I'll see what I can make happen."

With a murmured thanks, Sara closed and locked the door behind him.

That was when it struck her.

His infuriating smile wasn't nearly as infuriating as it first was.

Sara had a full day's work waiting on her, but she couldn't resist the lure of sitting outside on her porch swing.

She convinced herself it was for better efficiency. It offered the perfect opportunity to awaken and refresh her dulled brain cells. She had spent too many hours in front of the computer, she reasoned, and not enough time in the fresh air and sunshine.

Essentially, sitting on her porch was the same as getting more work done.

*Work smarter, not harder,* she reminded herself.

At times, she even spotted two officers outside, roaming somewhere along the perimeter of the trees.

Besides, who could work with all the racket outside? Between the dogs and the returning helicopter, she could hardly hear herself think. She decided, instead, to make her mind a blank slate. To breathe in fresh air, block out stale thoughts. To live in the moment.

The activity settled around noon. A few officers and volunteers remained to patrol the area, but in the absence of all the noise, it seemed suddenly quiet. Too quiet.

Now restless, Sara returned to her office and powered up her computers. The break had done her good, but not as much as she had hoped. She felt tense again, like she was waiting for the next shoe to fall.

It was because the search had proved fruitless, she decided. Even with all those departments, all those resources, and all those volunteers, Thomas Bernard was still at large. The thought was unsettling.

As the shadows of the day lengthened, a familiar truck pulled down her lane. Sara had bushel baskets and a nut gatherer in hand by the time Mason Burleson and another officer unfolded from the vehicle and approached the porch.

"Ready?" she asked, saving them the bother of coming up the steps.

"I guess so," the detective said, amused by her eagerness. "Miss Jennings, may I present today's pear picker, Gil Ingalls. Ingalls, this is Sara Jennings."

"Good evening, ma'am," the lanky TDCJ officer said.

"Word of warning, Ingalls," Mason said out of the side of his mouth, and just loud enough for her to hear. "She doesn't like to be called ma'am. Makes her feel old."

Sara bristled. "I never said that was the reason."

"My apologies." With the humor in his voice, it was hard to take his apology seriously. "May I ask what's the objection, then?"

"It sounds so formal. You've been here a half-dozen times. It's not like you don't know me from Adam," she groused.

Gil Ingalls raised his eyebrows, slid his partner a knowing glance, and wisely chose to remain silent.

"Point taken, Miss Jennings."

"Stop mocking me!" she snapped. She knew she was being irrational, but her nerves were frayed. The detective had been nothing but professional. He didn't deserve her unreasonable and unsolicited ire.

Mason turned his palms upward, clearly at a loss of how to appease her. "What should I call you, then?"

"My name is Sara." The frost in her voice didn't match the request. Being on a first-name basis suggested a friendly exchange. Her tone was anything but.

He tried the name out in his deep, soothing voice. "Sara. Nice name."

From the look in his eyes, she couldn't tell whether he was sincere or mocking her. Not that it mattered. She handed both men a basket and turned to lead the way to the orchard.

"Hang on there a minute." Mason stopped her. "We need to be with you at all times."

"I'll go first," Gil Ingalls volunteered. "You follow with Miss Jennings."

Normally, the walk down to the orchard was relaxing. She would take in the beauty of nature and fill her lungs with fresh country air. On a typical day, her stroll was peaceful and serene. Birds would twitter from limb to limb, their cheerful chirps lifting her spirits as high as the treetops.

Today, the woods were ominously quiet. No birds sang. No squirrels scampered about, searching for nuts and hoarding them away for the winter months to come. Even the breeze was hushed. The treetops barely stirred. Tension hung in the air.

With Officer Ingalls walking ahead of them, gun drawn, and Detective Burleson walking stiffly beside her, Sara imagined this was how the doomed must feel on the way to the gallows.

Sara couldn't help but throw a glance over her shoulder as they started down the incline to the orchards. The house was almost out of sight now. Crazy as it sounded, she felt untethered from her lifeline.

The pecan orchard was in the largest of two clearings. She thought of it as her secret haven. A secluded valley just for her. But today, the clearing felt more like the perfect place for an ambush. The huge pecan trees towered over her, calling attention to her vulnerabilities. She loved the massive old trunks, but a prisoner seeking cover could easily hide behind their thick diameter. She had always been fascinated by the thick, leafy boughs overhead, but now she realized they offered a natural camouflage of their own. Even for an inmate wearing white.

With her house out of sight and the birds still silent, it felt like they stepped into an abyss, isolated from the world.

Beside her, the detective had his hand poised over his gun, ready to pull it at a moment's notice. His eyes were in constant motion, scanning the area with hawk-like awareness.

Obviously, he felt the same sense of impending danger as she did.

"I'll be quick," she promised, her voice little more than a whisper.

"Stay close to me." His volume matched hers.

While Officer Ingalls circled the perimeter of the orchard, Detective Burleson shadowed Sara as she walked beneath the trees, peering upward to check the readiness of the crop. Most of the nuts were still tucked neatly within their tight green husks. A few husks had begun to unfurl, offering a peek of the brown shells they cocooned. Even fewer were fully opened.

The nut gatherer Sara carried featured an extensible handle and a hook on one end that she had designed herself. Using it on the opened buds she could reach, Sara rattled the lower limbs until ripened nuts showered down around them. She expertly cracked two nuts against one another, tossed aside the shells, and pulled the flesh from both pecans.

"Mmm." She savored the sweet, nutty taste of the state's native product. She gave the nut her nod of approval. "These are good."

She offered one to the detective, who popped it into his mouth even as his eyes scanned the trees beyond. "Very good," he agreed.

"I'll just check a few more. Probably those on the far west side." She pointed to the trees at the back of the orchard.

"Is it absolutely necessary?"

Hearing the caution in his deep voice, Sara's eyes flew to his. The familiar pleasantness had given way to wariness.

"I—I guess not." When he looked away to search the perimeter of the orchard, her eyes followed. Her voice fell to a whisper. "What? Do you see something?"

"No. But something doesn't feel right. I think we should start back."

"Okay. But we passed the pear orchard on the way. Can we stop there?"

"Probably," he said without promise, already turning to retrace their steps. He spoke into the radio clipped against his shirt's lapel, his voice low. Sara barely heard the replied, "10-4."

Unconsciously, Sara stepped closer to him. "Detective Burleson?"

Pulling his eyes back down to hers, one edge of his mouth lifted with a smile. "Since we're on a first-name basis now, call me Mason."

"The birds aren't singing. It feels like someone has been down here."

She noticed how he paused, ever so briefly, before replying, "We have officers still stationed nearby. They could have made a recent round through here."

"Maybe," she agreed. "Or maybe... maybe someone's still here."

They both knew she wasn't referring to law enforcement.

"Ingalls and I will come inside the house with you, just to make certain things are okay," he offered.

Sara rolled the nut gatherer on the ground as they went, collecting the few ripened pecans that had fallen.

"What about going into town?" she asked. "I need to go soon."

"Miss Mamie Hutchins does, too. Is tomorrow good for you?"

"That's fine."

"Text me when you're ready to go."

Ingalls joined them, flanking Sara on the other side. As they reached a well-worn path to the right, she asked, "My pears?"

Mason glanced behind them, judging the danger posed by the pear grove. It was a much smaller clearing, encircled by woods. Sending an unspoken message to his partner, Mason consented with a nod.

This time, Mason took point. Ingalls followed behind with Sara. The TDCJ officer helped her collect the nearly ripe fruit from the branches and the fallen, ready-to-eat pears from the ground. Together, they filled the better part of two baskets.

The entire time they were in the small clearing, Mason kept his gun drawn and his senses alert.

On the way back to the house, Mason offered to carry Sara's basket. The third basket only had a few pecans inside, so he stacked them together and carried them on one hip, leaving his gun hand free. Even though the weapon was now back in its holster, Sara noticed how his hand rested lightly upon it.

As they took the steps onto the porch, Mason told his partner, "I told Miss Jennings—Sara—that we would see her inside. You stay with her while I make the initial sweep." He turned to Sara. "Key?"

"Uh... it's unlocked," she admitted.

"What?" He stared at her incredulously, anger seeping into his voice. "There's a convict running loose, and you *don't lock your door*? Are you kidding me?"

"I—I seldom lock my door when I go down to the orchard."

"There's never been a killer on the loose, either," he reminded her in a cold, harsh voice.

In retrospect, Sara realized the folly of not always locking her door. The acknowledgement had more to do with Shawn than the convict.

In spite of that, she stubbornly challenged, "But you said there were officers still patrolling the area! And... And I was with you!" It wasn't much of a defense, but it was all she had.

"You can't take any chances, Sara. And you can't make stupid choices that put your life at risk."

He had a knack for pushing her buttons. She was sick of being ridiculed by a man. And no man, not even an officer of the law, could tell her what to do, or what or how to think. Not anymore.

"Now you're calling me stupid?" she flared.

He looked vaguely apologetic. "Maybe not stupid. Maybe just naive."

Sara's green eyes turned a stormy shade of jade.

"That's where you're wrong, Special Detective Burleson." The ice crackled in her voice as she addressed him by his official title. "I am anything but naive."

# Chapter 9

## Mason

"What was that all about?" Gil Ingalls asked as they pulled out of Sara's driveway fifteen minutes later.

"Damned if I know," Mason grunted. "I get the distinct feeling that Miss Jennings is hiding something."

"Like what?"

"I don't know."

"Then why the suspicion?"

"Call it instinct."

Gil made a show of looking back, as if he could see through the trees and pick up something his friend had missed. "Not sure what big secret she's supposedly hiding, but I guess it's possible."

"I didn't say it was a secret. But there's... something. She's been skittish from the minute I first knocked on her door."

"What do you expect? There's an escaped convict on the loose. Everyone's skittish."

"Not like this. Not like her."

"What do you mean?" Gil asked, finally interested in Mason's theory.

"I understand being cautious. She didn't just take my word that I was a law officer. I had to bring backup, and she made both of us turn our badges face down and recite the numbers."

"Smart on her part."

"Absolutely. But even after she knew we were officers, she wouldn't open the door wider than an inch. Even the second time we came, she only relented to five or six inches. She seems to have an aversion to letting people get too close to her. Yesterday, she offered me coffee, but I had to wait on the porch."

"Damn, man, how many times have you been out here?" Ingalls said, leaning as far away as possible to give his friend a full perusal.

"Enough to know she's hiding something," Mason muttered. He refused to rise to the bait of his friend's teasing.

"I didn't see any skeletons in her closet. And I literally looked in her closets," Ingalls pointed out.

Mason grunted, "And took your time doing it."

The prison officer grinned. "What can I say? I'm a fan of old architecture. The wife and I live in a brand spanking new modular home. These days, they replace character with chrome. Nothing interesting or unique about that."

"She does have a pretty cool old house," Mason agreed. "Which is another thing that strikes me as odd. Did you see all those computers she had? What's a high-tech girl doing living in the sticks?"

"Don't be a snob, buddy. With the invention of the internet—and especially since Covid struck—you can work from literally *any*where. Whether she lives in Apple County or the Big Apple itself, she can do her high-tech thing wherever she wants."

"I guess. She never did say what all those computers were about, though. She just said 'work.'"

"Are you seriously sitting over there sulking?" Ingalls demanded. "Have you got a thing for this woman? I saw the spark between you two, but I thought it more like a dynamite fuse. Maybe it was a different kind of fireworks."

His remark clearly irritated his friend. "Don't make something more of this than there is."

"Take your own advice, man. Maybe she does have more computers than most people. So what? It doesn't mean she's using them for nefarious purposes. You think she's trying to decode a bank's security system or something? Infiltrating an international database?"

"It's always possible. But no, that's not what I'm thinking."

"Then what are you thinking?"

"That she's scared." Mason chewed the inside of his lips. "Not about Bernard. There's something in her past. Something that's made her cautious and suspicious and, as she said, definitely not naive. She's hiding something, I can feel it."

"I guess we all have our secrets," his friend agreed. "At least hers are packaged nicely." The teasing returned. "But then, I don't have to tell you that, do I?"

Mason smoothly changed the topic. "Speaking of infiltrating... do you think there's something to the theory that Bernard had inside help?"

"If he did, it was from an inmate," Ingalls snorted.

"Sorry, I don't mean to step on your toes. I know you're an officer at Roscoe. But that gives you a unique insight as to what could have happened. *How* it could have happened. I just can't buy into the theory that another prisoner helped him pull this off."

"Yeah, I get it," Ingalls acknowledged. "I know a lot of people are saying that, but if Bernard had help, it had to have come from another prisoner. Warden Hye runs a tight ship. If you think he's rough on the inmates, you should see what he puts the guards and officers through. He has backups in place for backups. Even if a guard *wanted* to be dirty, he couldn't get past Hye's crazy security levels. The man is thorough to the point of being paranoid. Nothing slips past him, especially not a dirty guard."

"Then how do you explain Bernard's escape?"

"I can't. And I don't have to. I'm not on the internal investigation team at the Unit. I'm in the field on this one."

"We're almost back to mobile command. Where's your car?" Mason asked.

Ingalls rubbed a weary hand over his face. "Good question. I haven't slept in so long, I can barely remember my name." He fought back a noisy yawn. "Uh, over there, behind the tac bus."

The mobile command post had been set up in a field off County Road 147, not far from the crashed van. Even with the focus of the hunt gradually shifting to the west, officers still reported in at the original scene.

"I know what you mean, brother," Mason said, maneuvering around a collection of county and state vehicles, three tactical buses, a US Marshal van, two fire trucks, and one ambulance. The investigation called for every resource available. "Maybe tonight will be the night."

"We can hope." Ingalls opened the door as Mason stopped the truck and put it in park. With a deep sigh, he repeated, "We can certainly hope."

Mason watched his friend weave between vehicles to find his own among dozens of others. Like the rest of them, Gil was exhausted. Along with the physical burden, Mason knew the TDCJ officers and guards felt the added weight of responsibility on this manhunt. Their own agency had failed society.

In Gil's case, his own unit had failed. Spectacularly. Somehow, Thomas Bernard had managed to escape from the Roscoe Unit. Even with a tough warden like Hye, even with all his backups and over-the-top security measures in place, a dangerous inmate had outsmarted his captors and gotten away. It couldn't be an easy pill to swallow, especially for an officer as conscientious and dedicated as Gil Ingalls.

Mason and Gil went back for more than fifteen years. Their paths had crossed during the early days, back when they were both newly minted law officers. Through the years, they had seen each other at training sessions and meetings. For a while, before Gil signed up with the prison system, they had worked together in Tyler. Mason had even been an usher in his wedding when Gil married the love of his life, Isabella.

He knew the couple had endured more than their share of troubles during their marriage. First, there had been the matter of a jealous ex-husband from Izzy's early days. Then there had been the miscarriages. The final blow had come when Izzy was diagnosed with cervical cancer. A series of extensive treatments had followed, but the end result had left them financially strapped and unable to have children. But Isabella had survived, and that was better than many could say.

Mason made a mental note to keep an eye on his old friend. He knew Gil was the sort of law officer to take his unit's failure as his own. He didn't need to carry that sort of guilt on his shoulders, not after all he had been through.

And if he did, Mason would be there by his side to lighten the load.

# Chapter 10

## Bernard

He knew they were coming closer. With each day he stayed out, the law had another twenty-four hours of opportunity. Opportunity to capture him and put him back behind bars, a place Bernard had promised himself he would never go back to.

If he died during this escape, so be it. The Seven had it in for him. He was already as good as dead in prison.

Tucked inside his cocoon of trees by the creek, Bernard made certain the mud was still intact. He was covered in the filth from head to toe. As it dried and hardened, it fell off in small flakes and, sometimes, large hunks. He couldn't be too careful, not with all the activity in the area. Not an inch of skin or cloth must show.

The prison-issue white clothes were no longer white. Hiding inside the barrel, exiting the van on a dirt road in a duck-and-roll position, pushing into the dense undergrowth of leaves and roots, slipping and falling in the mud and the creek, and sleeping on a bed of leaves and dirt had taken care of that problem. Nature had turned his clothes a dingy shade of dull red and muted browns, staining them beyond recognition.

He did the same now for his skin, making certain the mud smeared evenly enough to camouflage his whereabouts among the brambles. An added bonus was the way red clay disguised human scent. Once he pressed freshly snapped cedar twigs and pine needles into the mix, even the tracking dogs would be thrown off.

Applying the slimy mud and clay mixture to every bit of exposed skin—even that at the back of his neck and over his eyelids—a thought crossed his mind. He tried hard not to smile, knowing it could crackle the mud already applied to his face. Keeping his expression stoic, he acknowledged that some people were stupid enough to pay for this shit, thinking a mud bath would make their skin tight and youthful again.

Bernard had no desire to be young again, not if it meant reliving his childhood. Once was more than enough for him.

With nothing left to do but wait out the search, Bernard kept alert, even as his mind wandered.

The first years of childhood hadn't been so bad. His parents tried doing right by him and his younger brother, even when money was tight. They had gone on picnics and visited the zoo and whiled away hours on the city's public playground. Their life had been simple, but in a not-so-bad way. And once a year, when his mom got her inheritance check in the mail from some seldom-mentioned aunt, they would go on a vacation and buy new clothes for the upcoming school year.

Neither were extravagant. Plain jeans and plaid shirts for school. Camping at state parks for vacation. Once, they even stayed at a motel in their own town just so they could swim in the pool and be served a free breakfast.

But those were the early years, before his father had his heart attack. After that, everything changed.

Bernard barely remembered the funeral. A bunch of people came and said nice things, and there was a huge meal at a church they never attended. They even let Momma bring the leftovers home, and that's what they had to eat for the next few weeks.

During those weeks, his mom was a mess. She spent most of her days crying or sleeping. He was the one who got his little brother ready for school. He was the one who walked him home from school every afternoon. He was the one who heated up the leftovers and made sure Danny took a bath every night.

He was the one who let Danny drown in the bathtub.

They made him go away for a while after that. Something about his mom not being fit to keep him, but he knew the real reason. They were punishing him for not watching his six-year-old brother. For letting Danny play in the tub while their mother sat in the kitchen and cried.

They sent him to the church where all the food had been. The nuns had taken care of him there and drilled into him the basic decencies and principles of life.

Love, joy, and peace.

Patience, kindness, and generosity.

Faithfulness, self-control, and chastity.

A mindful tongue and a dutiful heart.

By the time he came back home, his mother had made a new friend. Bernard hated Merv on sight, and the feeling was mutual. In no time at all, his mom and Merv were married, and Merv had taken over everything that once belonged to his father.

After that, life was miserable.

Merv had a bad temper, and anything could and would set him off. He believed in corporal punishment and used it often. He treated his stepson as his personal slave, and his wife much the same.

Once tolerable, even school became miserable. He spent more time in the principal's office than he did in the classroom. He didn't drop out because it would mean more time at home. Merv had never been one to hold a steady job. The inheritance checks gave him an excuse to quit whatever dead-end job he was working at the time, which made school the only escape his stepson had.

Over the next few years, anger festered in Bernard. He watched his mother shrink and shrivel, retreating into a shell of remorse and grief. She literally withered away, mourning her first husband and her child. And then they buried her, and the checks stopped coming, and Merv turned from mean to evil.

When Bernard finally had enough, he beat his stepfather within an inch of his life. He discovered that revenge felt good, even if it meant he spent a little time in jail. What was a few weeks behind bars, when it fed him three meals a day and helped settle a few debts?

Merv was only the first. Bernard had a long list of people who had done him wrong, and they all needed to pay. He worked his way through them, one by one.

He worked his way on to bigger crimes and bigger rewards. Revenge, he learned, didn't pay very well. But there were plenty of things that did, and Bernard wasn't afraid to try them.

Now, as the daylight faded and the sounds of the night crowded around him, Bernard realized it had been hours since he had heard the chopper, or even the dogs. In fact, he could hear nothing now, not even the sound of men talking or motors purring in the distance.

He knew they were still out there, still hoping he would mess up and reveal himself, but Bernard was smart. Smarter than a bunch of prison guards and hick deputies and pasty-faced lawmen. The higher the rank, the softer the man. Promotions made them lazy, and lazy made them stupid. Stupidity always led to carelessness.

Bernard was anything but stupid. He could wait them out. The silence was probably a trap. He couldn't see where they were in the dark, but in the daylight, he could keep better tabs on the people chasing him.

This was the second time he had changed hiding locations, with no one the wiser. But he still had one more move to make, and a major hurdle in getting there.

Somehow, he had to make his way across the highway.

# Chapter 11

## Sara

The sweet scent of pears, brown sugar, cinnamon, and pastry dough floated through the air as Sara pulled the bubbling cobbler from the oven and set it aside to cool.

With her baking done and her computer program well on its way to success, Sara felt a lightness she hadn't experienced in days. She was actually looking forward to going into town today, something she normally dreaded.

She showered and washed her hair, then dressed for her outing while the cobbler cooled. The forecast called for slightly cooler temperatures, so she pulled a trendy blue flannel shirt over her white t-shirt and jeans and applied a light brush of cosmetics. She never got too dressy when going into town, and she was determined that today would be no different. Just because she was seeing Mason Burleson today—that maddening, bossy, chauvinistic *man*—didn't mean she would go to extra care with her appearance. It was only a light coat of makeup, and there wasn't much she could do with her shoulder-length hair. Tying it back never worked and putting it up in a messy bun seemed like she was trying too hard. No, she would leave it just the way it was. It had just enough swing to make the style casually chic.

An hour before she was ready to go, she texted Mason as instructed.

*I'm ready to go into town if you are.*

Almost fifteen minutes later, her phone dinged with his reply.

*I'm tied up for the next couple of hours. I'll send someone to escort you ladies out.*

Sara refused to acknowledge that his words sent a sharp pang of ... what? ... coursing through her.

*Not* disappointment, she assured herself. More like irritation. He wasn't doing what he promised he'd do.

The words rang false, even to her. He never promised to personally take her into town. He had mentioned an escort, just as he did now.

She tapped back a short message.

*That's fine. Who?*

Another four minutes lapsed before he answered.

*I'll send someone you know. Gil, Pettaway, or Gray.*

She typed a quick question.

*Gil?*

His reply was just as quick,

*Ingalls. How long will you be in town?*

She thought of her short list of errands.

*An hour and a half, tops.*

Another two minutes, and he replied.

*Someone will be there within thirty minutes. If you'll wait for me at Bo's, I should be free to escort you home.*

Reading the words, Sara maintained a straight face. My heart didn't do that little flutter thing out of excitement, Sara told herself sternly. I'm just worried. Being escorted to and from Maypole is so far out of the norm, it's unsettling.

Nope. Had nothing at all to do with meeting Mason at the restaurant.

And to prove it, she sent back an oh-so-casual thumb's up emoji before dropping her phone into her purse.

Trooper Pettaway came for her. He circled the perimeter of the house before asking her to unlock her car by way of the key fob. With her safely stationed on the screened-in porch, he searched the vehicle's interior as well as the trunk. Finally satisfied, he gave her the all-clear, but she noticed how he kept his eyes moving at all times.

This time, Sara was certain to lock the door behind her.

With Miss Mamie Hutchins already safely stationed in his front seat, the trooper led the way out to the road and along the deserted highway. The only people Sara saw were a mismatched army of men and women, some in uniform, some in casual clothing, stationed every few yards along the south side of the road. They all stared into the woods, never looking her way as she drove behind them.

The sentries, she supposed, waiting for any sign of Bernard.

Once they reached the roadblock going into Maypole, the trooper waved her on and made a U-turn in the middle of the road. Sara proceeded slowly, amazed at how many vehicles and people she saw in the normally sleepy little town. There was a slew of law enforcement vehicles, two ambulances, several fire trucks, and a staggering number of news vans. Newscasters and camera crews gathered near the car wash, presumably for another update on the ongoing situation.

Day Five, and Thomas Bernard was still on the loose.

Despite the roadblocks and no doubt the posted warnings of a detour ahead, a steady stream of vehicles came toward her, only to be turned onto a side street and have their path rerouted. Shaking her head at their clueless behavior, Sara drove to the post office. She needed to collect mail from her PO box and send a few letters.

She couldn't say exactly why, but she found herself drawn to the used bookstore. Now that she knew it was the old *Hollister Drug Store*, she was curious about its beginnings.

The heady aroma of freshly brewed coffee and the sweet scent of vanilla greeted her, blending nicely with the unmistakable tang of old books. It was her first time to visit the establishment, but she immediately fell in love with it.

What wasn't to love about books and coffee, especially when the books were lined up on aged wooden shelves and displayed in glass-fronted cases? The coffee bar was obviously part of the original soda fountain, complete with twirling stools and antique bistro sets.

"Wow," she murmured in appreciation.

"Hello! *Welcome to Read it Again, Sam,*" a friendly woman said from behind the cash register. "Can we help you find a book? Make you a latte? We have both!"

"So I see." Sara was impressed, and her smile said so. She wandered over to the coffee counter, perusing the menu. "I had no idea you served coffee in here."

"You must be new in town," the woman guessed. Her mouth turned downward, ever so slightly. "Or just visiting."

"Actually, I've lived in the area for a year now. I just don't make it into town very often. I'm still learning where everything is." It was more than Sara usually offered about herself, but the woman had a friendly smile, and Sara could use that right now. This escaped convict business had everyone on edge.

"Oh, you really should visit all the stores on the square! We're trying to revitalize the town, and what better place to start than the courthouse square?"

"I understand this was originally a drug store. *Hollister Drugs*, I believe?"

"Well, yes, at one time. Before that it was a clothing store, and before that a feed store. It was built as a hardware store."

"Wow, that's quite a history!"

"After *Hollister Drugs* closed, it was a doctor's office for a short time. It's all there on the walls," she said, nodding to a display of old newspapers behind glass.

"If you'll make me a vanilla latte, I may take a look." Sara smiled.

"Help yourself."

Sara wandered over to the framed newsprints. There was a copy of every paper announcing the changing of hands, including a copy of the paper she had found behind the wood box. According to what she read, *Hollister Drugs* hadn't lasted very long, at least not in this location. By 1972, a Dr. Tom Benedict was setting up practice in the space.

It was the second headline of the week, topped only by news of a big theft at the local grocery store. According to the paper, a large sum of money was stolen just before the owner made his weekly deposit. It was one of a random string of robberies taking place around the county. The victimized businesses had few similarities, except that an undisclosed amount of cash was taken from each location.

With coffee in hand, Sara wandered along the aisles, scanning titles as she went. There was a wide mix of material to choose from. Romance novels to mechanical guides. Old textbooks to books of poetry. Music sheets to well-known thrillers. She spent a good half hour exploring before paying for her coffee and an old cookbook. She told the proprietor she would definitely be back.

The grocery store was her last stop before meeting Mason at the café.

Everywhere she went, people were talking about the escapee.

She overheard someone say their dogs had barked all night, certain it meant Bernard was nearby.

Another person said their sister-in-law spotted him down by her apple trees. By the time she called 9-1-1, he was gone.

Someone else heard he was seen in Austin.

A man swore Bernard was sleeping in his old barn. The hay had been disturbed, and some of his tack was missing.

Sara avoided the hearsay and went about her shopping, filling her shopping cart with staples. It should last her through the week and then some.

No need to come back into town, especially not with these crowds.

Despite law enforcement's pleas for citizens to stay inside their homes, it seemed everyone in the county was here in Maypole.

After paying and loading the bags into her car, Sara made her way back to the café on the square. Even at three o'clock in the afternoon, it was busy. The only place she found to park was across the street. Pulling into the space, she locked her car and started across, only to be met by a reporter.

"Excuse me, miss, but could I get a statement from you?" the woman asked, as her cameraman put a camera to his shoulder. "How is the escaped convict affecting your everyday life here in Maypole?"

"No comment," Sara said, averting her face.

"Please, miss. Our viewers want to know what it's like to live in a peaceful, safe little town that is suddenly anything *but*. Won't you spare us a moment to give your prospective?"

"I don't live here," Sara said, pushing past the woman.

"You don't?" The reporter was crestfallen. From the corner of her eye, Sara saw her give the cameraman the 'kill it' sign.

She was halfway into the roadway, hurrying to the other side, when she saw the second cameraman. Her feet faltered, stalling right there in the middle of the road. It just happened to be State

Highway 38, the main throughway in town. The cameraman was with another television channel, filming a panoramic view of the town's core. The lens captured her in its slow journey.

Her first instinct was to charge across the street and demand that he erase the film. But, what would she say?

That he didn't have permission to use her image? In today's day and age, with cameras in everyone's hands and on every street corner, was that even a legitimate argument anymore?

Would she tell him she didn't want her image broadcast all over who knew where, in fear that her ex-husband would see her and know her whereabouts? After a year of carefully avoiding any reference to her past, was a reporter really the person she wanted to share her secret with?

Nibbling on her lip, Sara debated her options. Was it worth making a scene? Would the film segment even make it on air? It was no doubt a filler, meant to offer a background view as some reporter did a voice over. She probably had nothing to worry about.

But still...

A horn honked behind her, reminding her that she stood in the middle of a busy highway.

"Sara! Watch out!" a man's voice called.

Confused, she didn't know where the voice came from. Worse, she didn't know where to go. A vehicle came from either direction, trapping her between them. The one that honked obviously saw her, but the other car's driver was more concerned with the activity along the street than he was with staying in his own lane.

Frozen in fear, Sara stood rooted on the yellow line.

The car swayed in her direction.

The pickup truck honked again. It sped up, trying to avoid a collision with the distracted driver.

Seconds before the car crossed the line—it came so close she felt the heat from the engine—someone yanked her arm and pulled her backward. Sara stumbled as her unknown savior dragged her to safety, and back to the side of the road she had come from.

"Sara! Sara, are you okay?"

Dazed, Sara looked into the worried depths of Mason Burleson's eyes.

"Sara, talk to me. Are you hurt?" His normally smooth voice came out rough. He bent at the knees so that his eyes were level with hers. "Are you okay?"

"I—I... Yes," she managed to croak out.

"God, that was close!" As she trembled, he wrapped her in his arms and held her tight.

People were staring at them. A concerned passerby stopped to ask if he could help. Mason thanked him but motioned him away. As a second person approached them, he released his hold on

Sara just long enough to flash his badge and utter a tight, "I've got this."

Oblivious to the narrowly avoided disaster, the driver of the blue car kept going. Horns honked in protest. People threw on their brakes. Traffic slowed and created a bottleneck. An audible buzz rose in the air as people pointed and murmured in outrage.

Yet, beneath it all, was the hint of anticipation. More drama to feed upon. Fresh blood for the circling sharks.

Mason saw the snarl of traffic and spoke into his radio. Within moments, a deputy hurried from the café to take control of the scene. Brandishing his badge and baton, he blew his whistle as he pushed his way to the middle of the stalled cars.

Halting traffic in either direction, the deputy motioned for Mason to bring Sara across the street.

Her legs wobbled as she allowed Mason to escort her between vehicles. Her face still wore a stunned expression, even as the traffic behind them slowly resumed.

The cameraman caught it all on film.

# Chapter 12

## Sara

They found the first available booth and sank into it.

"We'll have two cups of coffee. Strong," Mason told the waitress as she appeared almost instantaneously.

The woman peered at Sara in concern. "Are you okay, hon? I saw the whole thing. That car didn't run over your toes, did it?"

Sara looked down at her feet, trying to decide whether or not they hurt. Words were too much effort. She merely shook her head.

"Good," the waitress said with obvious relief. "That's good. I saw the whole thing happen." Her voice turned emphatic. "I hope they find that driver and give him a ticket! We have enough trouble going on in this town without a heap load of tourists coming in, rubbernecking and causing careless accidents! What is this world coming to?" She tsked as she patted Sara's shoulder. Her tone softened as she said, "Don't you worry about it now, hon. You're safe in here. Thank our Lord Jesus this nice officer was there to save you from being plowed over."

Sara looked at Mason as if seeing him for the first time. "Thank you," she whispered.

"Absolutely." Mason cocked his head toward the disappearing waitress. "You know her?"

"No." As her senses slowly returned, Sara thought to add, "Small town." She lifted her shoulders as if those two words explained everything.

Mason looked out the window to where the deputy continued to direct traffic. If nothing else, it made the drivers travel more slowly through town.

The waitress returned with two steaming cups of coffee and a tray filled with assorted pies. "I brought you each a piece of pie. On the house. We have apple, lemon, peach, and pecan. What will it be?"

"N—None for me, thank you," Sara murmured.

"Nonsense! Pie makes everything better. What will it be?"

"Pecan, then," she said absently.

"And you?" the waitress asked, turning her gaze to Mason.

"Apple."

"Here ya go."

"Thank you," Mason said, giving the waitress one of his charming smiles.

"My pleasure. Like I said, I saw the whole thing. What you did out there was real heroic, rushing out into the traffic and all." She nodded for emphasis.

"Thank you."

"What y'all are doing out there in the fields, trying to catch that no good for nothing escapee, is heroic, too. You never know what you might stumble upon. What ambush you could be walking into. Anytime you're in here, you ask for Beverly. That's me. I'll see that you're taken care of."

"I appreciate that, Miss Beverly."

"And we appreciate you," she assured him. She touched Sara's shoulder again before turning away. "You just sit there and catch your breath, hon. Take as long as you need."

"Thank you," Sara said. She reached for her coffee, only to slosh hot liquid over the rim. Her hands still shook.

"You're sure you're okay?" Mason asked, watching her closely. "You don't need to see a doctor, do you?"

She shook away his concern. "I'm fine."

Mason took a bite of his pie and then waved his fork toward the road. "Beverly's right. We don't need all these extra people in town. Even though we keep asking residents to stay indoors and to avoid the roadways, they just keep coming. If this keeps up, we may have to start issuing tickets for hindering law officials from doing their jobs."

"Catch Bernard, and that won't be necessary." Her tone came out harsher than she intended. Rubbing her forehead, Sara attempted an apology. "I—I didn't—"

"Forget it," he said, taking no offense. "I know you're still rattled from the near miss. Not to mention from the whole escapee ordeal."

Sara nodded. She pushed the pecan pie around on her plate without tasting it. "Thank you for sending Officer Pettaway."

"I told you I'd do my best to find you an escort into town. I'll go back with you, to check the house out."

She wanted to say it was unnecessary, but she couldn't bring herself to utter the lie. She lifted her cup again, this time managing a sip or two of fortification. "Is there anything new happening?"

Mason pushed out a heavy breath of air. "Unfortunately, no. We had hoped we could flush him out last night. A day of increased activity, followed by a night of laying low. But I guess he was on to us. Looks like he may be as smart as they say he is."

"If he's so smart," Sara said, her skepticism coming back, "why is he still in the area? A smart criminal would be long gone."

"You would think, but there's no evidence to support that theory."

He looked out the window. With the traffic pattern back to normal, the deputy directing traffic took leave of his post. Mason watched him weave his way back to the café.

Deputy Lewis came directly to their booth. He dipped his head in greeting. "Detective. Ma'am."

Mason thrust out his hand. "Thank you, Lewis, for taking charge of the situation."

"Glad to help, Detective. Ma'am, are you okay?"

Sara was still too dazed to take offense at the way he addressed her. "I'm fine, thank you," she murmured.

"That's good." The deputy looked toward Mason. "Did you happen to get a license plate number? I could put out a BOLO on him."

"That's not necessary."

"Are you sure? He almost hit a pedestrian."

"A pedestrian who was jaywalking," Mason pointed out. He darted a reproachful eye at Sara. "If we issue one ticket, we have to issue two. I think it's best we let the whole thing slide."

"Folks around here normally cut across the street like that, but I guess outsiders don't always know that," the deputy agreed. He looked at Sara. "You *are* a local, right? Don't you live out on Cora Miller's old place?"

"Yes, that's right." Her voice was tight, but her mind spun with questions. Why was a county deputy confirming where she lived? How did he even know that? Was she under some sort of surveillance?

"Pretty place," the deputy said conversationally. "Old man Miller kept the place running like a well-oiled machine. When he died, Miss Cora just naturally took over. She had a knack for growing things. Ran the farm as well as any man."

"Most women are nurturing by nature," she pointed out.

"I suppose so. But farming is hard work. Some women can't handle the physical labor, but not Miss Cora. She was one tough lady." He shook his head in admiration. "I remember how—"

Both men's radios crackled at the same time, cutting off the deputy's reminiscing.

"Apple County SO to Maypole Fire," the dispatcher said. "Grass fire on the southeast end of County Road 149, about two miles from the railroad tracks. Officers stationed nearby report seeing flames and heavy smoke."

Deputy Lewis looked at Mason. "Isn't that in the zone?" he asked uneasily.

The lines around the detective's mouth tightened. "Yes, it is."

Sara saw the look of concern that passed between them. "Do you need to go?" she asked.

"I'm on duty here in town," Deputy Lewis said. "Ma'am, I'm glad you weren't injured out there. Detective, let me know if I can be of any more help." He touched the brim of his hat in parting.

"The zone?" Sara questioned when they were alone.

"Our main area of focus. The one I mentioned yesterday, otherwise known as the Danger Zone."

"And I'm in it?" Her coffee cup wobbled again in her hand.

*Too much caffeine*, she told herself.

Mason didn't sugarcoat the truth. "Like I said, at the very edge."

She appreciated his honesty. "Do you need to go to the fire?" she asked again.

A muscle worked in his jaw. "They've only paged out one fire department. No reason to think it's something more than a simple grassfire."

"Then why do you look so worried?"

Mason stared out the window without answering. "There's a killer out there, still roaming free," he said at last. "Of course, I'm worried."

# Chapter 13

## Bernard

Bernard knew he needed a distraction. Something to keep his watchers occupied, while he made his move to the other side of the highway.

In the weak hours of early day, he cautiously stepped from his cocoon of safety after a restless night of waiting and watching. Nothing stirred. Bernard didn't see or hear anyone moving about.

He was stepping into the open, headed to the apple trees for more of the forbidden fruit, when a faint glow caught his eye. Drawing back against the trees, he studied the shadows of pre-dawn until he made out the shape of a man standing along a creek bank ahead. A cigarette dangled from the man's mouth, the end of it glowing red.

The man stood there for what seemed an eternity. He probably thought he was well hidden in the trees, undetectable to a prisoner planning a run across the open field.

The loud *pop!* startled them both. It could have been the backfire of an engine or the discharge of a gun. In the silence that preceded daybreak, it sounded like the roar of a cannon.

The unexpected noise made Bernard jump. He all but rustled the trees he hid within.

Upstream, the man jerked, dropping his cigarette onto the ground. After a brief pause—was he speaking into the radio clipped across his chest? — he loped off in the direction of the highway.

It could still be a trap. Bernard debated what his odds were. Deciding to risk it, he waited a few minutes before crouching low and wading up the creek. The cold water made him shiver, but it would cover his scent and hide his tracks. He didn't hear the hounds, but they could return at any moment.

Scanning the sandy bank, he guessed he was nearing the place where the man dropped the cigarette. Careful not to create a splash, his progress slowed to a crawl.

Unwilling to climb from the creek and expose himself, Bernard looked around for a long, thin branch. He found a lengthy stick that would suffice and snaked it up to rest along the creek's bank. He dragged the stick carefully along, raking through sand and grass, hoping to ease the discarded butt his way. The hardest part was being unable to stand at full height to see what he was doing. It was too risky, and this could still be a trap.

He made gentle sweeping motions, careful not to pull too hard and roll the cigarette off into the water. It was bad enough he had to drag it through sand.

When the stick caught and snagged, Bernard had a moment of pure fear, imagining he had struck a booted foot. He dared look up, fully expecting to stare into the end of a gun barrel.

Relief surged through him, causing his arm to jerk. The stick tugged on the item of resistance, raking it down the bank to tumble into the water.

It hit with a splash, too heavy to be a cigarette. Bernard ducked, hoping to hide from anyone close enough to hear. It also provided opportunity to rake his fingers along the creek bed.

When he came up with a disposable cigarette lighter, he could hardly believe his luck. It hadn't been under water long enough to do permanent damage.

Back at his makeshift camp, Bernard ate his last apple. It was still green and left his taste buds puckered, but it put substance in his belly. Now that he had a plan, he didn't need to go weak from hunger.

The old barn wasn't far away. Abandoned structures would be the first place officials looked, so holing up there had been out of the question. But he had gone inside yesterday morning, just to look around in case there was something he could use.

At the time, he thought he had no need for a rusted five-gallon can of diesel.

The cigarette lighter made all the difference.

Crawling on his belly through the dried grass, Bernard made his way to the barn. He wasn't stupid enough to approach the structure at his full five feet, seven inches. Like he had done in the creek, he kept low and depended on his instincts to guide him. He misjudged the angle and went a good thirty feet out of his way this time, but he eventually reached the ancient barn.

Bernard scouted out the area before easing inside, careful to open the doors just wide enough for his slight form to squeeze through. Dodging the stacked hay bales, he grabbed the can and hauled it out with him, unscrewing the rusted lid as he went.

He splashed the fuel behind him on his retreat toward the creek. It left a dotted line through the dried grass, but he had faith that the flames would jump from dot to dot. Already a nice breeze blew, promising the perfect recipe for a wildfire.

About fifty feet from the creek, Bernard flicked the lighter open and touched the flame to both the diesel-dampened grass and its drier counterparts. It caught fire slowly, threatening to extinguish itself before it gained strength. Bernard didn't tarry long enough to nurse the flames to life. He had to put as much distance between himself and the barn as he could before someone came to investigate the smoke.

Bernard made it to the creek and turned around to see the field behind him slowly igniting. With another good gust of wind, the flame should take hold and move along the dried grasses and the dotted line of diesel, snaking its way back to the old barn.

He shook the can he still held in his hand, feeling the last bit of fuel slosh inside. He knew diesel wasn't as explosive as gasoline, but he flicked the lighter one last time, dropped it into the rusted metal can, and flung it with all his might.

# Chapter 14

## Mason

Mason's radio went off yet again as they approached their vehicles.

"Are you sure you don't want to go?" Sara asked, motioning to the noisy apparatus clipped to his side. "I can get home by myself."

"Pettaway's already taken Miss Mamie back. I said I'd see you home, and I will." Mason's tone left no room for argument.

He shut her car door before getting into his own truck and leading the way out of town. He stopped at the barricade to gain access onto the deserted highway.

"What's the latest word on the fire?" he asked the officer who cleared them.

The rotund man grunted. "Not one. Still searching the barn for Bernard before they let firefighters in."

"I hope they catch the SOB," Mason said. "This has gone on long enough."

"I hear you, brother," the man agreed. "Take care."

"You, too, man."

Mason glanced in the rearview mirror as Sara followed close behind. It looked like her hands were still shaking as they curled around the steering wheel in a death grip.

She had a near miss today, no doubt about it. He still couldn't quite get the scene out of his eyes, seeing the way she stood in the middle of the road, frantically searching for a way out. Without a second thought, he had rushed through the traffic to tug her back to safety.

With a smile, he knew she wouldn't appreciate him referring to it as 'rescuing her.' Sara Jennings had an independence streak a mile wide.

He remembered the way she had trembled in his arms, and the shocked look that haunted her eyes.

In some strange way, Mason thought 'haunted' was exactly the right word. There was something in Sara's past that haunted her. He was certain of it.

She had been in a daze when they entered the café, and it had taken awhile for her to come out of it. She hadn't eaten the pie and drank only half her coffee. She made an attempt at conversation, but it wasn't until the reporter came in that Mason saw her spunk return.

He replayed it all in his mind.

"Excuse me, ma'am."

Mason had seen this same woman approach Sara earlier, just before the fiasco in the middle of the road.

With a cutesy expression, the reporter flashed a contrite smile that didn't reflect in her eyes. "Me again. I couldn't help but see what happened in the road. Would you like to make a comment this time?"

Sara's expression was one akin to horror. All she did was shake her head in fervent denial.

"Not even about this brave gentleman here who saved you?" The reporter tried again, indicating Mason with flourishing hand movements. "Surely you'd like to publicly acknowledge his heroic act!"

"Turn that camera off!" Sara had snapped. "Stop harassing me!"

"I only want to speak with you. Tell your story."

"No! You're the reason I rushed out into the street in the first place. I asked you to leave me alone. I'm not interested in an interview!"

"But—"

"But nothing! Erase whatever footage you have of me. If you don't, I'll lodge a formal complaint against you to your television station." Sara's jaw was set with a stubborn edge.

"But—But..." the woman sputtered.

"Ma'am," Mason had broken in, "I believe the lady has made her position clear. Erase the tape."

"I can't do that," the reporter argued. "I have an obligation to my viewers—" Her words cut short when he flashed his badge. In a stiff voice, she murmured, "Of course, Officer. Good day to you both."

Sara had dropped her head into her hands then, running her fingers through her dark hair. The tangled look suited her, just like the flannel shirt and white tee suited her.

But the girl-next-door look was at odds with the fear he saw in her eyes.

"That other cameraman got it, too, didn't he?" she asked in a defeated voice.

"I didn't see another cameraman."

"He was across the street in the other direction. I was caught between the two of them."

"*That's* what you remember most?" Her statement stunned him. "That you were caught between two cameras, not two vehicles?"

"I—no, of course not. It's just that..."

"The vehicles posed a much greater danger, Sara," he told her gravely.

She had said the strangest thing at that point. She dropped her voice, but he still heard the words. "I don't know about that," she had said.

In Mason's eyes, that was definite proof she was running from something. Or from someone. No one had that kind of fear in their voice, that kind of haunted look in their eyes, unless they were scared for their life.

Mason mulled over the thought as he drove past a half-dozen sentries, each stationed at intervals along the highway. Few looked his way, but the man sitting at the bridge turned at his approach and lifted his hand in greeting. Mason returned the gesture, grateful that the man was so near the two most vulnerable houses. Mr. Hewlitt's driveway was a half mile up the road and on the right. Sara's lane was just after his.

"She's hiding something," he confirmed to himself, unable to shake the feeling she was in some sort of trouble. "She has every right to be afraid, what with a convict on the loose and nearly being hit by a careless driver. But that's not it."

He glanced in his rearview mirror again. "This is deeper," he mumbled. "This was there first. I saw it the first day I met her, and I see it even more so now."

If he were being completely honest, if only to himself, he had to question his excessive interest in her past. As a detective, he was naturally nosy. Call it an occupational hazard, but he couldn't help but analyze people's reactions when they discovered he was with law enforcement.

Shifty eyes often meant the person felt some sort of guilt.

Hostility could mean they had prior experience with the law, and it hadn't been good.

Fear could mean either but usually indicated some level of guilt.

Gratitude usually meant a prior experience had been favorable.

Support implied they knew someone in law enforcement or could relate to the trials and tribulations officers went through.

Cautious acceptance signaled the person didn't quite trust the law but was willing to give them a chance.

Suspicion signaled that a person's trust would have to be earned, and it wouldn't be easy.

Sara's first reaction to him had been puzzling. Her eyes held a curious mix of cautious suspicion, mingled with fear. The fear, however, didn't seem to be of the law. She seemed suspicious of men in general. Maybe even of *people* in general. Sara Jennings wasn't exactly the warm, open, friendly type.

*What was the word for that?* Mason wondered, trying to decide how to characterize her personality.

Reserved. Yes, that was it. She held a part of herself back. She seemed on guard, afraid to let her shield down, lest she was caught unaware.

She seldom smiled, but when she did, it transformed her entire countenance. It softened her face and warmed the green jade of her eyes. It made him want to see more of that side of her personality and find out the secrets she held so close.

*Occupational hazard?* He wondered.

*Or attraction?*

Mason considered the question as they approached her driveway. No doubt about it, Sara was very attractive. Her personality had a few sharp edges, but their banter left him oddly energized. He found himself looking forward to their next encounter.

Wait a minute. *What was he saying?*

Mason shook his head to knock some sense into it.

Those encounters were only possible because a killer was on the loose. His obligation was to keep her safe, not develop personal feelings for her. He shouldn't treat her any differently from the way he did her neighbors.

But did he? He checked on her neighbors the same way he checked on her, but he'd never eaten cookies with them on the porch. Or walked them down to their orchards. Or escorted them home. Miss Mamie Hutchins had offered him coffee and a hot meal, but he politely turned down her generosity. So, why was Sara different?

"I'm intrigued because I know she's hiding something," Mason reasoned aloud. "There's more to Sara Jennings than meets the eye. And as soon as this Thomas Bernard ordeal is behind us, I plan to find out what that story is."

It had nothing to do with any attraction he felt toward her.

Nothing at all.

# Chapter 15

## Bernard

As he hurried up the creek bed, Bernard took less care than he had earlier. Already, he heard the wail of sirens arrive on scene. The sound of rushing vehicles and excited voices moved away from him, hurrying toward the old barn and the railroad tracks beyond. The wind was in his favor, a nice steady breeze that fanned the flames and pushed them ever southward. He splashed his way upstream, until he neared the highway.

He saw the sentry posted near the guardrail of the bridge. Orchard Creek meandered under the highway by way of a large concrete culvert before flowing freely again on the other side. All he had to do was distract the lookout man, cross under the bridge, and come out on the northern side of Highway 38.

The police-band radio blared out the most recent update on the fire, even though the man at the bridge was clearly not law enforcement. He held himself too casually, studying his phone as much as he studied the trees.

From what Bernard could hear on the radio, the fire near County Road 149 was growing rapidly and endangering a structure on the property. It was a hay barn but unknown whether or not the structure was occupied. Dispatch called for another fire department to assist, as well as troopers and a tac unit.

It went without saying that their fugitive could be inside the structure. That's why they asked all units to stage a hundred yards away and allow the tac unit to go in first.

Bernard barked out a humorless laugh, knowing the squawking radio would hide any sound he made. "Suck-ers!" he spat.

He debated for a moment on the best way to distract the lookout. He could make a run for it and hope the guy was too caught up in his phone to notice, but he hadn't come all this way to get sloppy now. He needed a better plan.

While Bernard sifted through different scenarios, the situation resolved itself. Again, luck was in his favor today.

First, Bernard found a discarded beer bottle. Most of its long neck was broken, leaving only a sharp and jagged edge in its place.

Second, the lookout put down his phone, left it and the radio behind on his folding chair, and stepped to the edge of the road. He eased the zipper down on his jeans, glanced behind him, and seemed to have second thoughts. Bernard watched as the man descended the embankment several feet and allowed himself privacy while taking a leak. From the highway, should a vehicle get through the restricted access, only the top of his head would be visible.

Bernard knew there was no time to waste. He rushed up the embankment, taking the lookout off guard. The startled man saw him in time to jump back, but not before he could grab his gun. He lost his footing and slid toward Bernard, rather than run away from him.

"What the f—" The vulgarity died on the lookout's lips as Bernard thrust the broken bottle upward into his abdomen.

Blood gushed from the man's wound as he looked into his killer's face. His expression changed from shock to fear, and then from pain to horror. As he crumbled to his feet, his ashen face wore no expression at all.

Keeping his head low, Bernard scampered the rest of the way up the incline, grabbed the police ban radio and the small cooler beside the chair, and slid back out of sight. He stopped his flight to bend over the dying man. His checkered shirt was torn and bloody, but Bernard could wash the worst of it off in the creek.

He jerked the gun from the sentry's holster and took the money and knife from his pants pocket. As Bernard roughly pushed him from side to side to wrestle off his shirt, the man's eyes fluttered open. He tried to speak. Only blood bubbles came out.

"It'll be over soon," Bernard assured him. Out of some weird reflex from the past, he passed his hand over the man's eyes to shield them from the sun. It was the only kind thing to do.

Too bad Sister Nancy had spent so much time preaching against bad manners and cursing, and so little time preaching against murder.

# Chapter 16

## Sara

Sara dutifully sat in her car while the detective circled her house. It gave her time to calm her nerves and regain her composure.

She *knew* she shouldn't have gone into town today! Her mail could have waited. She didn't need milk and bread that badly. She could have waited a few more days, until this madman was caught, and life went back to normal.

A short, humorless laugh escaped her. Normal? It had been so long since her life resembled anything close to normal, she had forgotten what normal actually was.

Sara knew what it *wasn't*.

It wasn't normal to leave your life in the city behind and move to a small rural town where you didn't know a soul. It wasn't normal to be practically a recluse at the age of thirty-four. It wasn't normal to have the reaction she had today with the reporter. It wasn't normal to live in constant fear.

It wasn't normal to live under an assumed name.

The tap on her window startled her, making Sara jump. The detective motioned for her to unlock the door. When she did, he opened the door like a gentleman and helped her out.

"What about my groceries?" she asked.

"You can carry the lighter bags in now if you like. I'll come back for the rest of them after I've checked inside."

He would be invading her personal space again. After the day she had, she wasn't sure she was up to it.

"Isn't that a bit excessive? If the doors and windows are still locked, I'm sure everything is fine."

His expression was mocking. "So, you actually locked your door today?"

Sara rolled her eyes. "Yes, I locked my door. I'm not a moron."

He pulled two plastic bags from the backseat and handed them to her. "Never said you were a moron," he replied mildly. "You left yesterday without locking your door. Wasn't sure if you'd do the same thing today."

"Yesterday, we only went to the back of the property. Plus, there were police officers in my yard! I didn't think it was necessary to lock the door."

"It's always necessary to lock your doors. Thomas Bernard doesn't play by the rules."

Suddenly impatient, Sara said, "Let's just take all the groceries in now." The sooner they got the bags in, and the house cleared, the sooner he would leave. “My milk will spoil. It already sat in the car while we were at the café.”

“I thought that was the purpose of the cold bag.”

“Yes, but the purpose of the nice, long handle is that you can sling it over your shoulder while carrying other bags in your hands. Here, hand it to me, and I’ll show you.”

Ignoring her sarcasm, he put the insulated carrying bag over his shoulder and took the two remaining bags in the same hand. As he locked and shut her car door, he purposely left his gun hand free.

On the porch, Mason lowered the bags he carried, took her keys to unlock the house, and told her to stand in the doorway.

“If you see or hear anything outside, come inside and lock the door behind you. Otherwise, stay there until I call for you.”

“What if you don’t call for me?”

She had meant the question as flippant, but his answer sent chills up her nape.

“Run. Don’t bother with the door. Run to your car, drive away, and call 9-1-1 on your way out.”

Instead of a smart retort, Sara mumbled, “Then you’d better call for me.”

After what seemed like forever, Mason walked into the living room. “You can come in now. I’ll get the groceries.”

When he returned, Sara was in the kitchen, a slight frown on her face.

He noticed immediately. “What’s wrong?”

"Uhm, nothing." She shook her head to convince them both. "Nothing's wrong."

"You don't look like nothing's wrong. Did you hear something?"

"No, it's not that."

"Did you see something out of place?"

Sara looked around, seeing nothing unusual. All the knives in the knife block were accounted for. The electronics were still there. When she had opened the mammoth of a refrigerator, no food appeared to be missing.

"No, everything looks normal."

"Then, what?" he pressed. He was a big believer in trusting one's instincts.

"It just... feels different, somehow."

"Feels different?" His tone was more inquisitive than condescending,

"I—I can't explain it. It just feels like... like someone has been here."

"I'll recheck the house. You stay here. Where's your gun?"

"There really is a Glock by the front door, and a Hellcat 9mm in this drawer. You go on. Check my office first. Make certain all my computers are there."

"How will I know?"

"You're right," she said, a rueful smile coming to her face. "I'll follow you in there."

A second search brought up nothing. The house, Mason assured her, was secure. He had even checked the attic.

"I guess I'm just edgy. The trip into town and all," she said.

"Not to mention being nearly hit by a car."

"That, too."

Mason's eyes strayed to the pear cobbler, still sitting on the counter where she left it to cool. "Is that from your orchard?"

"Yes. I made it this morning. I thought you and Officer Ingalls might like it."

A playful light twinkled in his dark eyes. "Maybe I should taste-test it first, before I offer it to my friend. Gil and I go way back. I wouldn't want to give him something that wasn't fit to eat."

"Is that your not-so-subtle way of asking for a piece now?"

"Only if it comes with coffee."

Sara frowned. "You just had coffee and pie, less than an hour ago."

"You're right," he agreed. "You didn't by chance buy the makings for a sandwich, did you?"

So much for getting him quickly in, quickly out.

"I know what you're doing," Sara told him.

"I'm trying to get a sandwich."

"No, you're trying to keep me company until my nerves settle down." She held her hands out in front of her, willing them not to tremble. "See? All settled."

"You sure put that one hand down awfully quickly," he noted, without pressing the issue. "But, seriously. I could use something of sustenance before I test out that cobbler. Have you eaten today? You didn't touch your pie."

"I, uh, don't remember."

"I'll take that as a no. Come on, one little sandwich for both of us. Then I'll be out of your hair."

"Aren't you on duty or something?"

"I pulled an all-nighter. I'll be back out there again tonight. I have about six hours of downtime, and I'd like to squeeze in a nap. But I can take a hint. I'll go back into town and grab a bite to eat."

He had already turned and started toward the door before Sara found her voice. "There's no need for that," she said in a quiet voice. "I'll make you a sandwich."

He turned with that maddening grin of his. "I thought you'd never ask."

"I didn't. *You* did," she said pointedly. She went to the refrigerator and looked at their options. Like she suspected, there was only one. "Turkey okay with you?"

"Sure." He eyed the behemoth behind her. "Are you sure that thing still works?"

"Unfortunately, yes. And it weighs a ton. There's no moving it."

Mason watched as she pulled out the makings of a simple meal.

"Tell me what to do, and I'll help," he offered.

Sara pointed to a cabinet. “The plates and glasses are in there. I’ll put everything out so you can make your sandwich the way you like it.”

“What are we drinking?”

“There’s tea in here and water in the tap. I’ll take water.”

They worked in silence, each making their own sandwich and carrying it to the kitchen table to eat. It occurred to Sara that he was the first guest to sit at her table.

Mason was the first to speak. “So.” He made it a statement in itself. “I couldn’t help but notice you have an unusual number of computers.”

“I suppose.”

“I’m not sure we have that many back at the office, and I work for the government.” He eyed her in jest. “You don’t have some weird computer hoarding fetish, do you?”

She almost laughed. It came out more of a snort. “Hardly.”

“Please tell me you aren’t a computer thief,” he deadpanned.

“I’m not.”

Mason waited for her to pick up the conversation from there.

She didn’t.

He gave her a prompt. “This is where you explain why you have a dozen computers in your house.”

“For work.”

Getting nowhere, Mason bit into a chip. "You're not much of a conversationalist, are you?"

"That's why I like my computers. They don't ask a lot of nosy questions."

"But you obviously have to feed them information for them to work correctly."

Sara narrowed her eyes. "Is that what all the questions are about? Are you working?"

"I'm working at having a nice conversation with my lovely, if not unwilling, dinner companion. And I'm failing miserably."

Deciding to give him a break, she admitted, "You're not catching me on my best week."

"I get that. Bernard has a lot of people on edge."

After a significant pause, she volunteered more. "I'm working on a big project for my company. Up until last night, it wasn't cooperating. I think I may have finally worked out the kinks." She pulled in a hopeful breath. "Most of them, anyway."

"That sounds promising. Who do you work for?"

"Myself."

"Ah, an independent contractor." He nodded with approval and perhaps new admiration.

She made no comment, letting him draw whatever conclusions he wanted.

Behind her, the refrigerator groaned. The vibrations rattled the glass bottles inside and made a terrible knocking sound against the floor.

"What is that racket?" Mason asked in alarm. His hand automatically went to his sidearm.

Her reply was casual. "That's just my refrigerator. It's a little uneven. I have to give it a good shove every now and then."

When she started up, he stopped her. "I've got it. Maybe I can straighten it up a little."

"Good luck with that. Like I said, it weighs a ton."

Mason pushed and tugged on the huge old appliance, noting that it was, indeed, uneven. He looked beneath it and then behind. Ignoring a dust bunny or two, he spotted a potential problem.

"I think I see what's going on," he said, squatting down at the back of the refrigerator.

"I know what's going on. The floor is structurally sound, but it does sway a bit under the weight."

Mason grunted as he continued to push and tug on the oversized device. After a considerable amount of time and effort, he pulled something from beneath it.

"I found your culprit," he said. Rising, he brought her a slightly water-stained book, similar to the cookbooks left in the cupboard. "This was beneath a back corner. It may have originally been to stabilize it, or it may have fallen there. Either way, I hope it takes care of the rattle."

"Wow. I never even saw this." She picked up the book in amazement. "Thanks."

"Only time will tell if it works. If it makes it worse, I'll put it back." He shrugged as if it made no difference to him.

"Now I'll owe you another cobbler," she murmured.

"Make another batch of cookies, and we'll call it even," Mason told her. He looked at his wristwatch. "I may have to take a raincheck on that cobbler. If I want to get any sleep, I'd better get going."

"Take the cobbler with you. Just make sure Officer Ingalls gets a piece."

"I'd never cheat a friend. If he happens to come along before I finish it, I'll gladly share." His brown eyes twinkled again.

"How generous of you."

He motioned toward the table. "Can I help you clean up?"

"I've got it. You go catch a nap. I'll put some paper plates and forks in with the cobbler."

When she handed him the plastic bag, she reminded him to keep it upright.

He took it, his hand barely brushing against hers. Both tried ignoring the sparks that flew between them. "I appreciate the sandwich."

"I appreciate the escort to and from town," she replied.

He knew he was stalling. He knew he had to go.

"I'll be sure and share this with Gil."

"He was the one to pick the pears, after all."

That maddening smile reappeared. "Does that mean I get a pecan pie?"

"Don't push your luck," she warned, but with a half-smile.

She walked him to the door.

"Lock the door behind me."

"I will. And I won't open the door to strangers, and I won't go outside, and I won't take any stupid chances. Is that what you want to hear?"

"It's a start."

Once he was gone, the house seemed unusually quiet. Empty. To ward off an unexpected wave of loneliness, Sara turned on the television.

She cleaned up the kitchen and poured another glass of iced water. The last thing she needed was caffeine.

It wasn't time yet for the six o'clock news, so she picked up the newly discovered book and carried it into the living room. She hoped it was another cookbook, filled with more handwritten entries to delight her taste buds.

At some point, the book had gotten wet. The first few pages were stuck together and illegible. By the time she found a readable entry, she realized it wasn't a cookbook at all. It was a journal.

The writing looked vaguely familiar. She couldn't tell, at first, if it had been penned by a man or woman. From what she could tell, it was a chronicle of seeds purchased, planting times, cultivation notes, and harvest details. A farmer's record of farm crops.

A few pages in, the writing stopped. Sara assumed the blank pages meant she had reached the end. As she set it aside, she almost dropped the book. Catching it by the back cover before it hit the floor, she saw more writing in the back half of the pages.

This, obviously, was written by a woman. It took only a few pages to realize the writer was Cora.

She had met someone. Cora only referred to him as "R," hinting to Sara that he was a secret lover. Forbidden, either because of their stations in life or because of her rumored involvement with Samuel Foote.

It was clear from reading the entries that Cora wasn't in love with the up-and-coming merchant, even though their futures had been loosely tied together since childhood. Something about an arrangement their fathers had and plans for the orchard's expansion. The mysterious R, however, enchanted the young woman.

The first entries were innocent enough. Cora wrote about shy, curious glances. Catching one another's eyes beneath leafy pecan boughs. A brief exchange of words over a proffered cup of water. It took a few entries before Sara realized R worked for them.

Maybe the theory of their different stations in life was closest to the truth.

There was a gap in the entries and then a large headline. *"He's back!"* With these entries, Cora wrote of a few stolen kisses. A picnic by the creek. How thoughtful R was, bringing her small presents. A tortoise-shell hair comb and candy. On another occasion, pencils and pens tied with ribbons. A bold and passionate kiss as they dared consider a future together.

Silly R, Cora had written. He thinks money will make the difference. He thinks Pa won't accept our courtship until he proves he can provide for me. Doesn't he know I do most of the work in the orchards? Pa's health is ailing. With the boys gone, it's up to me to work the fields and take care of the business dealings. If I have to, I can provide for R, the same way I provide for Pa. I have money of my own. The farm has been good to me.

After another gap in writing and a boldly proclaimed *"My beloved R is back!"* Sara concluded that R was a seasonal worker on the farm. Without him there to brighten her days, Cora found no reason to write in her personal journal.

After flipping through the pages a few times, Sara suspected the only entries Cora made during those bleak times concerned planting and harvesting. When the mysterious R returned, so did the flourishing cursive.

Her praise for him filled the pages. R was doing well for himself, earning and saving money for their future. To prove it, he brought a bag full of cash for her to see. He even left it in her care for safekeeping. One more harvest, he predicted, and he could ask for her hand in marriage. Blinded by love and the thoughtful gifts he brought her, Cora gave herself wholly to him.

The entries didn't include full dates, but Sara sensed they spanned several years. The words on paper matured along with the woman who wrote them. The flowery phrases gave way to hints of frustration. More than once, the name Samuel appeared. Cora wrote about obligations and old promises as much as she did dreams of the future.

Sara could almost feel the resignation as it crept into Cora's heart, turning her from a starry-eyed twenty-something to an on-the-verge-of-spinsterhood thirty-something.

R continued to work for Miller Farms, even after Leroy Miller passed away. The couple couldn't reveal their years-long love affair for fear of it ruining Cora's reputation. In the mid-seventies, more than her virtue was at stake. Despite women's lib, a woman's personal life very much affected her professional life. If people suspected a social scandal, her business would be ruined.

The promise of 'one more harvest' never seemed to materialize for the star-crossed lovers. R insisted they needed more money in case business suffered when she married a migrant worker. Even a duffel bag filled with bills wasn't even.

Not with Samuel Foote in the picture, he claimed. Not when the businessman was pressuring Cora to finally marry him and make good on their fathers' arrangement.

Sara almost cried when she read Cora's entry about accepting Samuel's proposal. She obviously loved the mysterious and somewhat elusive R, but the businesswoman had to be practical. She needed the stability Samuel could offer. Between the two of them, they could keep Miller Farms prospering for years to come.

Cora delayed the wedding, so she could have one more harvest with her lover. She knew it was wrong, but she couldn't help herself, so the journal stated. One more taste of love and passion before the reality of a loveless marriage jaded her forever.

Sara turned the page to continue reading, but the title sequence for the local news drew her attention.

There was still no good news about the escaped convict. As Day Five drew to a close, unconfirmed reports placed Thomas Bernard in various locations around the state, but officials believed he was still in the area. While every lead was thoroughly investigated, the search in Apple County continued at full force. Residents were asked to remain cautious and alert and to stay off the roadways to allow emergency personnel through.

In other news, there was a fire still burning within an area of interest concerning the search. So far, there was nothing to suggest Bernard started the fire or that he had perished in its midst.

Also, with increased traffic around the town of Maypole and the snarl of traffic created by roadblocks, residents were complaining of safety issues. Just that afternoon, there was a near-miss as a woman attempted to cross the road and was almost struck by a distracted driver.

Sara stared in horror as her own image appeared on screen. The story wasn't even from their local news team. It was compliments of an ABC affiliate in Dallas.

Covering her face with her hands, she moaned aloud, "No! No, no, no. This can't be happening!"

And yet, it was. They didn't identify her by name, but it was no doubt her. While she may have declined an interview, several witnesses had jumped at the chance to be on television. They complained about the increase in traffic and the dangers it posed, on top of worrying about an escaped murderer in their midst. One witness raved about the officer's heroic act of rescuing the helpless woman from grave bodily harm.

Sara didn't have the energy to resent the 'helpless' claim. At the moment, she felt exactly that.

The journal fell away, completely forgotten, as Sara curled into a ball and wondered how long it would be before Shawn found her.

# Chapter 17

## Sara

Sara first met Shawn in college.

The moment she laid eyes on the tall, lanky basketball player, she was mesmerized. She was embarrassed at the way her gaze followed the athlete up and down the court—especially since she was there on a date—but she had no control over her eyes. They seemed glued to number twenty-two.

She passed it off to her date as an avid interest in the sport when, in fact, she had never been particularly fond of basketball. The squeak of rubber soles against the hardwood floors wore on her nerves. She never understood the rules of passing or what the painted markings on the floor meant. Fouls and penalties were a mystery to her.

But watching Shawn Angelos play changed all that. She was too caught up in his graceful moves to notice the squeaky shoes. The way he jumped, the way he hung suspended in mid-air before the ball made a mighty *swoosh!* through the hoop left her in awe. The way he slung dark hair out of his eyes left her mesmerized. She became dizzy, watching him race up and down the court. Or maybe it was her pulse. Her heart drummed in excitement as she watched him. He was always the fastest, always the best. Shawn Angelos was amazing.

In just one game, she became his biggest fan.

Sara started attending all the home games after that, just to get a glimpse of the good-looking player. He wasn't handsome, not in the traditional sense. He had a hawkish nose and deep-set eyes. Against his dark hair, his skin was shockingly light. But his legs were long and lithe, his forearms strong, and his body fit and lean.

Fate was with her the next semester. She actually had a class with the mighty Shawn Angelos! Sara was elated. She knew he caught her gazing at him, but she supposed he was accustomed to it. He certainly had all the girls in the classroom fawning over him.

Near the end of the semester, the professor assigned a project to be done by two-person teams. The professor chose the duos, and by some grand stroke of luck, Sara's name was paired with Angelos'. It was the first time she had even spoken to the man, and now she was assigned one-on-one time with him.

During that first session, she was too tongue tied to speak. Her adoring gaze inspired a slow, sexy, somewhat-cocky smile from the basketball star. All Sara noticed was the sexy. She overcame her nerves by the next session. By the fourth one, they were laughing over cappuccino at an off-campus coffee shop. Sara thought of them as study dates, even when random girls interrupted them, ignoring her and openly flirting with the man she was with. Even when Shawn flirted back.

Sara never minded that she did most of the work on the project. A win for her meant a win for him. It looked good on his GPA, which was oh-so-important for his continued scholarship. Plus, the more work she did, the more time Shawn had to perfect his game.

Their work—her work—earned them the top grade. To celebrate, Shawn treated her to dinner. It was almost like a real date, especially when he kissed her at the end of the night.

Summer break came, and Sara resigned herself to not seeing her idol for three long months. She couldn't believe her luck when he called a few weeks later, asking if she'd like to catch a movie.

As they stopped for a quick bite afterward, he talked about the mini-mester he had enrolled in, bemoaning a full semester of work crammed into such a short amount of time. Sara volunteered to help. If it meant spending more time with him, she was all in.

By the fall semester, they had fallen into a comfortable routine. They met a couple of times a week, usually at a coffee shop or a fast-food restaurant. Their relationship was platonic, sprinkled with casual good-night kisses and comfortable banter.

Sara resigned herself to Shawn's roving eye when they were together, and to the endless parade of admirers, mostly female, who thought nothing of breaking into their private conversations. Sometimes, Shawn even invited his fans to join them. Sara was forced to smile and act as if their presence didn't chip away at her self-confidence and stab at her heart. Obviously, what she felt for Shawn wasn't reciprocated.

By mid-semester, as all things basketball consumed him—practice sessions, non-conference games, and of course his adoring female fans—Sara faded into the background. Faced with the inevitable, Sara accepted that their time together was over.

Her friends convinced her that she needed a distraction. They set her up on numerous double dates, until she finally found the one guy who piqued her interest. His name was Craig, and the two of them had quite a bit in common.

He wasn't Shawn, but he was the perfect distraction. They spent the holidays together and made plans for a ski trip over spring break. Sara thought she glimpsed a possible future with the computer science major.

The re-emergence of Shawn Angelos changed all that. A devastating knee injury put him out for the end of the season and nixed the team's hopes for making the playoffs. Despondent and facing surgery, Shawn called his old friend Sara. Could she possibly swing by to do him a favor?

One favor turned into two. Two favors turned into three. When he begged her to stay with him at the hospital—over spring break—she couldn't say no. Craig didn't like it, but he appreciated the loyalty she showed to a friend in need. He drew the line when Shawn asked Sara to stay with him at his off-campus apartment and nurse him back to health.

After a heated argument, Sara and Craig parted ways. For the next three weeks, Sara slept on Shawn's couch. During that time, a dozen girls stopped by to cheer the ailing basketball player. They were more about taking pictures, signing his cast with hearts and mushy sentiments, or showering him with kisses and praise than they were about bringing his meals or running him back and forth to doctors' appointments. They certainly weren't about helping him with class assignments.

Girls weren't the only ones to visit. Sara met his teammates and closest friends. She was surprised when they accepted her into their circle so easily. Even after Shawn healed, and she returned to her own apartment, they invited her to join them for pizza night or drinks at the pub. She became one of 'the guys.'

At the end of the semester, just before the senior players graduated, the guys invited Sara to join them for a night of clubbing. She donned one of her few party dresses, a short little red number that left one shoulder exposed. She piled her long hair up into a messy bun and added dangling earrings.

The guys saw her differently that night, including Shawn. It could have been the excessive amounts of alcohol they all consumed. It could have been the dress she wore. It could have been her surge of self-confidence, inspired by their admiring remarks. It could have been the flirty way she danced with them.

Whatever it was, it made Sara feel special.

And it made Shawn jealous.

She was dancing with Pete, moving with the beat of the music, his hands on her twitching hips as their bodies moved inevitably closer to one another. He was lowering his head to kiss her. She was raising hers to accept.

Shawn suddenly jerked his friend away, sending the shocked couple reeling. Shawn swooped in and caught Sara in his arms. He never looked back to see how Pete fared. He twirled Sara in a dizzying dance, lifting her completely off the floor and landing her several feet away.

"What the hell was that?" Shawn demanded. The crowd on the dance floor separated them from his friend. "What do you think you were doing back there?"

"I was dancing," she answered. The alcohol had lowered her inhibitions. Holding her hands over her head and letting her hips sway to the music, she only laughed at him. “Lighten up, Angelos. Dance with me.”

She had taken to calling him Angelos several weeks ago, the same way the rest of the guys did. Shawn seemed to notice it for the first time, and he didn’t like it. He grabbed her by the arm and shook it. “Stop it, dammit! Call me Shawn, the way you always do. Stop acting like you don’t know me. You’re here with *me*, dammit!”

“With you?” Sara stopped dancing, ignoring the people who bumped into her from behind. “With *you*? You barely know I exist!”

He slung his dark hair from his eyes, his jaw in a stubborn set. “I know you exist, all right. And I know you’re *my* girl, not theirs!”

“Yeah?” she challenged. “What makes me *your* girl?”

Shawn pulled her roughly to him, fitting his body in tight around hers. “This, dammit!” he said, lowering his face to hers.

And then he kissed her, and nothing and no one else in the world existed. It was just him and her, alone on the crowded dance floor. Alone in the universe, for all she cared.

Foolish Sara. She mistook his possessiveness as a sign of his love.

That had been her first mistake.

# Chapter 18

## Sara

She couldn't wallow in self-pity all evening. She needed to run the computer program one more time. If there were still no hitches, Sara could call the Dallas company and set the date for a soft install. It would require spending several days in the city, training personnel, and making certain their trial runs went as smoothly as hers, but a change of scenery might be good for her.

Assuming, of course, that Thomas Bernard had been caught. Sara didn't relish the idea of leaving her house for any length of time. What if the convict decided to break in and camp out in her living room?

There were also her pecans to consider. The pears had run their course, so losing the last few wouldn't cause any great harm. But she needed to keep an eye on the maturing pecans, so she could hire help for harvest.

"I need to go back to the orchards tomorrow," she reminded herself aloud. "Day after next, at the latest."

She was up late, letting the computer program go through its sequencing. She washed a load of clothes while she waited. With time yet to kill, she dared a peek at her social media pages. They were under her business name, *SJ Innovations*, but she feared Shawn would see through the alias and find her, anyway.

There was nothing on her own pages, but there was plenty on social media about today's near-miss. People shared the news channel's clip, adding their own impressions to their post. *Prayers for this poor woman*, some said. Or, *This guy can rescue me any day!*

Seeing her face plastered over the internet at least a half-dozen times, Sara turned it off. She could only pray that Shawn wouldn't see the clips. Her hairstyle was different, and the color was darker now, but she still looked much the same as she had before.

She often wondered how that was possible. She was nothing like the girl she had once been, so how could she look the same?

There were subtle differences, of course. Her green eyes were more solemn now, and worry had etched its way into the grooves of her forehead. Sometimes, she thought her lips had forgotten how to smile. Fear was her constant companion. The perpetual loss of sleep had left permanent smudges beneath her eyes.

At one point, she had been desperate enough to consider plastic surgery. If she changed the slope of her nose or the angle of her jaw, would he still recognize her? Surgery was so drastic.

Yet, was the route she had taken any less so? She had abandoned her old life. She no longer spoke with old friends. She cut ties to her family. She quit her job, moved halfway across the country, and left no forwarding address. When Shawn found her, she moved again.

When the random acts of disturbance in a new city began—the two-a.m. fire alarm at her apartment building, the break-in at work, the phone calls when no one said a word—she knew he had found her again.

The next time Shawn managed to track her down, she moved again. And this time, she had her name legally changed.

Bridgette Donaldson Angelos ceased to exist, and Sara Jennings was created.

But when her car was broken into a few weeks later, she worried he had cut through the red tape and found her. Managing to get out of her lease agreement, she found a cute little duplex to rent. When someone broke into her car yet again, she decided Ft. Worth was no longer a safe city to live in.

She would find somewhere nice and quiet, some place so out of the way and so small, Shawn would never think to look for her there.

She was driving through Apple County, headed to Louisiana to install a computer program for a newly built hospital, when she happened to stop in Maypole for a bite to eat. The town was so small and innocuous, so ordinarily *simple*, she decided to stay. The sleepy little rural town was the last place Shawn would come searching for her, especially under her assumed name.

But Thomas Bernard changed all that. His daring escape captured the news industry and drew coverage from around the nation. While most people were curious, the nosiest of people made it their mission to experience the drama firsthand. The distracted driver who almost hit her today and the cameraman who captured it on film made perfect examples of that fact.

The last thing Sara wanted was to draw attention to herself and the new life she had built. That's why she seldom went into town. Seldom talked about herself. It was why she didn't try to make friends. Why, until just this afternoon, no one had ever eaten at her table.

Today's events had destroyed all her hard work. The news coverage hadn't identified her by name, but they had identified her by sight.

Not even her new name would matter now.

Not if Shawn knew where she lived.

Her telephone rang at 2:22 am. The sound filled Sara with terror.

She reached into the nightstand and pulled out her pistol. Her hand trembled as she checked the chamber to make certain it was loaded.

It was Shawn. She knew it. Who else would call on her landline?

She only kept the number because the real estate agent suggested it. Cellular coverage was often spotty here in the country, he said, especially without wi-fi calling enabled. Since the electricity was also prone to outages, the internet wasn't reliable. The agent highly suggested keeping the landline and the ancient old wall phone in the kitchen. Only later did Sara discover that, during inclement weather, the telephone lines were no more predictable than the electricity.

The timing couldn't be a coincidence. Two-twenty-two was 'their' number. The two of them, plus Shawn's old basketball number.

He used it in passwords. He used it on his specialized license plates. He requested it at every hotel. Before they could move into their first apartment, he insisted on finding a complex with unit 222 available.

He proposed to her at 2:22 am on February the twenty-second.

When at all possible, especially on away games, he called at 2:22. Morning or night, and often both.

Her landline ringing exactly at 2:22 could only mean one thing.

Shawn had found her.

Going back to sleep would be impossible. What if he were calling from nearby? Shawn could be very persuasive. She had no doubt he could convince the patrolmen guarding the roadblock to grant him access. He would play the part of the worried husband, desperate to get back home to his wife. And he could bust down her door at any moment, taking three and a half years of pent-up rage out on her.

Sara piled her pillows up against the headboard and sank back into them. She tucked the covers in close around her, hoping to ward off the chill invading her from the inside out. In her lap, she cradled the gun, a flashlight, and her cell phone. She needed to be prepared.

Thirty minutes later, her cell phone rang. She almost didn't answer, until she saw Mason's number on the screen.

"Hello?" she answered.

"Sara? It's Mason. I hate to wake you—"

"I wasn't asleep."

"I'm sorry."

There was a significant pause on the line.

With her nerves already fraught, Sara's voice came out sharp. "You called me at almost three in the morning to say you're sorry that you *didn't* wake me?"

"I'm sorry you haven't had any sleep yet tonight, because... you definitely won't sleep once I tell you the news."

A sense of doom settled in alongside the chill. "It's about Bernard."

"I wanted you to hear it from me before you heard it on the news. We can't keep this quiet for long."

The way he stalled, she knew it was bad. "Just tell me what it is, Mason. What's happened?"

"We think Bernard started the fire to create a distraction. He managed to get past the sentry and, presumably, make it to the north side of the highway."

Her words were matter of fact. "My side."

"Yes. But we don't know which way he went after that," Mason was quick to say. She knew he tried injecting a positive spin on the situation. "He could have gone further west. Most likely, he's hoping to make it to the next highway and then on to the interstate."

"But if he stays in the creek, he'll pass right by my house. Almost in the orchard." She had the craziest image of the man somehow massacring her pecan trees.

"And we'll have people stationed there to watch for him. You'll see increased activity, including the bird and the dogs."

"You saw how dense the trees are around the creek. You can't even see it from several places. You can't wade upstream, either. There are roots and brush and beaver dams all up and down. Especially the section that runs along my property. The only access point is right there in the orchard."

"Then that's where we'll be."

"Don't you dare damage my orchard!"

"What's more important, Sara? Catching this monster or saving your pecan trees?"

Her answer came quickly. "Both. And he's not stupid enough to come out if two dozen armed men are waiting there with rifles."

His reply came out edgy, roughened by lack of sleep and worry. "We're trained professionals, Sara. We know how to stage an ambush."

"Then why is this man still on the loose?" she charged back. "What is this? Day 6? This is to the point of embarrassing! A dozen law enforcement agencies, and this criminal is still roaming free."

"I agree. Bernard has been at large far too long. But TDCJ has their own guidelines of dealing with escapees, and we have to follow along."

"Why don't the Texas Rangers take over? They're the premier law enforcement in Texas. Why aren't they here?"

"They are. Now."

Sara picked up the way he added the word 'now.' "There's more, isn't there?" she asked.

She heard his heavy sigh. "I'm afraid so." After a brief hesitation, he told her the truth. "He didn't just slip past the lookout. He killed him."

A gasp of horror escaped her. “You—You’re not serious.”

“I’m afraid I am.”

“What about you being trained professionals? What good did that do the sentry?”

“Unfortunately, many of the men watching along the highways aren’t licensed lawmen. Some are members of fire departments or former military, but with such a large perimeter to patrol, some of the volunteers are ordinary citizens.”

“And this was an ordinary citizen.” It wasn’t a question.

“Yes.”

The cell connection buzzed with more than silence. Tension hummed along with it, as well as dread.

After a long moment, Mason asked, “Are you still there?”

“Yes. I’m just... absorbing it all.”

“It’s a lot to absorb. But I didn’t want you to be blindsided when you hear it on the news. Or to be frightened when you see increased activity around you.”

“Have you warned Mr. Hewlett? He lives on the other side of Orchard Creek.”

“I’m calling him next.”

“Thank you, Mason, for letting me know.” His name fell easily from her lips, as her tone finally softened. “It’s... definitely unsettling. Scary. But I’m glad you called me.”

She thought she heard a smile in his voice. "Even if it was in the middle of the night?"

"Like I told you, I wasn't asleep."

"I understand. None of us are getting much sleep these days." Now she heard a frown. "Or nights, whichever it is."

Without thinking, Sara shook her head and said, "It's not that."

The moment the words were out, she wanted to call them back. She normally guarded her words so carefully. She measured every statement, making certain it left no room for cross examination. Making certain her answers were tight, allowing no peek into her past.

Tonight, fear made her careless.

Fear of the unknown, not knowing if Bernard was headed her way. Not knowing if he would see her as a threat to be dealt with.

And fear of the known, certain that Shawn had found her again. Knowing exactly what he was capable of, and that he wouldn't see her as threat, but as a challenge. Knowing he would seek revenge.

"Then what, Sara?" he asked softly. "Why couldn't you sleep?"

His deep voice was so concerned. So deep and comforting. Sara had the craziest urge to confide in him, but that was crazy. Now wasn't the time for bonding. Now wasn't the time to tell anyone her secret.

If she didn't survive Thomas Bernard, there was no reason to fear Shawn Angelos.

She shook away the foolish idea of telling him the truth. "My phone rang," she told him truthfully. "Wrong number."

"Humph. Bad timing. Two o'clock phone calls are rarely good."

"Hence your call."

He made no apologies. "You needed to know. Again, he's probably headed to the highway, but you need to be on guard. Have your gun close and your outdoor lights on."

"I've got my gun in my lap."

"It wouldn't hurt to let Bruno bark every now and then."

Her lips curled slightly upward. He knew the dogs weren't real, but he hadn't called her out. Not directly. "Not a bad idea," she admitted.

"Look, I have to go. Take every precaution you can. If there's somewhere you can go, I urge you to do so. I can't stress how dangerous this man is, especially now. He's getting desperate."

"I'm staying," she said stubbornly. "But I'm not an idiot. I'm prepared."

"That's good. Stay that way. There will be a lot of activity around you tomorrow. Don't be alarmed, but don't let down your guard, either. Anything can happen when you corner a criminal."

His words didn't exactly inspire confidence. "Are you *trying* to keep me awake?"

"I'm trying to keep you safe," he assured her in his deep rumble. "I've got to go now."

"Mason? Thank you for letting me know."

"I promised to keep you updated. I never break a promise if I can help it."

# Chapter 19

## Mason

Mason had managed a three-plus-hour nap after his search-turned-sandwich at Sara's. It wasn't much to carry him through the night, but it was better than nothing.

Now, a long, hard day had morphed into a long, hard night.

On the way back into town, Mason noticed the sentry wasn't beside the bridge as he had been on the way in. He thought nothing of it. Sometimes, the lookouts had to answer nature's call. Sometimes, they just needed to stretch their legs. Stakeouts sounded a lot more exciting than they actually were. More often than not, they were boring and tedious and difficult to stay awake through. Moving around was sometimes the only thing you could do to keep from falling asleep.

Shifts changed as evening descended. Station 24 West was the one at the bridge near Sara and Mr. Hewlett's houses. Dispatch radioed the volunteer lookout and asked if he needed relief. The static-filled reply came back, "Nah. I'm good."

Around midnight, the lookout's wife called the sheriff's office to say her husband wasn't answering his cell phone. The dispatcher again reached out to him on the radio. "Chuck, you still doing okay out there? Ready for me to send a car?"

It was mandatory that sentries were dropped off and picked up in case Bernard got the drop on them and stole their vehicles. During the overnight hours, alone in the dark with a killer on the loose, it had to be an eerie feeling. Particularly for volunteers, it showed real courage to sit out in the open, knowing a convict could be nearby.

It took a moment for the lookout to reply. "Told you. I'm good."

"Your wife says you aren't answering your cell phone."

Another pause before static almost overrode his voice. "Battery died. Tell her don't wait up on me."

Nearly two hours later, someone mentioned Chuck wasn't answering his radio. He had been out there for over twelve hours, they noted, and he needed a break.

Mason had volunteered to check on him. He was riding with Gil, making rounds over the back roads, and checking in with sentries as they came across them.

Fog had moved in overnight. It hovered over the creek and low-lying areas in a thick blanket. Along the roadways, it rose as wispy, patchy tendrils, thicker in some places than others. As the TDCJ pickup neared the bridge over Orchard Creek, the air grew thicker and appeared as a fine mist through the truck's harsh headlights.

The lights fell across a visibly empty chair near the bridge.

Mason shifted uneasily in the passenger seat. Hadn't there been a small cooler there this afternoon? He hadn't noticed on the way out from Sara's, but he could have sworn he saw one when going in.

"Something doesn't feel right," Mason murmured to his friend. "Radio the station, tell them our 10-20. Tell them we're doing a welfare check on Station 24 West."

Gil relayed the information as Mason opened the door. Gun drawn, he cautiously approached the empty chair.

The smell immediately hit him, caustic in the thick autumn air. The pungent, rancid stench of death.

He motioned for his friend to join him. "We have a problem," he told the lanky officer as he approached.

"What is that smell?" Gil asked, his nostrils flaring. "It smells like..." His sentence broke off as he recognized the scent of blood.

"We need to spread out. Find the guy who should be in this chair." Mason took lead on the scene. Judging from his friend's widened eyes, he was in no shape to do so.

Still in a daze, Gil meandered along the highway, following the beam of his ultra-bright flashlight. While he stood at the guardrail to peer down at the concrete culvert, Mason walked in the opposite direction, careful not to trample potential evidence.

It was difficult to see in the night fog. He moved slowly, examining every fuzzy bump in the condensed air. He could only see a few feet down the embankment, which meant he had to go down to see anything more. He went well out of his way, working his way back toward the bridge in hopes of preserving the scene.

A seasoned lawman, even Mason acknowledged the uneasiness settling over his bones. The safety of the truck and of his backup were well above his head, hidden somewhere in the fog beyond. He was walking along the bar ditch, all but invisible to anyone on the road, with only his gun and his wits to protect him. Not only was there a murderer on the loose, but feral hogs and snakes were bad in this area. He was in the very pit of danger, following the scent of death.

The acrid odor grew stronger. Mason stood still, moving his light methodically along the embankment's slope.

There. Was that something?

He approached with care, skirting around the suspected area. Several feet away, he saw it was only a clump of dirt and dried grass, but the smell here was stronger. It smelled like someone had gutted a wild animal nearby.

Or a man.

Mason's senses tightened as he probed the misty area beyond with his light. Was that other lump something?

At first, the lookout's dark skin blended in with the shadows. Between the fog and the dark of night, most things appeared in monochrome. Without a shirt, the man's bare chest stood out no more than his blood-stained jeans.

Wait. Was that a boot? A leg? Mason crept closer, choosing where to step. When he was certain he saw a body sprawled out on the ground, he spoke into his radio. His first call was to his friend on the closed talk-around circuit.

"Ingalls, get down here. I found the source." Flipping to the SO channel, he called in his findings.

Mason snapped several pictures on his cell phone, cataloging the scene before he moved in closer. He took pictures of the ground he was about to step across, lest he unknowingly contaminated the scene. Donning gloves, he approached the body.

He had no doubt the man was dead. Too much blood had leaked onto the ground beneath him. His intestines hung as much outside his bloated body as they did in, exposed by a deep and jagged stab wound into his abdomen. Flies already buzzed around him.

Mason took more pictures as Gil's lanky form appeared in the mist. He made his way down the embankment, less careful than his friend now that they knew where the body was located.

"Careful," Mason cautioned anyway. "We don't know which way Bernard approached from. Presumably from the left since the wound angles that way, but he may have sneaked up from the other direction."

The TDCJ officer skirted the perimeter, stopping not too far from his friend.

"Oh, God," he said. His expression was one of pure horror. "Oh. My. God."

"I know. It's pretty disgusting," Mason agreed solemnly.

"This wasn't supposed to happen," Gil said, backing away in revulsion. "He was a volunteer. He doesn't look any older than us."

"I know. It's a true shame." Mason looked down at the dead man, shaking his head in empathy. "He was trying to protect his community, but Bernard butchered him in cold blood."

"I... I think I'm going to be sick."

"Then get away from the crime scene!" Mason barked.

His tone came out harsher than he intended, but Ingalls was a seasoned officer. Staring death in the face was never easy but eventually, a person became hardened to it. It was the only way to maintain sanity. Mason knew this wasn't the first victim

Gil had attended; they had worked murder cases together in the past. This friend needed to suck it up and get his act together. Contaminating a murder scene with the responding officer's own vomit was unacceptable.

While Ingalls emptied his stomach several feet away, Mason heard sirens wail in the distance.

"We need to spread out!" OIG Director George Lehman roared. His arms moved wildly about his body. "We have to find this SOB, and we have to find him *now*!"

"How?" someone dared ask. "The fog is getting thicker. I can hardly see you, sir, and you're only ten feet away."

"Then you'd damn well better part the fog and walk through it!" his superior snapped. "This man has made a mockery of the TDCJ, and I. Will. Not. Stand. For it. Do you understand me?"

Mason understood that an innocent man was dead, and all the pompous director worried about was how this damaged his reputation. Mason shook his head in disgust, knowing the fog hid his reaction. He couldn't even pretend respect for this man.

Gil sidled up to him. "This man is a real piece of work," he muttered.

"He's a piece of something, all right," Mason agreed.

In front of them, Lehman still spouted out orders. "I want five-man teams to spread out, an arm's length apart, scanning every inch of this creek bed. One team on either side. Another team needs to move down along the highway to the next station, then fan out and push north. Meanwhile, another team needs to cover the distance in between."

"It looks like he's been dead for several hours, sir," someone dared to say. "Don't you imagine Bernard has had a good head start by now?"

Lehman's voice filled with rage. "I don't *imagine* anything, Officer. I don't deal in guess work or assumption. I deal in cold, hard facts. I want *proof* that Bernard has moved on. I want every inch of this territory covered. *If* and when—and only then! —will I conclude he's had a head start and left the area. Do I make myself clear?" He roared the last question.

As a detective, Mason stayed with the body. Gil joined one of the search teams, even though they all knew it would be fruitless. Unless they literally stumbled upon Bernard's person, there was no seeing him in this fog.

When he had a moment, Mason excused himself from the two others guarding the murder scene. Lehman's vehicle had already pealed out and headed back toward command.

Stepping aside for some privacy, Mason pulled out his phone.

One of his first thoughts had been of Sara. Mr. Hewlett, too, and Miss Mamie Hutchins. He felt he owed it to all of the residents in harm's way to inform them of this new development, no matter if Lehman liked it or not. It was the right thing to do.

He was surprised to learn he hadn't awakened the dark-haired spitfire. He assumed she was working, until she admitted it was more than just the escaped convict that kept her awake at night. When he questioned her meaning, she clammed up.

But Mason was determined. He was a detective, after all. It was his job to ferret out the truth and find out what people were hiding.

And now, more than ever, he was positive that Sara had something to hide.

# Chapter 20

## Bernard

The luck he had that afternoon carried over into the night.

After killing the lookout post, Thomas Bernard had easily gotten to the other side of the highway. He paused at the creek only long enough to wash the worst of the blood from his hands and the stolen shirt. With the shirt halfway clean, he wadded it up and stuffed it inside the cooler. His stomach had begged him to see what was in the cooler's depth, but his instincts told him not to tarry.

He pushed into the woods, not knowing when the body would be discovered. Even with the advantage of carrying the police radio, he couldn't risk the sound being overheard. He kept it so low he had to strain to hear it. And with all the newfangled electronics and tracking devices these days, he couldn't be certain his movements were covert. For all he knew, they could trace his every step once they realized the lookout was dead and the device missing.

Bernard followed a steady northwest path, seeking a dense thicket to hole up in. Eventually, he would turn east toward the creek, where he knew his scent could be more easily masked.

When he found a thick enough place to hide, Bernard found his way through the brush and the dense undergrowth. Discovering a small patch of worn-down, chewed-down saplings, he sank thankfully against a cushion of pine needles and crushed leaves. From the looks of the pellets he found, his new bed once belonged to a deer.

He listened for movement around him and heard none. He tuned into the radio, going through the channels to make certain he didn't miss any new developments in the search. Most of the suckers were still at the fire, sifting through what was left of the old hay barn and making certain the embers didn't reignite. There was no mention of the murdered volunteer.

Only then did he give in to his empty stomach and see what was inside the cooler. He couldn't believe his luck when he found a veritable feast inside.

A sandwich with thick, hand-cut slices of sugar-cured ham and all the trimmings. A bag of potato chips. A candy bar. Two bottles of water, one Gatorade, and a small thermos of lukewarm coffee. Half of the coffee was already gone, and the rest he gulped down in just a few sips.

He ate the candy bar and chips. The chips were crispy and, at least for now, no one was around to hear the crackle of cellophane packaging. And the candy bar would melt, so he really had no choice. The delectable-looking sandwich would have to wait. With a pout of sorrow, he hid the temptation back inside the cooler, spread the sentry's shirt across it so it would dry out, and drank half a bottle of water.

Bernard ventured out of the thicket to study the lowering sun. He followed its westward trek, judging the best angle to head to ensure he went the opposite direction. He made note of other tree lines and potential thickets. Noted there were no houses, and only one deer stand. He would need to avoid any possible game cameras installed, but it was doable. And as luck would have it, he only saw one herd of cattle grazing in the distance.

Satisfied he had a plan of action, Bernard lay down to rest.

As dusk fell, he heard the radio at his ear crackle. "SO, calling Station 24 West. You doing okay out there, Chuck? Need relief?"

There was just enough daylight left to see the reflective tape across the radio, identifying it as 24 West. Keeping his voice to a nondescript mumble, he replied, "Nah. I'm good."

He hoped the reply bought him a little more time. He guzzled down the rest of the water and found a place further among the trees to relieve his bowels. When he heard a rustle in the bushes behind him, he hoped it was just a disgruntled deer, returning home to find it already occupied.

Satisfied that his luck had held, Bernard took off his prison-issued shirt, ripped the short sleeves from the seams, and put it back on. The plaid shirt was dry enough to wear on top of it, even with its ragged rip and the lingering stain of blood. The front pockets were intact, so he could tuck the last water into one pocket and the radio into the other. He ripped his shirt sleeves into thin strips, making certain some were only an inch or two long. Stuffing them into his pocket, he stepped back out, the stolen gun in hand.

He eased westward, finding the nearest trees. He 'snagged' one strip of his shirt onto a low-lying limb and trampled the ground underneath, staging what looked like a stumbled step. He went further west, repeating his method. This time, he even spared some of his precious water to wash the small strip of material, so that it was relatively white once again. He zigzagged in the woods, coming close to the field of cattle, and staged two more snags of material. He let one float free in the air. As his luck held, he saw moonlight reflect on the strip floating away with the westward breeze.

Bernard found his way back to his hideout, which was no easy feat in the dark. He hadn't heard anything more on the radio, so he chanced getting another night's rest. A light haze of fog had moved in, so between the false leads and the lowered visibility, he reasoned it was a safe risk.

The radio went off a few times, but it wasn't until midnight that he took notice. They were calling for Chuck, asking if he was ready for relief.

Bernard hesitated. Hadn't he answered to that name before? But what if there was another Chuck? He waited for someone else to reply. When no one did, he keyed the mic to brush off the dispatcher's concern.

"Your wife says you aren't answering your cell phone," the dispatcher persisted.

He tried to think of a suitable answer. He wiggled the antenna, hoping the crackle of static would help disguise a voice that clearly wasn't Chuck's. "Battery died," he muttered. "Tell her don't wait up on me."

He knew his time was up. They would be on to him soon. Someone would check on the sentry and find him dead. The search would be on for real, then. He had to move, and he had to move fast.

Bernard pulled the sandwich and the Gatorade from the cooler, replacing them with the radio. Using true control, he ate exactly half of the sandwich. The other half went into his shirt pocket. Cradling the energy drink and the gun in one arm and the cooler in the other, Bernard stepped from his hideout one final time.

He couldn't believe his luck! The fog had intensified, wrapping everything in a swirly haze. The closer to the creek, the thicker the fog would be. Both were in his favor.

When officials discovered the dead body, they would search all around the creek first, even though it would be difficult to see the noses in front of their faces. When they fanned out in other directions, they would eventually find his false trail. And all the while, Bernard would be traveling eastward, back toward Orchard Creek. Again, it would be shrouded in fog, making his task even easier.

Taking a moment to get his bearings in the foggy night, Bernard pointed himself in the eastward direction he had scouted earlier in the day.

With all his might, he flung the cooler and the radio toward the west. Knowing they would scatter and possibly break to pieces. Not knowing where they would land, but hoping it was far enough away to lead his trackers astray.

As the fog swallowed him up, Bernard marveled again as his streak of luck continued.

# Chapter 21

## Sara

Sometime before daylight, Sara drifted off to sleep. She awoke to the sound of dogs barking, but there was no roar of the low-flying helicopter.

Maybe, she thought drowsily, it was a good sign. Maybe they had caught him in the wee hours of the morning.

She had been awake most of the night.

She knew Shawn would call again.

She knew she needed to rest.

Two days ago, she had taken advantage of the police presence and sat outside on her porch. Yet Mason had cautioned her to stay on guard, even now.

With a sigh, Sara turned over and went back to sleep.

By the time she awoke, the murder was all over the news. All over social media.

As Sara made coffee and turned on the television, the constant coverage almost sent her back to the sanctuary of her bed.

She had turned on the TV just in time to catch the live update from the TDCJ spokesman.

"... afternoon, Chuck Dunn, one of our volunteers in this search for Thomas Bernard, was brutally attacked on the side of the road near his look-out station on State Highway 38 West. After what appears to have been a very brief struggle, Mr. Dunn was fatally stabbed in his abdomen. From preliminary reports, we believe a broken beer bottle found nearby was used as the murder weapon. Although it is yet to be confirmed, we are working on the assumption that Thomas Bernard is responsible for Mr. Dunn's death. Chuck Dunn was a very brave and family-oriented man, and we are forever indebted to his service to this community.

"We are also looking into the theory that Bernard set the fire off County Road 149 to serve as a diversion tactic. While resources were busy putting out the grass fire and searching a structure that was destroyed in the blaze, Bernard may have used the opportunity to move nearer to the highway. The attack took place at the bridge crossing over Orchard Creek, approximately nine and a half miles west of here. We believe Bernard then crossed to the north side of State Highway 38 and is headed northwest, presumably toward the interstate.

"Upon discovering Mr. Dunn's body at approximately two a.m. this morning, we immediately launched a search party. Dogs and a helicopter were also called in but due to heavy fog, the helicopter was unable to launch, and the ground search was temporarily suspended. We resumed the search as the fog cleared, but evidence discovered about one hour ago suggests that Bernard is moving in a northwestward direction. We will continue searching the northern stretch of Orchard Creek for much of today but with these new developments, we are more convinced than ever that Bernard is making his way to the interstate. Residents near the Wayside community are urged to use extreme caution as Bernard moves that direction.

"That said, all residents of Apple County, especially those in the grid from the northern section of Orchard Creek over to Wayside, should be on high alert. No gun was recovered from Mr. Dunn's body, leaving us to believe that Bernard is now in possession of at least one, if not more, firearms. Please keep your vehicles and homes locked, stay inside your home as much as possible and avoid trips into town, and don't hesitate to call 9-1-1 if you see or hear anything suspicious.

"I'd like to thank—"

Sara turned off the news, unable to stomach any more. She got it. A monster was on the loose, and they were no closer to finding him now than they were six days ago, when this entire fiasco began. She didn't need to hear it a hundred times to know the danger she was in.

What they didn't tell—what they couldn't tell because, of course, they didn't know—was that she was in double danger. Thomas Bernard, plus Shawn Angelos.

And for the life of her, Sara wasn't certain which was more dangerous.

News of the murder and Bernard's apparent move across the highway left Sara feeling edgy and out of sorts. She put her nervous energy to work, dusting, sweeping, and mopping her entire house. With the massive refrigerator now level, she searched for dust bunnies that could have been hiding alongside the journal.

The only thing she unearthed was a torn-out section of a newspaper. It was an advertisement for a new rotary-style nut harvester, intended to roll over the ground and collect nuts such as pecans, walnuts, and the like. It was similar to the one Sara used now, but cruder. She marveled at the tiny price tag associated with the early prototype, wondering if the improvements made over the past fifty-plus years justified the current, much higher price tag.

She stuck the advertisement on the counter and continued sweeping. Where did all this sand come from? She swept yesterday as the cobbler baked, but she certainly couldn't tell it today. If having company added this much work, Mason may have been the first—and last—person allowed in her kitchen.

The vigorous housework helped dispel some of her energy, but it also left her hungry. She decided that wiping down the cabinet fronts could wait until she ate a bite of lunch.

When she opened the refrigerator, the movement caused a draft, sending the torn-out ad back to the floor. Just before it disappeared under the monstrosity for another few decades, Sara snagged one corner and pulled it free.

"I'll just put you on the front of the old beast, instead of under it," she told the paper smartly, securing it there by a magnet. She tilted her head, studying her handiwork. "I guess it might help if I put it right-side up and not upside-down and backwards."

She started to flip the paper over, but even upside-down, the headline caught her attention. Adjusting it quickly, she saw the article on the other side. It reported more thefts in the area. Thieves had broken into several houses and taken cash only, leaving the electronics, jewelry, and other valuables untouched. There was no date on either side of the torn-out paper, and no way of knowing which side Cora had meant to keep.

The entire time Sara ate, her mind wandered to the piece of paper. Had Cora been interested in the handy nut harvester, or the article about the thefts? Something about it nibbled at her mind, but to be honest, there were a lot of things nibbling away at her sanity. The computer program. The call at 2:22 this morning. The call thirty minutes later. The news of the murder, and that Bernard was now on *her* side of the highway. The way she had become so… familiar with the handsome detective in such a short time. She hadn't allowed a man anywhere near her since Shawn. Yet, yesterday, Mason Burleson had eaten with her at this very table.

Restless again, Sara washed her dishes, took the time to dry and return them to their rightful places, and wiped off the table. She could start on the cabinets, but she should run the computer program one last time.

She decided to read more of Cora's old diary while she waited for the program to run through its paces.

Where was she? Oh, that's right. Cora had delayed her wedding to the respectable Samuel Foote to have one last fling with the questionable "R" character. She quickly found her page and picked up reading where she left off.

*I told R about Samuel's repeated proposal, and that I had finally accepted. R was devastated. He begged me not to go through with it. He said I would never know the lengths he had gone through to be worthy of my hand in marriage. He spoke about hours of back-breaking labor, and the risks he had been willing to take for me.*

*He asked me to give him until the end of the year. He needed to return to Mexico to tell his family goodbye, one last time. He asked me to keep the money safe that he had saved for us, not knowing I had put aside a nice nest egg of my own. He would be back for the money, and for me. There was something so desperate in his voice, something so urgent in his voice, that I couldn't deny his request. I promised I would wait for him.*

*It pains me to admit this, but I didn't exactly call off my wedding to Samuel. I stalled. I told him I would marry him in the new year, but that I needed time after harvest to make the proper wedding plans. His mother offered to help, but I insisted it was something I wanted to do myself. The poor man believed me.*

*The end of the year came and went, and I heard not one word from my true love. It was clear that R wasn't coming back, so there was no reason to continue stalling. Samuel and I set a date.*

*But fate had other plans. I could no longer hide my secret love affair with R. Samuel was furious. He said some horrible things about me. Most were true, but they hurt all the same. He called off the wedding just one week before we were to walk down the aisle. We've not spoken to one another since.*

*I told people I went away on vacation, but that wasn't true. I didn't want to see or speak to another soul during that time. I just wanted to be alone as I rebuilt a new life for myself, one without a man in it. Because if my suspicions were true, R was either dead or in jail. Those were the only things that could have kept him from coming back for me.*

*Georgia was my only friend then. She was a sweetheart, doing all my shopping for me. Getting the supplies I needed. Helping me make my one big splurge, a beautiful bedroom set.*

*If I was starting a new life, I wanted a new setting.*

The telephone rang, jarring Sara from her reading. She grabbed the phone on her desk without conscious thought. Only after hearing the silence on the other end did she realize it was the house phone that rang, and that it was 2:22 in the afternoon.

Sara slammed down the receiver and jerked the cord out of the wall.

She was too upset to read any more of the journal. Besides, the program had finished without any glitches, so she could call and set up a tentative date for Dallas.

With that done, she considered returning to her housecleaning. What she *really* wanted was to walk down to the orchards, but she knew it was out of the question. She settled for a few exercises and a couple of loads of laundry.

She still needed a distraction, so she decided to cook dinner despite the early hour.

Sara always bought the value-size ground beef and split it into portions perfect for a single user. A meatloaf would make good use of the meat she hadn't yet divided and would be enough for several meals. The rest she could separate, wrap well, and put into the freezer.

She wondered, yet again, if Cora had been lonely in the years after her affair with the mysterious R. She had the farm to keep her busy, but hadn't the nights gotten cold? Had she died alone, wondering what her life would have been like if she had made different choices?

An hour and a half later, Sara was still rattled from the phone call. Her hands were unsteady as she ripped open a package of instant potatoes into a serving bowl. They were the add-water only kind, so she ran two cups of water through her coffee pot, poured it over the dehydrated flakes, and stirred. *Voilà*. The perfect side dish for meatloaf.

Her cell phone chirped with a message. It was from Mason.

*If you hear someone knock, it's me.*

Even with the head's up, Sara had her gun handy as she peeked out the window. She put it away before unlocking and opening the door.

"Hey," she said, thinking how tired and haggard he looked. Even with smudges of fatigue beneath his eyes, the day-old growth of his rusty blond beard looked rakishly sexy.

*Not,* she convinced herself, that she noticed. It was merely an observation of how tired he must be.

"Hey." He gave her a hopeful smile. "I couldn't by chance beg a cup of coffee, could I?"

She hesitated just long enough for him to notice. "I can drink it out here on the porch," he offered. "I just need something to keep my eyes open."

In the distance, she heard the dogs barking. Her driveway was once again littered with extra vehicles. Hardly the brief respite the detective clearly needed.

"Would an early dinner work?" she asked.

"Food would be a Godsend," he admitted. For the first time, she noticed how he sagged wearily against her door frame.

She didn't take time to think it through. She just said, "Come on in. Lock the door behind you while I check the meatloaf."

"Meatloaf? I just hit the jackpot!"

"It should be almost ready."

"Can I wash up first?"

She was tempted to say no, that venturing further into her house was too intimate. She kept the thoughts to herself. Not only would that be beyond rude but fruitless. He had already been through her house, searching for intruders and making certain she was safe. How could she possibly say no now?

"You know where it is," she murmured.

By the time Mason joined her in the kitchen, his face was splashed clean, and he looked somewhat more awake. She heard his stomach grumble as he took an appreciative sniff of air.

"When was the last time you ate?" she frowned, setting microwaved green beans beside the bubbling hot meatloaf.

"The sandwich you fed me, plus some of the pear cobbler. It was delicious, by the way."

"And you've been up all night?"

"I caught a couple of hours after I left here, but yeah. I've been up most of the last forty-eight hours or more."

"Sit down and eat," she instructed. She saw the way his eyes lit up, then dimmed. "Don't wait on me. I'll get our drinks."

He didn't wait for further encouragement. "You're sure?" he asked, already pulling out a chair.

"Sure. Tea, or water?"

"Tea. I need all the caffeine I can get."

Mason helped himself to a large portion of the meatloaf. He politely cut a smaller section for Sara and put it on her plate. He was in the process of adding vegetables to their plates when she delivered the drinks.

"You didn't have to fix my plate," she murmured. It was a totally new experience for her. Shawn had never been so thoughtful.

"You didn't have to feed me," Mason replied. The grin returned. "But I'm sure glad you offered."

She gave him a few minutes to shovel in forkfuls of food before she questioned him.

"Any word, yet?" she asked. "I caught the morning update. It sounds like they think he's moving northwest?" There was the unmistakable ring of hope in her voice.

"Possibly."

"You sound... doubtful. Why is that?"

"Bernard is a smart man. By all counts, he's a very cunning criminal. He doesn't make a lot of stupid mistakes."

Sara broke in before he finished. "Then how did he land in prison?"

"I didn't say he *never* makes a mistake. Two of the biggest ones he made was killing a woman with connections to a crime syndicate and trusting the wrong person with sensitive information.

His associate turned on him and helped send him to the pen."

Sara read between the lines of what he hadn't said. "What stupid mistake did he make, or not make, this time?"

Mason paused to weigh his words. "Can I trust you not to share what I'm about to tell you? It hasn't been released to the public yet."

"I think by now you can see that I have little to no contact with the outside world."

He cocked his head in curiosity. "Is that a new thing since Bernard escaped, or your norm?"

"My norm," she admitted with hesitancy. "I like to work without distractions."

"Friends aren't normally considered distractions," he pointed out but not unkindly.

The conversation was getting too personal. Irritation sharpened her voice. "Are you going to tell me, or not?" she asked.

"This goes no further than this table," he reiterated.

"You made that clear."

"The media knows that Bernard stole the lookout's weapon. What they don't know is that he also stole his radio."

"We're talking police radio, not music. Right?"

"Right." He paused to shove another forkful of meatloaf into his mouth.

"You're saying he can keep one step ahead of the search," Sara noted.

"In a way. I remember seeing a cooler beside the lookout when we drove past yesterday afternoon, but—"

"Wait. *That's* the man who was killed?" For some reason, the news surprised her.

Intellectually, she had known he was the lookout over Orchard Creek. Emotionally, it was jarring to think she had actually *seen* the man who was murdered. It made his death that much more real. That much scarier.

"Unfortunately, yes. The thing is, we didn't find the cooler at the scene of the crime. We assume Bernard stole it, along with the gun and the radio."

"And this is important because...?"

"For one thing, if the cooler had food inside it gives him something of substance. More substance gives him more energy. More energy gives him more strength."

"That's true," she murmured thoughtfully. The last thing this monster needed was the strength to murder more people. "The other thing?"

"This is the part the media doesn't know. The cooler was found about a mile northwest of here."

"He emptied it and left it behind?" To her, it seemed logical. Why carry extra weight if it wasn't necessary.

"Maybe. The thing is, he left the radio inside it."

"So, he dropped it." It was an easy enough assumption.

"Maybe." He repeated the sentiment as he savored a bite of mashed potatoes.

Sara frowned, not understanding the note of caution in his voice. "Maybe the law was getting too close. Maybe he needed to cut his losses and move on, unhindered."

Mason offered another, more chilling theory in a quiet voice. "Or maybe he knew the radio could be traced, and he wanted to create a false trail."

"What—What are you saying?"

"Brass seems to think it's a positive sign that he's moving out of the area. They found pieces of clothing on a northwestward trek, supporting that theory."

"But you have trouble with that theory." It was an observation, more than a question.

"They found pieces of his white, prison-issued shirt."

"And?"

"There wasn't a shirt on the lookout when we found him. We assume Bernard stole it. Gash, blood, and all."

Sara drew in a sharp breath at the visual. Mason muttered an apology.

After pushing green beans around her plate with her fork, Sara made an educated guess. "You think Bernard planted false evidence. You think he left a fake trail on purpose."

Mason was impressed with her hypothesizing. "From what I could tell from the pictures, it was one of those lunchbox-style coolers, the kind where the handle slides down the side to expose the contents. The cooler's hinges were severely damaged but not enough for the top to come open completely. The radio was still wedged inside. In my opinion, that much damage couldn't happen from dropping the cooler."

"So how would it happen?"

"Someone could have thrown it."

Sara closed her eyes and nodded, understanding his implications. "In the direction opposite of the way they were headed."

"That's my theory, yes." Mason pushed back his empty plate. "But brass doesn't see it that way. If today's search doesn't turn up something along the creek, they plan to intensify efforts to the northwest."

Sara hated that her voice came out in a squeak. "And abandon this area?"

"Not entirely, but the focus will move further west."

"Like you said, Bernard is cunning. If he set up false leads to lure them westward, then he could, conceivably, be headed back this way."

"He could, but I'm having trouble making sense of the *why*. He could stay in the creek bed to mask his scent, but the creek curves and twists, actually taking it further from any major roadway. His safest bet would be to head northwest and hope to reach the interstate."

"Not being from here, he may not know the creek's path," Sara pointed out.

"I have a gut feeling Bernard didn't just pick this area by chance. He could have easily gone east toward Louisiana."

"But the interstate is closer. It makes sense he would head in that direction."

"I don't know. He sure seems to know exactly where to hide. He's managed to stay under the radar for six days now."

"You think he had inside help."

"It's the most obvious explanation, and one that is definitely being explored."

Sara stood and cleared the table. What was left of the meatloaf wouldn't go far now but, somehow, she didn't mind.

"Why are you telling me this, Mason? Why should you trust me to keep this information to myself? Are you sharing it with my neighbors?"

"I should," he agreed. "I should tell Mr. Hewlett and Miss Mamie. The three of you stand to be in the most danger, as well as anyone else who lives further up the creek."

"From my understanding, there's a big ranch north of here. The owner's house fronts another highway, which leads over to the interstate."

"That's my understanding, as well," Mason agreed. "The only structures between here and there are a few outbuildings."

"So, are you telling my neighbors?" she repeated.

"I'm under orders to keep the details confidential."

Sara turned back to face him. "Yet you broke those orders to tell me. Why?" she asked bluntly.

His solemn gaze met hers. "I'm asking myself that very question."

Sara came back to the table and sat beside him. "I won't tell. You have my word."

He spoke in his deep voice. The one that inspired such blind trust and confidence. "I know that. That's why I told you." Keeping his eyes on hers, Mason reached out and touched her hand.

After her initial start, Sara sat unmoving, allowing him to maintain contact. Welcoming a man's touch seemed so foreign to her, no matter how innocent.

"One day, Sara Jennings," he told her quietly, "I'd like to get to know you better." He saw the flash of fear in her eyes, and the way she started to jerk her hand back. "But for now," he continued, injecting a professional note into his voice, "my job is to keep you safe. I don't agree with my higher-ups and their strategy, but I'm not in a position to challenge them. All I can do is stay alert and refuse to let my guard down. I have no intentions of abandoning the search in this area, official or not."

When he removed his hand from hers, she felt oddly lost. She quickly tucked both hands into her lap. "You still haven't answered my question. Why not tell my two nearest neighbors?"

"You want an honest answer?"

"Of course."

Mason chose his words carefully. "It's not that I don't trust them. True, they have more opportunity to let secrets slip than you do, seeing that both of them are very social people. But that social circle also means... they have a better support system than you do. I'm sure they have friends who check on them frequently, who are familiar and aware of their comings and goings."

Sara bristled. "And you're saying I don't have that?"

"I'm willing to bet my life on it," he told her, matter of fact. His voice softened as he said, "The thing is, I'm not willing to bet *your* life on it."

His statement left her speechless, so Mason continued.

"I'm taking it upon myself to be the one to look in on you. The one to keep track of your comings and goings. Since you don't have your own support system, I'll be it."

He knew she was a private person. He knew that hearing such a proclamation overwhelmed her. She was unaccustomed to depending upon others. Most likely, she was unaccustomed to having people care about her, too. Knowing that he appointed himself as her support system probably embarrassed her.

Mason knew, too, that it was time for him to leave. He pushed back from the table.

"Sara, that meatloaf was delicious. You're quite the cook, and I appreciate your generosity. It would be easy to make this a habit, but I'll do my best not to take advantage of your cooking skills."

"It seems like the least I can do." Not quite an afterthought, she added softly, "Considering."

"Still, it was exactly what I needed to keep me going."

"What about that coffee? Do you still want a cup?"

He glanced at his wristwatch. "Yes, but I really should go. Do you have a to-go cup?"

Sara opened a cabinet door and pulled out a travel mug.

"You don't have a paper cup? I'd hate to take a good, insulated mug."

"You can bring it back. If you don't, it's no big deal. I have plenty." She didn't point out that it was a promotional item, imprinted with her *SJ Innovations* logo.

The coffee took only minutes to brew in her Keurig machine. In no time, Sara fastened the top and handed him the insulated mug.

"Thanks again for dinner."

Sara trailed behind him toward the door. "Thanks again for giving me an update. Especially an off-the-record update."

"The thing is," Mason said, turning to face her, "I think Bernard set law enforcement up, and top brass has fallen for the bait. I don't plan to be lured in so easily, and I don't want you, or anyone else, to have a false sense of security. Not while that monster is still out there."

"I'll keep my guard up," Sara assured him.

Mason believed her. If anyone was guarded, it was Sara Jennings.

As he reached to unlatch the locks, he made a casual comment. "You can still hear the dogs barking in the distance. It would stand to reason that your own dogs might bark in response, don't you think?"

Understanding the covert message, Sara inclined her head. "*Touché*."

Mason stepped out onto the porch. "One more thing," he said. "There's a possible storm headed this way. Some sudden development down in the Gulf that could bring rain and lightning our way. The rain would be particularly bad because it could hinder the search for Bernard. Wash away what little traces we have, real or not."

"That's not good," she murmured.

He thought she meant about the rain. But she meant the storm itself.

Sara hated storms.

# Chapter 22

## Sara

Mason was almost to his truck when she hit the button on her SJ's Big Dogs device. She saw his half smile as he turned his head back toward her. She let it cycle a second time and made a point to repeat it again later in the evening.

In the meantime, she watched the local news. The latest press conference spoke of the continuing search underway in two distinct areas of interest. The prison spokesperson parceled out a few more details surrounding Chuck Dunn's life and death, offering a timeline of how and when things happened.

Now that she knew what to listen for, Sara could tell how he skirted around most issues, offering only partial truths and incomplete theories. No mention was made of the stolen cooler, the trail of white snips of material, or of the missing police radio.

As a rerun of her favorite game show came on, Sara's mind wasn't on which suitcase held the coveted million dollars. She was thinking of the events over the past twenty-four-plus hours.

Was it only yesterday that she had gone into town?

Only yesterday that the news reporter had captured her face on film and splashed it all over national television?

Only since 2:22 this morning that her worst nightmares had been confirmed—that Shawn had located her yet again?

Was it all within twenty-four plus hours ago that Bernard set the fire, murdered a lookout, and made his daring move across State Highway 38?

Had she invited Mason to sit at her table not once, but twice, within a day's time?

Had her entire life changed irrevocably over a course of so few hours?

The answer was obvious.

Yes.

It was one of life's hallmarks. A single event, catastrophic or miraculous, could change a person's world forever.

This may not have been a single event, but it all happened in a single day. And Sara knew her life would never go back to the way it had been before.

Was this how Cora had felt all those years ago, Sara wondered. Her last diary entries had been about resigning herself to a new fate. Her dream of a life with R was shattered. Even her business alliance and arranged marriage to Samuel was ruined. She was forced to start over with a new plan for her life.

Something about those last entries still bothered Sara. What had Cora meant when she wrote *'if my suspicions were true, R was either dead or in jail?'*

Her interest piqued, Sara went to her office and searched for local thefts that had taken place during the 1960s and 70s. She found several hits. The decade-long string of crimes was one of the few criminal acts to go unsolved in Apple County.

One theory had it as the work of traveling hippies. During the late 60s and early 70s—the very years the thefts took place—hippies were a big thing, even in a small community like theirs. Hippies were known for their nomadic lifestyles and noncompliance to tradition. Wild and free, they claimed. Living off the land and brotherly love. In reality, nothing in life was ever free, including the drugs they openly embraced. Many people believed hippies traveled through the area undetected, except for these nefarious forays into town.

With the spike of inflation during those same years, yet another theory—one much less popular and therefore one seldom explored—was that money-strapped merchants and homeowners took advantage of insurance policies by making falsified claims. After one had successfully pulled it off, others followed suit. Soon, it had become a 'wave' of unexplained crimes that were *expected* to happen each year.

Sara frowned as she read the various theories. None made sense to her, so she worked on one of her own. She studied the dates, comparing them to some of the entries in Cora's journal.

In the late summer of 1966, *Mercer's Dry Goods* was broken into. Thieves took clothes, a locket, pencils and notebooks, and possibly some candy.

In one of her early entries, Cora wrote of a romantic picnic with her beloved. He bought her a hair comb and a box of candy.

Another time, he brought her a thoughtful gift of pencils and pens, tied with ribbon. A book she used to hold her recipes. A necklace of some sort, one never described in detail. Had it been a locket?

The mysterious R was a migrant worker. Had he dressed in his work clothes on their romantic ventures? Or had he stolen more suitable clothing to wear when wooing the boss' daughter?

Then there was the matter of all that cash. He brought it to Cora for safekeeping, but where had it come from? He claimed he worked extra hours and saved every penny he made, building a nest egg for their future. Did migrant workers make that much money, particularly if they were in the States illegally?

Cora seldom listed complete dates in her journal, but when Sara checked the dates in the newspapers with the timelines in the diary, the two seemed intertwined. Money was reported stolen in a mechanic shop in Bonnie. R had shown up with the first proof of his worth. Money was taken from a gas station in Jonestown. R delivered a stash of cash for Cora to tuck away.

Another search told Sara that the rotary nut roller, as shown in the advertisement she found, was patented in 1971. She wasn't sure when the device hit the shelves, but the flip side of the torn-out ad told of local homes being hit by thieves searching for cash.

In 1972, the biggest theft of all took place. Apple's only grocery store was broken into just prior to making their weekly deposit. In one of Cora's latter entries, she wrote of a duffel bag filled with cash.

Was R the thief? Was that what Cora meant by 'her suspicions?'

Was that why R never returned? Had he been thrown in prison for his crimes? Nothing was reported in *The Apple's Core* about it, but perhaps, if he were indeed a citizen of Mexico, the arrest had taken place there. If not for these crimes, perhaps for ones committed on that side of the border.

It was a reasonable assumption. And it would explain why he never returned for the cash. Or for Cora.

Sara felt sorry for the woman who had lived here before her. From all accounts, she truly loved R and believed he would come back for her. When he didn't, she must have been devastated. She said as much in her diary. She just wanted to be alone during that painful period of her life. She needed solitude while building a new life for herself. Her only friend had been Georgia, whoever that was.

The *one big splurge* explained the bedroom set that now occupied Sara's guest room. Apparently, it had been Cora's consolation present to herself. Perhaps she spent some of her own savings. Perhaps she had dipped into R's pilfered stash. Either way, she saw it as a new setting for a new life. That's why it didn't match any of the other furniture, or even the style of the house itself. Cora's splurge had been a feminine bedroom set for a woman who worked as hard as any man.

Sara hit her Big Dogs button again as darkness settled in for the evening. She thought she heard a rumble of thunder in the distance, so she hit the button again, and then again. She would do anything to drown out the sound of an approaching storm, especially at night.

Closing her mind to her own troubles, Sara concentrated on Cora's.

At the end of her life, as she died here in this very house and most likely in her four-poster bed, had she wondered about 'what if?'

What if she had married Samuel as planned? Would she have been happy or miserable?

What if R had come back for her? Would their future have been as rosy as they believed, or would reality have painted a different picture?

The truth was no one ever knew what their lives would have been like on the path not chosen.

Sara tried distracting her mind as she prepared for bed. She hummed a tune as she arranged her gun, flashlight, and cell phone on the bed beside her. She tucked the covers in tight around her, determined to get a good night's sleep.

With the house phone unplugged, she wouldn't be disturbed again at 2:22.

But as she drifted off to sleep, her own 'what ifs' haunted her mind.

What if she had never gone clubbing that night with the guys? What if she had worn something less flashy?

What if she had never gotten involved with Shawn?

What if she had never married him and hadn't discovered the dark, evil side of the basketball star?

If only she could go back and undo the past...

It was storming in her dream. A wet, stormy Friday night. One she would never forget, no matter how hard she tried. It lived everlasting in her nightmares.

Sara—or, at that time, Bridgette—had just gotten home from work. It had been a late evening at the office, finishing up work on a big project, so she called Shawn to tell him to eat without her. She would pick up something along the way.

How was she to know the boss would order in an elaborate meal? Or that it would include a fully stocked bar to help celebrate completion of a job well done? How was she to know she would be one of the last to leave and that Shawn, her ever suspicious and highly jealous husband, waited for her outside the parking lot? How was she to know he misread the mostly empty parking spaces and the way her boss walked her out, offering to share his umbrella with her?

Driving home, the rain fell heavier, and visibility grew lower. Bridgette got stuck behind a minor wreck on the highway.

Shawn made it back home long before she did. His fast, reckless driving was the stuff of legends gone wrong.

By the time she sloshed her way up to the apartment where they lived, soaked to the bone and teeth chattering, he had worked himself into a full rage. A drunken, righteous fit of anger fueled by insecurity and possessiveness. A typical Shawn reaction to anything that involved Bridgette and her career, particularly when her boss was involved.

The lights flickered as she opened the door. Or maybe it was a jagged flash of lightning. The storm was getting worse, and the radio warned of possible power outages.

"Just what I need," Bridgette muttered, kicking off her rain-soaked shoes at the door.

The flash came again, but this time it came from *inside* her head, if that were even possible. But as she fell to the floor, blindsided by the force of Shawn's punch, she knew it wasn't only possible, but happening.

"How dare you! How dare you cheat on me!" he bellowed. For good measure, he kicked her while she was down, all the while hurling horrible names at her. Accusing her of all sorts of sultry acts. Belittling her. Taunting her. Kicking her again.

"Shawn! Shawn, stop it!" she shrieked, managing to scuttle backwards away from him.

He was so drunk that when he attempted to kick her a third time, his feet flew out from beneath him, and he landed on his butt. The pain only made him that much angrier.

"Where are you going?" he demanded. "I'm not done with you! But when I am, you'll regret the day you ever dared cross Shawn Angelos."

"I—I didn't cross you, Shawn! I don't even know what you're talking about." She tried pulling herself to her feet, but the hems of her pants were slick. With rain or blood, she wasn't sure, but she knew if she stayed down here any longer, he would surely kill her.

She made another attempt to stand, only to have him reach out a hand and snag her ankle. "Stay down, b—"

She kicked his hand away, surprising him into temporary silence.

Above them, the storm raged, and the lights flickered. As the apartment plunged into darkness, Bridgette scrambled to her feet. Holding in a whimper, she felt her way along the wall. Everything around her was pitch black. She couldn't see where she was going, but she knew she was headed in the wrong direction. The door was the other way. *Behind* Shawn.

She only had two choices. The bedroom, where she could barricade herself inside until he kicked the door down. He had done it before, and he would do it again. Or she could try to make it out onto the patio, and...

And, what? They lived on the twelfth floor. On an ordinary night and without the pelting rain, she could maybe, *perhaps* maybe... climb over the railings to the adjacent patio and beg their neighbors for sanctuary. *If* they were home. And if they were willing to get involved. This was hardly the first time Shawn had flown into a rage.

But on a night like this? She wasn't sure she could manage anything in this tumultuous downpour. Not in the pitch dark. Not with the only lights she saw being the ones zigzagging in her head. Not in this much pain.

"You want to go outside?"

His hot breath came out of nowhere, heavy against her face. The vile odor of stale booze and heavy garlic, combined with the pain in her throbbing head and her bruised body, made her want to vomit. It was all Bridgette could do not to gag.

"Good idea," Shawn said, as if she had answered. "Let's go outside." He grabbed her roughly by the arm and hauled her toward the sliding glass door.

"N—No, Shawn. It's pouring outside."

"You didn't seem to mind it earlier, when you were outside with your lover!" he spat.

"What—I don't even know what you're talking about."

"I was there! I saw you with him, huddled beneath his umbrella like two lovers walking in the rain! You said you were working late, but you lied!" In his drunken state, he had trouble unlatching the fastener on the door.

"We *were* working late. The entire team. You can ask Laura. Or—Or Louisa. We were all there."

"I only saw the two of you!"

"I had to go back in and turn off the lights. I was one of the last ones to leave, but I swear, we were all there."

"Liar! You were there, alone, with *him*! I can smell the wine on your breath, you lying, conniving bitch!" He finally managed to get the door open. A cold swoosh of blowing rain swept into the apartment.

"Kelvin catered a meal for us. For all of us. To celebrate a job well done."

"You're lying! He catered a meal for the two of you. I. Was. There." With each word, his face came closer to hers, until she was tempted to bite that slightly hooked nose of his. Long before now, she had decided that Shawn was no longer a good-looking man. Liquor and despair had soured everything that had ever been good about his life. "I saw you! I saw you with my own two eyes!"

He twisted her onto the patio, forcing her out into the cold, relentless rain. When her foot slipped on the wet tile, he trampled it as he half-pushed, half-carried her closer to the rail.

"Say it, Bridgette!" he demanded. "Admit you're having an affair with your boss!"

"B—But I'm not! I'm not!"

"Then what you took so long to get home?" he demanded.

It was hard to talk with his hand holding her by the throat. He used it as leverage, pushing her back against the railing as they both struggled against the blowing rain. "I—There—There was a wreck. Shawn! Shawn, you're ch—choking me!"

"Need a drink of water?" he sneered. His hand slid upward, forcing her chin toward the sky. He slammed his body up against hers so she couldn't move. Then he used some unknown pressure point—or maybe it was just raw strength, she thought in a daze—to force her mouth open. She couldn't even bite down. She couldn't close her mouth. The rain poured into it and straight down her throat, choking her in a different way.

Her beg for mercy came out as a gurgle.

Below them, the city was in a state of confusion. Traffic lights were out. Streetlights flickered with bursts of battery-powered backup. Somewhere up the block, a transformer blew, sending sparks into the inky night sky. The rain continued to sluice down, filling Bridgette's mouth with more water than she could swallow. Very soon, she would drown there on the patio, forced upright by her husband's unrelenting body as he held her mouth open.

She teetered on the verge of collapse. When her knees gave way, the sudden change of position loosened Shawn's vicious grip. He pulled back then, allowing her to collapse on the patio floor.

Lightning flashed across the dark night sky.

Thunder rolled, ushering in fresh gusts of wind and rain. Horns blared and brakes locked up, screeching their protest.

Bridgette was oblivious to it all. Her lungs had too much water and not enough air. She coughed and gagged and desperately fought to breathe. Driving rain plastered her clothes to her skin. When she finally gagged to the point of emptying her stomach onto the patio tile, Shawn gave her a disgusted kick and turned his back on her.

He locked the door and left her there for the night.

When the neighbors saw her there the next morning, huddled into a sorrowful ball in one corner of the patio, she was unconscious. The ambulance rushed her to the hospital, where she was treated for contusions to the neck and throat, a concussion, two cracked ribs, a sprained ankle, and pneumonia.

When she was released from the hospital three days later, Bridgette filed for divorce. She never returned to the condo or to the life she had once shared with Shawn.

And to this day, she could barely tolerate the sound of a storm.

Sara awoke with a start. A noise had penetrated the nightmare, bringing her back from the other side. She hated it there. The place that was a dream, and yet not. A place she remembered all too well. A place she only went in her subconscious, because facing the demons of her past when wide awake was unbearable.

She lay there for several minutes, willing herself to breathe normally. Straining to hear whatever it was that woke her. Searching the murky shadows for any sign of movement.

The only thing she saw was the flash of lightning outside her window.

She heard the thunder then. A low rumble that built into a shuddering crescendo.

That's when the nightmare truly began.

# Chapter 23

## Bernard

The fog had been a lifesaver. He knew a helicopter couldn't fly in such low visibility. The dogs may not have been hindered by the weather, but their handlers were. Most likely, the search would be suspended until the fog cleared.

It took him longer to make the eastward swing than it would have on a clear night, but that was fine. He had plenty of time. If he arrived at the creek too early, the dogs would be there. He needed to wait them out, even if it cost him most of the day. He just needed somewhere to hide when he got closer to the creek.

Finding the deer stand proved Lady Luck was still with him. It offered a safe haven, and with a view, to boot. From up there, he could see for long distances in all directions.

Bernard used his stolen knife to cut several cedar boughs from nearby trees, careful that the shorn nubs weren't easily visible. He swept the area around him with the boughs, littering the ground here and there with aromatic shavings. If the hounds should make it this far, the strong smell of freshly cut cedar would knock them off his scent.

Bernard climbed the ladder and checked the stand for varmints. With the coast clear, he crawled inside and proceeded to smear the window openings with sticky cedar sap. The smell was stout, and the prickly stems made him itch, but it was a small price to pay for avoiding the hounds. He even left the last bough in the stand with him. As the scent dissipated, he could always slice off more shavings.

Feeling confident, Bernard pulled out the other half of his sandwich.

With the fog cleared and the sun out, there was nothing else to do now but take a nap and wait.

The distant sound of running dogs stirred him awake. Bernard reached for the gun and prepared for what may come.

Nothing did.

The dogs were far away and heading west. No search teams moved noisily in the woods or crossed the empty fields. The fools had fallen for his red herring. While they ran off in the opposite direction, finding the false clues he planted, Bernard would head back to the one place they would never look for him.

He could smell rain in the air. Clouds rolled in and bunched into dense clusters, the bottoms dark and heavy with moisture.

A heavy sprinkle dotted the dirt around the deer stand and pinged against its tin roof. Dusk was moving in fast, along with a storm.

He left the empty bottle from the energy drink behind as he crawled from the stand and down the ladder. He returned to the cedars to do his business, hunched his shoulders as the sprinkle turned into a true rain, and continued his journey to Orchard Creek.

The building thunderstorm was another stroke of incredible luck. The sky darkened and thick clouds rode in on a low rumble of thunder. Lightning flickered in the distance. The storm provided him with the perfect cover.

If he got out of this alive—and he always did—Bernard would buy a lottery ticket. With the streak he had going, he would surely hit the jackpot.

Jagged streaks of lightning illuminated his path as he drew nearer. It was almost too easy.

He found the window with no problem. He waited for the next roll of thunder before he eased the window up and climbed over the sash. He landed with more of a thud than he intended, but Bernard hoped the noisy storm masked the sound.

Bernard closed the window as he waited for his eyes to adjust. Once he could see through the murky darkness, he moved through the door to the left. The first thing he saw was the bathroom.

He eyed the facilities and listened to the raging storm around him.

*Why not?* he thought, shrugging to himself. The storm would hide any sounds he made.

He knew the only occupied bedroom was on the opposite side of the house. He could lock the bathroom door, take a quick shower to warm up, and sit on an actual toilet for a change. It was too sweet of a deal to pass up.

And if the dame woke up and found him... well, he still had the gun.

Man, he *definitely* needed to play the lottery when this was over.

# Chapter 24

## Sara

The storm played tricks on Sara's mind. She thought she heard noises in the house. Thought she heard the creak of the refrigerator's monstrous door as it defied aged metal hinges. Thought she heard the slightest rattle of... something.

Must be the windows, she decided. The glass panes rattled in tune with the thunder's raging melody. She was safe and warm—dry—in the cozy haven of her bed. There was nothing to be afraid of.

Somewhere around early dawn, Sara stirred.

It wasn't a sound that woke her. It was a sense.

A sense of someone nearby. A sense of someone watching her.

At some point during the night, she had turned over, putting her back to her phone. And to her gun.

Sara moved slowly, hoping not to call attention to herself. She raised her head just enough to look toward the door. Shadows made it impossible to see into the hallway or her office beyond.

Her eyes shifted to the window in front of her. Still closed. The curtain undisturbed.

The other window was to her back but was too narrow for a person to crawl through. She hoped.

Trepidation tempered any sense of confidence she felt. She couldn't shake the feeling of being watched.

Pretending to be asleep, Sara mumbled incoherently as she rolled to her back. Her fingers skimmed the covers for her gun.

"Looking for this?" a man's voice asked.

With a screech, Sara scrambled into a sitting position, pressing backward against the headboard. A man sat in her reading chair with one leg crossed over the opposite knee, casually twirling her pistol. In the weak morning light, it was difficult to see details, but she knew he was too short and wiry to be Shawn.

"Who—Who are you?" she demanded.

"Really?" he scoffed. "You have no idea who I am? I thought my name would be plastered on every television and every newspaper in the nation by now. Not to mention social media."

"You—You're Bernard." Her breathless statement wasn't a question.

"That's right. Thomas Ramon Bernard." He said his middle name with a flourish, rolling his 'r's.

"Why are you here? What do you want?" She pulled the covers up to her chin, as if the fluffy linens could somehow protect her.

"Want? I want a lot of things. Helped myself to some of them," he boasted. "A nice hot shower. A sandwich. That was some mighty tasty meatloaf, by the way. You make it?"

Sara nodded. Her voice had escaped her.

"Good. You can make me another one."

"No."

He stopped the gun at mid-twirl. Faster than Sara could blink, he pointed the barrel directly at her. "What did you just say to me?"

"I—I'm out of ground meat," she lied.

"Then make me something else." He said it as a challenge.

Sara made no comment. Her mind raced, searching for a way of escape. If she could reach another gun... Or her phone...

She slid her hand beneath the comforter, trying to find her cell phone. Maybe he hadn't seen it when he took the gun. Maybe she could send a text to Mason or dial 911.

"We could always call and order delivery," her uninvited guest suggested. He waved something in his other hand. The movement activated her cell phone screen, casting light across his sneering face.

He looked meaner in person.

"I didn't make coffee," he went on, almost conversationally. "Didn't want the smell waking you. But you're awake now, so you can do the honors."

"I need to get dressed." Anything to stall.

Bernard disagreed. "You'll be fine just like that."

He flipped the lights on without warning. He must have swiped the remote control from her nightstand when he took her gun. After the initial burst of blindness, Sara's eyes adjusted to the bright light.

She darted her gaze toward the door.

Bernard's gruff tone held the same warning as his words. "Don't even think about it." He waved the gun. "Get up."

Sara was slow to rise. Was there nothing she could use as a weapon? She pushed her feet into the slip-ons she kept at the side of her bed, her eyes still looking for something, anything, to help her escape.

The box of tissues wouldn't help.

Unless she could make him choke on a cough drop, those were just as useless.

The tube of lip balm was a possibility if she got close enough to stab him in the eye with it. Sara palmed it, just in case.

"You don't need that."

At his sharp comment, she put the tube back on her nightstand. She hadn't relished getting that close to the man, anyway.

"Quit stalling," he growled, "and make me some coffee."

She could find a better weapon in the kitchen. That's where the knives were and where she kept her Hellcat 9mm. Without an objection, Sara started that way.

"Don't try anything funny. I have a gun pointed at your back. Try to make a run for it, and I'll drop you in your tracks."

She had no doubt of that fact. She noticed the way his plaid shirt hung on his slender frame. The dark stain around a jagged rip confirmed this was the shirt he had taken from the slain sentry. It still looked damp from last night's storm.

She realized then that the rain had stopped. Weak morning light pushed through her kitchen curtains and promised a sunny day ahead.

Bernard's gun on her back promised only darkness.

"I like it strong," he said. "With bacon and eggs."

*Now she had to cook for the man?* The thought galled her, but it bought her extra time. Sara moved to the monstrous old refrigerator to gather ingredients.

"If I feed you, will you leave?" she asked.

Bernard made a show of looking around the kitchen and to the dining room beyond. "I don't know," he said whimsically, "this place is awfully cozy. Sorta feels like I was meant to be here. I may just decide to stay."

"They'll catch you, you know."

"They haven't yet."

She couldn't argue that fact. Day Seven, and he was still on the loose. Not only had he eluded officials for a full week and moved about at will, but he had murdered a man and was now seated at her kitchen table.

Absorbing the enormity of it all, Sara felt lightheaded as she moved to the stove.

"Fried," he instructed her. "They don't give you that in prison. They give you that fake scrambled crap and don't even season it. I like mine with lots of black pepper."

Sara worked on autopilot. She started to microwave the precooked bacon but decided against it. If she could swing the skillet hard enough, there was a chance of knocking him unconscious. It would still be hot from the burner, and there would be grease left from the bacon, even after frying the eggs.

It could work.

Bernard was one step ahead of her. "Put it on a plate. Leave the skillet on the stove."

Mason was right. The man was smart and just cunning enough to predict her every move.

"Leave the plate where it is," he instructed, "and sit in this chair."

Sara did as told. She watched as he produced a length of thin rope and a roll of duct tape. She kept tape in her laundry room, but she only remembered having rope in her shed.

"Put your hands behind your back. On the outside of the rails."

After tying her to the chair with rope, Bernard poured himself more coffee and brought his plate to the table. He then shoveled in two fried eggs and four slices of bacon like he hadn't eaten in days. Which, she considered, he probably hadn't, except for the meatloaf sandwich he had a few hours ago.

Sara tried to ignore his sloppy eating habits as she contrived ways to get away.

"I need to use the restroom," she said abruptly.

"Wait until I finish my coffee."

"But I need to go now."

"I said to wait."

While he noisily slurped his coffee and used his finger to sop up the last drop of yellowy yoke, Sara squirmed in her chair. "I really need to go."

The squirm was real. She hadn't used the restroom since last night.

"When I finish, you can use the john in the back."

So much for her hopes of crawling out the window. Only a child could squeeze through the tiny square in the utility room bath.

Which, apparently, he knew, meaning he had roamed through her house while she slept.

"And don't think about escaping. There's nothing in there you can use as a weapon," he told her. "I checked."

He took his time before standing, rubbing his belly with satisfaction and stretching both arms above him. Already, Sara's arms ached from the awkward position hers were in.

Just when she thought it would be too late, he came around to untie her. "You can close the door," he said, nudging her toward the small bathroom with the gun, "but if you don't answer when I knock, I'll shoot my way in. And don't think I won't."

Sara took care of business before doing her own search.

He was right. There was absolutely nothing she could use. The best she could do was spray air freshener in his eyes and make a run for it. If she wasn't fast enough to get away, she knew he would make good on his threat to shoot her.

For now, she had to go along with him, the same way she used to go along with Shawn. The secret was letting him believe he was in control.

Bernard was waiting for her as she came out.

"Back in there," he said, motioning to the kitchen. He once again secured her to the chair. This time, he used the duct tape.

"I'm going to ask you a question," he told her, "and you'd better answer the right way. If you don't..." The gun he waved under her nose finished his sentence for him. "*Comprende*?"

Sara nodded.

"Where's the loose floorboard?"

The bizarre question took her by total surprise. "Excuse me? The loose *what*?"

"Floorboard." He tapped his foot against the wooden plank at his feet. "A loose floorboard. Tell me where it is."

It sounded like he had a loose screw, not a loose board. "I have no idea," she said with a puzzled frown.

"Wrong answer." He jerked one of her shoulders further back and taped it to stay in place.

"It—It's the only one I have!" Sara protested. "I don't know what you're talking about."

He jerked on the other shoulder, making her position even more awkward. The pain shot all the way to her lower back.

"I'm talking about one of these. Right. Here." He kicked his heel against a board, his voice harsh. "One's not nailed down good."

"They told me the foundation was solid when I bought the house."

"When did you buy it?"

"Last year."

"What about the old hag you bought it from?"

"I bought it from a real estate agent. A—A man."

"What about the woman who owned it before you?"

"Cora Miller? I never met her." Even though pain shot through her like sharp needles, she felt the need to defend the woman she only knew through journal entries. "But she kept the house and the farm well-maintained. If there was a loose board, I'm sure she took care of it."

Bernard's face turned dark. "Don't make me rip them all up. Tell me where the loose board is!" He kicked the leg of the chair, jarring her enough to make her cry out in pain.

"I told you! I have no idea."

Bernard studied her for a moment. "Maybe you're right," he murmured thoughtfully. He shifted his gaze to the room behind her, studying its walls. Before sheetrock, there had only been wooden boards. "Maybe I had it wrong. Maybe it's a board on the *wall*, not the floor." He returned his eyes to hers. "Where is it?"

"Where is what?"

"The loose board!"

"There's not a loose board."

"You're lying."

"Why would I do that?"

His dark eyes glittered with malice. "Maybe you have a death wish."

She truly believed dying by Bernard's bullet would be preferable to dying by any of Shawn's twisted means. But she couldn't tell him that, or else he wouldn't believe he had the upper hand.

At this point, neither of them had much to lose.

"I just don't know what my walls have to do with you being here."

"There's a loose board somewhere in this house. There's something behind it that belongs to me."

"What is it?"

"I'm the one asking the questions," Bernard raked out. "Not you."

"If I help you find it, *then* will you leave?"

He gave her a smile that was as chilling as it was disgusting. He had horrible dental hygiene. "Scout's honor."

It went without saying that he was no scout. And they both knew that when he left, he would leave her body lying in a pool of her own blood.

But with nothing to lose, Sara pretended to believe him.

"If you untie me, I'll help you find it."

"Do you think I'm an idiot?" He grabbed a fistful of her hair, yanking her head upward. "Is that what you think?"

"N—No."

"Then what do you think?"

"That you're hurting me!"

"That's only the beginning, little girl." His smile scared her more than his words. He appeared to enjoy every minute of his sick little game. "Unless you tell me where the loose board is, I'll rip every piece of hair out of your head." A quick tug plucked a dozen strands free. "By the roots," he added, tossing the wad of dark hair into her face.

Tears stung her eyes, but Sara didn't cry out. She wouldn't give him the satisfaction.

"I don't know where it is," she told him.

"Then we'll start in there," Bernard decided, motioning toward the dining room. "Move."

"You'll need to untie me."

Bernard's mouth twisted with his version of a smile. "No," he countered slowly, "I don't."

It was a slow, torturous journey. Sara waddled her way into the adjoining room, bent at the waist, toting a chair on her back with her hands still tied behind her. The effort left her huffing for breath.

When she straightened her aching back, gravity jerked her down. She landed with a thud. For one terrifying moment, she thought she would topple over backward. Eyes closed, Sara took a moment to gather her thoughts.

Opening her eyes, she saw the tools on her dining room table.

Sometime in the wee hours of morn, while Sara was caught between a raging dream and a raging storm, Bernard had been a busy man. He had raided her tool shed, finding a hammer and a small crowbar.

To her horror, he took the crowbar in his hand and turned to the wall in front of her.

"Is it this board?" Bernard asked. He slammed one end of the crowbar against the white-washed board. A picture on the wall trembled.

He moved to the board below it. "Or is it this one? Or maybe this one?"

The crowbar left small indentions in the first two boards.

The third board cracked.

Sara cringed with each bash. The framed print toppled down. Shards of glass littered the floor, crunching beneath Bernard's booted feet as he moved along the wall. The boards refused to give beneath his angry punch.

He moved to the next wall.

"Maybe *this* will be faster." He held up the crowbar's forked end.

Nails groaned beneath the strain. After decades of being buried in the studs, they wouldn't release without a fight. The board was the first to give, popping in half and catching Bernard by surprise. He staggered backward, before taking his anger out on the remaining jagged edges.

He attacked a second board.

"W—Wait!" Sara called out.

He turned to her with a sneer. "Suddenly remember something, little girl?" he goaded.

"You're looking in the wrong place."

Malice glittered in his dark eyes. He stalked toward her, the crowbar raised. "You've been holding out on me? You know where it is, and you lied to me?"

"No. I don't know anything about a loose board."

"Then how do you know I'm in the wrong place?" He held the crowbar higher, poised to strike.

"Logic."

"You think you're so smart, do you?" He used the back of his hand to slap Sara across the face. Hard.

Sara tasted blood on her lips. Stars erupted behind her eyes, but she held the tears at bay. Her refusal to cry always infuriated Shawn.

"Tell me!" he demanded. "Tell me what your so-called logic is."

She tried speaking, but nothing came out. It hurt to open her mouth. She ran her tongue along her teeth, swearing he knocked some of them loose. Unable to use her hands, Sara swiped blood and drool against the crumbled t-shirt she had slept in.

After clearing her throat, she managed to say, "Too high."

Through her peripheral vision, she saw him whirl around and slam his crowbar into a board near his knee. The entire wall shook.

"Here?" he leered.

Sara dipped her pounding head, nodding to the floor. "Lower."

He glared at her. To be such a smart and cunning man, he obviously hadn't considered the laws of gravity.

"You could save us both a lot of grief if you'd just. Tell. Me. The. Truth. Where is the loose board? Which room?"

"I. Don't. Know."

Bernard came closer, focusing on her knees. "Do you know what it feels like to have a kneecap bashed in by a crowbar?"

"N—No." In spite of herself, Sara's voice wavered.

"You're about to find out. I'm giving you one last chance. Tell me where the board is, or I'll start with your knee, and then I'll tear out every single board in this house."

Sara had to wipe away another mouthful of blood. Her chin lifted. "I can't tell," she said with deliberate slowness, "what I don't know."

From the depths of Bernard's pocket, Sara's cell phone rang. He pulled it out to see the screen.

"You have a man?" he asked, turning it so she could see Mason's name scrolling across the top.

She evaded his question. “I should answer. If I don’t, he’ll come to check on me.”

The look Bernard gave her was one degree below chilling.

“And when he does,” he told her, “I’ll blow your brains out.”

# Chapter 25

## Sara

Sara recoiled from his harsh words. The look in his eyes told her he meant them.

"We'll take our chances," Bernard said, silencing the call and stuffing the phone back into his pocket. "Tell me what you know about this house."

The question took her by surprise.

"Uhm, typical farmhouse." She cleared her throat and tasted blood. Her brain still quivered from the force of his blow. It took a moment to recall simple details. "Four bedrooms. Built in the early 1900s."

"What about the owner?"

"All Millers, until me."

"The last one. Cora Miller."

"What about her?"

"How well did you know her?"

"I told you. I didn't. She passed away before I bought the house." It hurt to talk—hurt to think—but she pushed out the words. "That's how I bought the house. She was the last of the line." More blood dribbled from the corner of her mouth. "Can I go rinse my mouth? Change shirts? This one is covered in blood."

"So is mine," he said, giving her a slow, evil smile. He plucked at the dark stain made by his victim's blood. Dismissing it as unimportant, he returned to his inquisition. "Did you re-model the house when you moved in?"

"No." She didn't bother adding that she loved the house exactly as it was. Why give him more fuel to destroy her beloved home?

"You didn't paint?"

"Two rooms."

"No loose boards?" he persisted.

Was the man deaf? She spoke louder, so he would hear. "No. Loose. Boards."

"Then where is it?"

It was a rhetorical question. In frustration, Bernard hurled the crowbar across the room. It crashed against the wall, knocking an antique mirror sideways on its heavy old chain.

The crowbar bounced off the wall and hit Sara in the shoulder. She yelped in unexpected pain.

He ignored her to pace the room. "I know it's here somewhere. I'll rip every inch of this house apart until I find it!" he vowed to no one in particular.

"My—My shoulder," Sara whimpered.

He whirled around to threaten, "I'll rip it apart, too!" He went back to pacing, talking more to himself than to her. “It has to be here somewhere. He said I’d find it. He said it was here.”

Sara saw the anxiety creep across his face. The fear. The uncertainty.

None were good. A nervous animal was a dangerous animal. And Thomas Ramon Bernard was definitely an animal.

Sara used a soothing, how-to-approach-a-wounded-animal voice with him. “Tell me what you’re searching for. Maybe I can help you find it.”

His voice was sharp. “I’m not cutting you loose.”

“I know that. But that doesn’t mean I can’t help you figure this out.”

“Why? Why would you do that?”

“If I do something for you, maybe you’ll do something for me.” She would have shrugged, but both shoulders were taped at an impossible angle.

“And what’s that?”

She dared look him in the eye. “Maybe you’ll let me live.”

For a long moment, Bernard stared at her with cold, dark eyes. He was trying to intimidate her. Daring her to wither beneath his icy glare. When she didn’t, he assessed her more closely.

“I’ll think about it,” he said abruptly.

He left her alone in the dining room as he ventured into the living room, tapping on boards and randomly banging one or two with the hammer. He made his way into her office, doing the same. Sara cringed when she heard something topple to the floor.

*Please, not one of my computers! Not a monitor!*

Framed prints and knickknacks she could do without. Her computers were not only her livelihood, but her identity. Her new identity, at any rate.

Bernard banged and tapped his way through the bath, into her bedroom, looped around into the kitchen, and came up behind her in the dining room. In all that time, Sara hadn't attempted an escape. She was too tired and in too much pain. She used the time to rest and to think of a way out of this mess.

So far, she had nothing.

To her surprise, Bernard pulled up a chair and sat in front of her.

"What did you have in mind?" he asked.

When Sara stared at him with a blank expression, he elaborated, "You said if you could do something for me, I might do something for you. What can you do for me?"

"Maybe nothing," she said with honesty. "I don't know what you're looking for."

He seemed to be weighing his options. "Someone hid something in this house," Bernard told her, "a very long time ago. I came to collect it."

"What was it?"

"A man's life savings."

Sara did well to swallow a gasp. The journal. R's hidden stash.

"If—If there's a safe in the house, I've never seen it." She spoke the truth.

"Not a safe. A hiding place. Hidden behind a loose board, so I was told."

Again, she told the truth. "I've heard nothing of a hidden fortune."

"How stupid are you?" he demanded. He raised his hand as if to strike her again. "It was hidden. A *secret* hiding place."

The blow never came, but Sara knew it was only a matter of time. Bernard was a ticking bomb, just waiting to explode. She had to find a way to defuse him.

She needed a distraction. A plausible excuse while she found a way to escape. She had once seen a television program that illustrated how kidnap victims could break through duct tape. The instructor said to yank upward with all your might. Or... was it to push outward? Sara supposed it could depend on how one was taped to the chair.

Come to think of it, the example had shown the hostage's wrists taped to the armrests at their sides. Nothing had been mentioned about having their arms tied behind their back.

Still, if she could get Bernard out of the room, she could try.

"There's a box in the attic," she blurted out. "I've never looked through it. Maybe—Maybe the fortune's in there."

"Sure," Bernard sneered, his voice dripping with sarcasm. "Like most people keep thousands of dollars in a box in their attic."

She would have shrugged if she were able. "Better than tearing down a wall to get to it."

Bernard studied her again with his cold, cunning gaze. "Assuming I believed you"—his tone said it was doubtful—"how do you get to the attic?"

Sara leaned her head to the left. A thin trail of blood leaked from the corner of her mouth. "Stairs. In the front bedroom, next to the bath."

"I didn't see no stairs."

"There's a door."

"Where's the box?"

"You'll see it. It's the only one up there."

"No Christmas decorations up there?" he taunted.

Sara didn't bother admitting she had given up decorating for the holiday years ago. Shawn hated all things cheerful. His open disdain ruined the joy of trimming a tree with shiny baubles and listening to Christmas carols. His allergies made hanging fresh boughs of cedar a thing of the past. He scorned the idea of Santa Claus, a persona he claimed was unnecessarily cruel to underprivileged children. And since her ex-husband didn't believe in Christ, even a nativity display was out of the question.

She refused to tell a monster like Thomas Bernard that she had celebrated this past Christmas for the first time in years. That she had put up a small tree she had cut herself, here on her beloved land, and decorated it with handmade ornaments. Dried slices of cinnamon-laced apple, pecans painted like Santa, paper snowflakes, and strings of popcorn, all lovingly created as a new beginning for her new home. The escaped convict would never understand the pleasure of such a simple act.

"Just the one box," she repeated.

He considered her answer. "Maybe I should check it out."

She only nodded, trying not to appear too eager. If she could lure him up to the attic, perhaps she could escape her bindings and reach one of her guns.

At the sound of a vehicle, Bernard hurried to the living room window. He peeked through the same tiny sliver of view Sara always used. When he saw the truck pulling into the lane, he hissed, "What's the law doing here?"

"I told you he'd come."

"Who?"

"I didn't answer the phone, and now he's here. He won't go away until he sees that I'm okay."

She indicated her blood-smeared shirt. "Which I'm not."

She could see the wheels turning in Bernard's mind. He moved quickly, untying her arms as he instructed, "You'll wash your face off. Change shirts. And then you're going to get rid of him. If you don't, I swear I'll kill both of you."

He ripped the tape from her arms without warning. Hair and quite possibly skin came off with it. If that weren't bad enough, a cry leaked out as sensation flooded into her arms. There must have been a thousand sharp needles pricking and shocking her nerves back to life. As normal blood flow resumed, her arms hung like lead at her sides. She couldn't make them move. Even her legs had fallen asleep while she sat bound to the chair.

Bernard tipped the chair forward to spur her into action. Sara stumbled as she came to her feet, every part of her aching. Her shoulder and face were the worst of it.

"Hurry it up," Bernard barked. He shoved the gun into her back as he prodded her forward. He herded her into the bathroom between her bedroom and office, wedging himself into the door frame so she couldn't escape. He found a washcloth and tossed it in the sink. "Wash the blood off your face."

Sara looked into the mirror, horrified at the red whelp across her cheek and her split, swollen lip. She had vowed to never look this way again, not at the hands of any man, and yet, here she was.

Anger simmered in her eyes as she gazed at the pathetic sight she made.

"Wash up!" he hissed again.

She looked only marginally better with her face cleaned up.

Bernard reached into the dirty clothes hamper and pulled out the first shirt he came to. "Put this on."

"It's dirty."

"But it's not covered in blood." He handed her the shirt. When she reached for it, he held one edge, forcing her to look him in the eye. "Yet."

His one-word warning was clear.

Sara turned away to change shirts. The modesty did her little good when he could watch every move through the mirror.

They heard the truck door slam. Any moment, Mason would step onto her porch and knock, expecting her to answer.

Bernard motioned her into the hall. "I don't care what you have to tell him. Just get rid of him." He pressed the gun into her back as they walked to the door. "Don't try anything smart. Remember, I'll have a gun in your back."

"He'll want me to open the door."

"Don't."

"Then he'll *know* something is wrong."

"Come up with an excuse."

"He won't give up until I open the door. Believe me. I've tried that before."

"Fine. But if you give him as much as a wink, I'll splatter your brains into his face. And then I'll kill him, too."

"G—Got it," Sara said.

They reached the door just as Mason knocked.

"Sara!" his voice called from the other side. "Sara, it's Mason."

For a moment, her voice was frozen in fear.

"Sara? Are you okay? I tried to call, but your phone went to voicemail."

She swallowed hard, trying to think of an excuse.

"Sara, answer me! Is something wrong?"

She heard the suspicion in his voice. Imagined the way his sharp gaze darted around, looking for signs of danger.

"If you don't open this door…"

Bernard nudged her with the gun.

A pathetic noise came out first. Sara had to clear her throat before she could speak. "I—I'm fine."

"Why didn't you answer when I called?"

"I was… asleep."

"Can you open the door? I have your coffee mug."

"Keep it."

"I brought it back."

When she still didn't open the door, she heard cautious intuition in his voice. "Sara, what's wrong?"

"I—I'm not dressed."

"At all?" A hint of humor, and perhaps interest, crept into his voice.

"Just pajamas."

His deep, warm voice urged her, "Open the door, Sara."

Bernard's hot breath fell against her bruised cheek. "No. Funny. Business," he breathed. "Open the door and get rid of him."

Keeping the chain intact, Sara opened the door a fraction of an inch.

Assuming she would stand aside, Mason pushed on the door, frowning when he met resistance. "What's going on, Sara? Are we back to this again?"

"I—I told you. I'm not dressed."

"I'll wait in the kitchen while you get dressed. I was hoping for a refill in my cup."

She could see just enough to know he held the mug up with a hopeful smile.

"Not today. I'm not feeling well."

He leaned forward, peering into the tiny slit. "Sara, is that a bruise on your face? Are you all right?" His hand moved to his service weapon, even as Bernard's gun pressed into her back.

"I had a little accident," she said. "I look a mess."

"What happened?"

"It—It was silly, really," she claimed. "My feet got tangled in Bruno's leash. I fell and banged my cheek."

She could almost hear the breath escape him. Going still, Mason repeated, "Bruno's leash?"

"Yeah, I know. Clumsy me. I fell. At the back door."

"Are you sure you're okay?"

"Y—Yes. I'm fine," she assured him. She quickly added, "But I don't want you seeing me like this."

He nodded curtly. "I understand."

To his credit, his gaze never wavered. He didn't turn to scan the area. Didn't try to peer through the shade at the side of the window. He kept his eyes trained on hers, reassuring her with a steady confidence in his dark gaze.

"There's no need to come back this afternoon," she volunteered. "I need to work on my computer program."

"How's that coming?" he asked, almost conversationally.

"I hit a snag." As the gun thrust deeper into her back, she tried hard not to wince. "It—It's just a programming glitch." She babbled off some computer lingo, guessing neither man knew what she was talking about. She wasn't even sure she did, at this point. She finished off with, "I'm working on a back-door safety feature so that no one can access the program without authorization."

"Sounds like you have it all worked out," Mason murmured.

"I'm sure it will work," she agreed. "I just need to get back to it."

"Okay. Raincheck on the coffee?"

"Of course."

When she would have closed the door, Mason's voice stopped her.

"Sara?"

She held her breath, praying he wouldn't blow things now. She closed her eyes in a silent plea, hoping Bernard couldn't see.

"Take care of that cheek."

"I will." Eyes opened now, she stared intently into his concerned gaze. "Thanks for stopping by."

She quickly closed and locked the door. Ignoring the tip of Bernard's gun still in her ribs, she sagged against the door in relief.

She prayed that Mason understood her message.

# Chapter 26

## Mason

Mason walked slowly back to his truck, studying the ground beneath him for footprints. After last night's storm, it would be hard to track a bleeding elephant, much less a set of human footprints.

As casually as he could, he turned his face up toward the morning sky, pretending to study the lingering clouds. His eyes, however, searched Sara's yard and the trees beyond. Nothing was visibly out of place, but he knew something was wrong. Terribly wrong.

Sara hadn't sustained injuries by way of an imaginary dog. He couldn't see much through the narrow opening, but Mason knew she hadn't gotten those bruises in a fall. Someone had hurt her.

Bernard? Or an unknown assailant? Perhaps a domestic partner? He knew no one lived with her, but that didn't mean she didn't have a boyfriend or husband elsewhere. If a worried lover begged to check on his loved one, would a sympathetic sentry let him through the roadblock?

Not for the first time, Mason realized how little he knew about Sara Jennings.

The most logical answer was that Thomas Bernard had managed to plant a false trail and slip away, yet again. With everyone searching in the opposite direction, the escapee had probably looped back toward Orchard Creek. It was the last place officials—at least the top brass—would look for him. Lehman had decided the trail led to the west, and nothing could persuade him otherwise.

Mason silently cursed the foolish man for succumbing to Bernard's manipulation. He had fallen for the red herring hook, line, and sinker, as the old saying went. And now Sara paid the price.

The question was how and why Bernard had come back.

The 'how' was easy enough. He must have traveled during the storm, knowing it would erase his tracks and mask any sounds he made. The search was temporarily put on hold during the storm, other than the few vehicles parked at sparse intervals along the roadways. Bernard would have suspected as much and had taken advantage of the opportunity.

The real question was *why*? Why had he come back here? More specifically, why to Sara's house? Did she have some connection to the escapee? Was he someone from her past? Was he the reason he saw such raw fear in her eyes?

As Mason started his truck and pulled out of the driveway, he did the math in his head. Sara was in her early thirties. Bernard was forty-seven. While it wasn't entirely impossible, it was highly unlikely that the man was her father. He had been in prison or some form of confinement for most of Sara's adult life, so a romantic relationship between them wasn't any more likely. An older brother, perhaps? An uncle or cousin?

Or a complete stranger?

His gut told him Bernard was a stranger to her, but he still couldn't understand the *why*. Even if she was the wrong person in the wrong place, why had Bernard come back? It didn't make sense.

Mason turned out of Sara's driveway but didn't go far. He stayed on the shoulder of the highway, pulling off-road when he spotted a cluster of trees. They would do for cover. He radioed dispatch to inform them he was conducting a welfare check at this location. After killing the motor, he traded his cowboy boots for a pair of knee-high muck boots. He tucked his back-up pistol into the top of the right boot, unsheathed his long-range rifle from its case, and locked the door behind him.

As he slipped through the woods, Mason replayed the strange conversation with Sara.

Sara claimed she had gotten tangled in Bruno's leash and had fallen at the back door, but he knew that wasn't true. Bruno was a figment of her imagination or, in this case, a figment of her SJ's Big Dogs gadget.

And when had Sara ever been so forthcoming with information? He normally had to pry even the simplest answer out of her. Yet this morning, she had babbled on about her computer program. He hadn't understood most of it, except the part about a safety feature. He knew most programs had 'back-door' access for troubleshooting purposes.

To top it off, she had answered with a quick 'of course' when he asked for a raincheck on the coffee. Her normal answer would have been more along the lines of a cautious 'We'll see.' Sara rarely committed to anything that required personal connection.

The only thing that made sense was that Sara was giving him clues.

Mason took a roundabout route to the west, going beyond the house until the trees thinned, and he found himself in the pear orchard. The house was now behind him, just over the hill.

He took a moment to ponder the best approach. There were more trees on the east side of the house, though none close enough to provide cover. The carport would offer some camouflage if he could stay low and skirt around Sara's car. He could possibly make it to the back door without being seen.

*Back door.*

Sara's covert message suddenly clicked into place. She was telling him to use the back door. To come in from the back and rescue her, because she was in some sort of trouble.

Mason approached with extreme caution, moving as stealthily as possible. He kept to the trees as much as he could, then crouched low as he sprinted toward the carport. He rested behind the side of her car, listening for sounds from inside while he caught his breath. He checked his weapons before daring to creep forward.

He eased the screen door open, wincing with each squawk of the rusty springs. Ever so slowly, he twisted the doorknob. Locked.

He used an old trick to loosen the locking mechanism before giving the door a gentle nudge. When nothing happened, he tried again. There was either another lock he couldn't see from outside, or something heavy blocked the entry. He couldn't risk forcing his way inside, for fear of making too much racket.

He would have to find another way in.

# Chapter 27

## Sara

She was once again tied to the chair in the dining room. Her ankles were bound together by duct tape. Her arms were behind her and taped at the wrist. For added security, a rope bound her to the chair at her waist.

Try as she might, there was no breaking the tape.

Bernard was in the attic. She could hear him up there now, looking for the box that had been left behind. Sara had no idea what was inside, but she was certain it didn't hold the fortune he sought or even a clue to its whereabouts.

How would he take the news? Would he fly into a rage and kill her in anger? Or would he take his frustration out on her, one break at a time? Her kneecaps smarted, just thinking about it.

*Think, Sara, think.* Bernard would be back any moment, and she still hadn't found a way to escape.

Belatedly, she realized the mistake she made when sending Mason the covert message. How could she have forgotten about the wood box she had shoved against the door? Even if he understood her secretly coded words, he couldn't get in. She had unwittingly ruined her chance days ago.

Without Mason, what were her other options? Sara had to come up with something, and soon.

Time had run out. Bernard was already stomping down the stairs. He appeared in the living room moments later, carrying a cardboard box covered in dust. Sara watched his approach, her eyes wary.

*What now*, she wondered?

Bernard dropped the box onto the dining room table, sending dust particles into the air. Unable to cover her nose from the onslaught, Sara did her best to bury her sneeze in her shirt.

Bernard didn't worry about such niceties. She dodged the spray as much as she could.

Without warning, he moved behind her, made a slicing sound, and set her hands free.

"You open the box," he ordered. "I don't like dust. But no funny business. I'll have the gun on you the whole time."

"O—Okay."

Sara tucked most of her face into her shirt as she unfolded the box's flaps. She let the dust mites settle before pilfering inside.

"These look like clothes of some sort," she reported.

"I can see that," Bernard said in a sharp bark. "What else is in there?"

"Uhm... more clothes."

She pulled the first garment out, surprised that it was so small. "The—These are baby clothes," she said in confusion. The style and material told her they weren't from the timeframe in which Cora and her brothers had been born. Even more telling, one set had tiny little cartoon characters on it. From what she understood, *Scooby Doo, Where are You!* wasn't popular until the early to mid-seventies. Sara knew that because a recent client used the character as his password, claiming Scooby Doo was his favorite cartoon as a child. She knew how old the client was, making the seventies a safe bet.

"There's crocheted baby booties in here, too, and a tiny blue blanket." Sara pulled the items out reverently, careful not to tear the tissue they were so carefully wrapped within. Someone—Cora?—had taken extreme care to pack the items away.

Sara's mind fervently sifted through the few facts she knew about Cora.

*Only daughter among seven children.*

*Engaged to one man, but in love with another.*

*A decades-long affair with her forbidden lover.*

Questions swirled in her mind.

Had Cora become pregnant with the mysterious R's child?

Had Samuel Foote discovered her secret and broken off their engagement just before the wedding?

Had Cora gone away to have her baby? Hadn't there been some talk of a much-deserved vacation in Galveston?

It all seemed plausible. Holding the tiny clothes in her hand, it was the only thing that made sense in Sara's mind.

*What happened to the baby?* Sara wondered. It was a boy, from the looks of it. Had the child died at birth?

Bernard motioned impatiently with his gun. "What else is in there?"

"Not much. Some sort of card..."

"What is it? What does it say? Does it tell where the money is?"

"Not unless it's in Georgia," she murmured, turning the paper over in her hand.

"Georgia?" he bellowed. "What the hell is my money doing in Georgia?"

"It's not," Sara was quick to assure him. "It's a name. Georgia." She held up a torn business card that had seen better days. "Georgia on My Side. It's a play on words, like the song Georgia on My Mind."

"There's no *play* going on here, missy. Does it say where my money is, or not?" he demanded.

If she told him the truth, would he kill her on the spot? Maybe if she stalled long enough, Mason would come.

She chose to tell him a bald-face lie. "I—I can't be certain. This could be some sort of code."

"Code? Like a secret code?" Bernard looked intrigued.

"I can't be sure, but maybe."

"Why? What else does it say?"

Her eye was steadily swelling, blurring her vision and making the faded print hard to decipher. Not that she would tell *him* that.

"It looks like a handwritten telephone number." Seeing his face fall, she added, "Or, maybe the number to a combination."

His expression immediately changed. It could have been excitement. Could have been greed. To Sara, his expression looked like pure evil. "Combination? Like to a safe? Or a lockbox?" he asked. He started to move closer, but another sneeze held him back. All the smoke and grass and cedar had been bad enough on his sinuses these last few days, without a ton of old dust. He stood just far enough away to avoid the worst of it.

"It's possible," she lied.

"What else is on there?"

"It's torn. I can't make out what it says."

That, too, was a lie. She could see well enough to make out the words 'Discreet Services' and 'Licensed Midw—'. The rest was torn, but it didn't take much imagination to guess it said midwife. This Georgia person was a licensed midwife.

Just the thing a businesswoman having a scandalous affair in the 1970s would need for a quiet, discreet birth in her own home.

Sara's mind ferreted out other pieces of information stored within her memory bank.

In the journal, Cora said that Georgia had been her only friend. She had done all her shopping for her, or something to that order. She had even helped Cora buy the fancy bedroom set.

*If I was starting a new life, I wanted a new setting.*

The last words Sara had read from Cora's journal. There had been more, but she hadn't read them yet.

At the time, Sara thought the words meant Cora was starting her life fresh. A single woman who didn't need a man to lead a happy, fulfilling life. But what if she had meant it in a more literal sense?

What if the new life she was starting was that of her soon-to-be-born son? Sara knew that Cora had died here in this house. Had her child been born here, too? In the same bed?

Sara couldn't help but gasp at the revelation.

Bernard pounced on her reaction. "What? Did you find something?"

"N—No."

"I don't believe you." He pointed the gun, gang-banger style, at her head. His face contorted in anger. "You're hoping to find the fortune, aren't you? You plan to keep it for yourself!"

"No!" She raised her arm as if to shield herself.

He slapped her arm down. The unexpected action jarred her aching shoulder, but he hadn't shot her. Yet.

"You saw something on that card," Bernard insisted. "Give it to me. Now."

Sara did as she was told. He took it from her hand and skimmed over it, seeing nothing of help.

"This don't tell me crap," he complained, tossing it back to her. "Why did you sound so surprised over it?"

"I, uh, recognized the name. Georgia was a friend of Cora Miller's, the woman who lived here before me."

Bernard narrowed his eyes. "I thought you said you didn't know her."

"I didn't."

"I swear," he told her, "if you're lying, you're going to live just long enough to regret it."

"I'm not lying."

"Because if you are, I'll make good on my promise to break both your kneecaps. And then I'll work my way up, until the last thing you hear will be your skull breaking wide open."

Sara was taking a gamble, telling him about the journal. But if it bought her time until Mason arrived—*if* he arrived—it was worth the risk. "I found her journal," she admitted. "In it, she said Georgia was her only friend. This must be her."

"A journal? Why didn't you tell me that to begin with, you stupid woman?" He backhanded her again across the face. The force almost sent her toppling, chair and all. "Where is it? Where's this journal? Maybe it tells where my money is hidden."

Sara grabbed for the table with her unbound hands, trying to steady herself. Tears drowned what limited vision she had in her swollen right eye. Bloody snot dripped from her nose. Drool collected in the corner of her mouth. She was too weary to wipe any of it away.

She was a blubbering, slobbering mess.

For once, she didn't think she cared.

"I won't ask again," Bernard growled. "Tell *me* where it is, or tell my crowbar. Your choice."

"I—I'm not sure."

"Guess." It was an order.

"I think... beside my chair." She motioned toward the living room. He had struck her hard enough to rattle her brain. It was hard to collect her scattered thoughts when every inch of her body ached. "No, wait. That's not right. Uhm, by my bed."

"On your nightstand?"

"Yes. No." She tried to shake her head, but it was too heavy to move. "No, not there."

"Make up your mind!"

"I can't... It's hard to think. My head hurts. I—I think it's on my desk." She put her hand to her head. Maybe if she held it, it wouldn't split in two. "Yes, it's on my desk. In my office."

"If you're wrong, I'll take my crowbar to your computers. One blow for every wrong answer you gave me."

"It's on my desk. I remember now."

"Let's go get it."

"Untie me."

His eyes glowed with that sick, evil glimmer. "Bring the chair," he countered.

It was another miserable trek. She wondered if she was up to the challenge. She shuffled her feet, one tiny step at a time, the chair still heavy upon her back. Her hands may have been free, but the rope at her waist meant she and the chair were inseparable.

With both her head and her heart pounding after the first few painful baby steps, she didn't care that she left a trail of bloody slobber behind her. She thought she might puke.

Or die.

At this point, Sara wasn't sure which would be better.

# Chapter 28

## Mason

Mason kept low as he crept around the house. The carport was attached to what appeared to be an add-on, and not original to the main house. The windows in the addition were smaller and made of aluminum frames. They were either too small for his broad frame to crawl through, or too high to reach without help. The windows in the rest of the house were larger, meant for plenty of air flow before the invention of central air.

If he wanted in, Mason would have to use one of them.

He knew Sara had locked all the windows. He and Ingalls had personally double-checked. But it didn't keep him from triple-checking now, on the off chance that Sara had opened one again.

After all, if it *was* Bernard inside, Sara wouldn't have granted him access through the front door. He had come in elsewhere.

When he found the unlocked window on the back east corner of the house, Mason wasn't sure if he should be thankful or furious. He was grateful to have a way inside, but angry that Sara had been foolish enough to loosen the latch.

Propping his rifle against the house, Mason eased the window up a fraction of an inch. He had no trouble seeing inside, even though no lights were on. Plenty of natural light poured in through the lacy white curtains.

Across the room, he saw that the door was slightly ajar. He hoped the mostly closed door muffled the sounds of his clumsy advance. It took some doing, but he finally managed to pull himself over the window ledge and into the room. The rifle stayed behind.

The first thing Mason noticed was the muddy footprints on the hardwood floor.

*Damn!* It had to be Bernard.

Edging around the four-poster bed, Mason was careful of where and how he stepped. One creaking board could give him away.

He knew the house's simple layout. The common rooms were aligned in a row, flanked on either side by the bedrooms. There were no hallways, just bedrooms connected by a bath. The front bedrooms opened into the living room, the back bedrooms into the kitchen. The newer addition was built off the kitchen's back door.

Mason had to be careful, not knowing Bernard's whereabouts in the house. He paused beside the door to the bathroom, listening for movement. He heard faint voices coming from the center of the house.

Creeping toward the other door, the one that opened into the kitchen, he strained to hear the conversation and the exact location it came from. The dining room or living room, most likely. Either way, both rooms had a clear view into the kitchen, save for the narrow support around their load-bearing openings.

“I swear,” a man’s voice snarled from unknown depths, “if you’re lying, you’re going to live just long enough to regret it.”

“I’m not lying.”

A tight smile puckered Mason’s lips. With her usual spunk, Sara didn’t allow Bernard to intimidate her. He could imagine the stubborn lift of her chin as she refused to cower, even to a known murderer.

“Because if you are, I’ll make good on my promise to break both your kneecaps. And then I’ll work my way up, until the last thing you hear will be your skull breaking wide open.”

Anger boiled up within him, filling Mason’s ears so that he missed Sara’s words. What he did hear was Bernard’s nasty snarl in reply.

“A journal? Why didn’t you tell me that to begin with, you stupid woman?”

A resounding *smack* filled the morning’s stillness.

It took every bit of Mason's resolve not to storm the room and take vengeance on the man cruel enough—and foolish enough—to strike Sara. But acting on emotion would only get him and Sara both killed. Mason had to put his personal feelings aside for now. But later, one way or another, Mason would make Bernard pay for daring to lay a hand on her.

Looking around, Mason contemplated his options. If he could be certain of Bernard's position in the room, he could sneak up from behind and get the drop on him. But he had no way of knowing which way Bernard faced or whether he would stay in one place. Already, Bernard was saying something about a journal, and Sara was trying to remember where it was. Any move on their part could expose Mason's presence in the house.

"It's on my desk," he heard Sara say. Her voice sounded weak and strained. "I remember now."

"Let's go get it."

"Untie me."

Mason frowned. Bernard had her tied up. That made extracting Sara from the situation more difficult, but not impossible.

If the journal was on her desk, it was a safe assumption they were headed for her office. But Bernard's next statement, something about bringing the chair, puzzled Mason. He didn't dare peek around the corner, but the sound of shuffled, plodding footsteps hinted that Sara was in extreme pain. More than likely, she was tied to a chair she now carried on her back.

Another thing Bernard would later pay for.

It seemed to take forever, but Mason eventually heard the shuffling sounds fade. Bernard spoke, his voice coming from Sara's office at the front of the house. Mason took it as his cue to make a move.

Quiet as a deer moving through a meadow, Mason made his way across the kitchen. He hesitated at the doorway into Sara's bedroom, listening for voices. Satisfied that he wasn't in Bernard's line of vision, he slipped into the room.

"Is that it?" Bernard asked from the other room.

"Y—Yes." Just the one word sounded breathless.

"Open it," the convict ordered. "Tell me what it says."

Calculating that the trajectory of Bernard's voice meant he was standing near the desk and facing away from him, Mason crept into the bath connecting the two rooms. It put him close enough to easily hear their voices.

Bernard's, at any rate. Sara's came out faint and hoarse.

"I—I can't. I need to catch. My breath."

"I said to read it!"

Sara was slow in answering. "Which part? The front... is planting schedules. The di—diary spans years. It would take—" Her gulp was audible before she panted out the rest. "—take all day."

"I've got the time."

"Do you?" Mason heard a hint of Sara's fighting spirit strengthening her voice. "They'll come back, you know." After a few ragged breaths, she managed, "Still looking."

Unfazed, Bernard's voice was cold. "Then you'd better read fast."

"Give me a minute," she panted. "I—I need water."

"There's a bottle on your desk. Drink that."

Mason could hear her gulping down the much-needed refreshment. At least Bernard hadn't come this way to seek water. It was a small break, but a break, nonetheless.

After a long moment, Mason heard paper shuffling. When Sara spoke again, she didn't sound as hoarse.

"I stopped here. Cora didn't say where the money was hidden, just that her lover—someone she called R—gave it to her."

"To hold onto." Bernard's tone was pointed. "He gave it to her for safekeeping, not to spend. He told her to keep it until he came back."

"How can you know that?" Sara asked.

"I told you. I ask the questions, not you."

Mason heard something crash to the floor, as if Bernard had taken his hand and swiped it across the desk, pulling everything in his path to the floor.

Judging from Sara's cry of dismay, he had done just that.

When she spoke again, Sara's voice sounded small. "According to this, he never came back. Cora waited for years, but R never came back."

"What did she do with the money?"

"It didn't say."

"Then you'd better keep reading. And you'd better hope it tells, or you won't like the outcome."

Sara did as she was told, reading from the journal in a halting voice. She was having difficulty speaking. Her tongue sounded thick, and her words were often slurred. If she stopped too long to catch her breath, Bernard would prod her to continue.

Mason couldn't hear or understand some of what she said, but he heard a few lines.

"Georgia was a true peach. No pun intended. She took care of all the arrangements. She had me write postcards that someone will mail from the coast. I wrote about a wonderful, relaxing vacation by the ocean, when nothing could be further from the truth. I'm stuck at home, in bed, waiting for a man who will never come and a baby I cannot keep. Dear Georgia has taken care of that, too. She knows a nice couple who can't conceive. They want a child so badly, and she assured me they will be good parents. I'll send money each year, of course, to see that my son never wants for anything. It breaks my heart to give him away, but I know it's better this way. My baby deserves more than I, a single mother, can give."

Bernard's response was surprisingly vocal. "The hell you say!"

"I—I'm just reading what I see," Sara defended herself.

"That Georgia woman lied," Bernard insisted gruffly.

"I wouldn't know. That's just what it says here."

"Well, I do know. It wasn't like that at all."

Mason imagined Bernard may have waved his gun as he instructed, "Keep reading."

A different date denoted a new entry.

"He's such a beautiful baby! Dark eyes, like his father. Fair skin, like mine. A beautiful blend of us both. Living proof of our love. Ten perfect fingers, ten perfect toes. Dark curls that wrapped around my finger the very first time I held him. A tiny little cry that wrapped around my heart and will forever hold it. I love this baby with my whole heart. I know I'll never be complete again. Part of me will go with my son when he leaves."

Bernard barked out a sharp order. "Skip the mushy parts. Find the part about my money. Find out where she hid it."

Mason caught a few words here and there as Sara skimmed through the journal, but his mind was racing ahead.

This explained why Bernard had come back here, to this specific house. He believed there was money hidden here. If he didn't find the answers he sought in the journal, he might very well kill Sara. There was a reason for the old saying, 'don't shoot the messenger.'

He needed a diversion. Something to pull Bernard away, so that Mason could separate the criminal from Sara. He didn't want her hit in what was sure to be crossfire. One thing was for certain. Bernard wouldn't go down without a fight.

Very quietly, Mason looked around until he found something useful to draw the criminal's attention. With secret weapons in hand, he slipped back into the kitchen, edging his way into the dining room. Hiding as best he could, he pulled his phone from his pocket and dialed Sara's number.

He heard Bernard's sharp voice. No doubt, he saw the name flash across her screen. "It's your boyfriend again. What the hell does he want this time?"

"M—Maybe I should answer," Sara suggested.

"Maybe you should shut up!" Bernard was clearly rattled. "I told you to get rid of him. Did you tip him off?"

"Would he be calling if I did?" she tossed back.

Mason hung up before the call went to voicemail. Instead, he tapped out a message.

> *Watch the leash the next time you take Bruno for a walk. Or get Hondo to chew your feet free.*
>
> *Oh, and good news. They spotted Bernard close to the interstate. Looks like he's headed toward Big D.*

Bernard laughed with glee as he read the text aloud to Sara. "The idiots think I'm long gone from the area. Ain't nobody coming for you now, little girl. We've got all day to read that journal."

Mason tapped out a second message to mobile command, requesting backup. *Covert,* he instructed.

Sliding the phone back into his pocket, he hit the SJ's Big Dogs button.

"What the hell?" Bernard demanded in a voice that rose to a near squeak.

Mason tossed the full can of hairspray into the living room. As it rolled across the floor, he was already halfway back to Sara's office.

A volley of gunshots reverberated throughout the wood-sheathed walls.

Then came the explosion.

# Chapter 29

## Sara

As soon as Bernard read the text message aloud, Sara knew Mason was sending her a message. Somehow, he knew her feet were bound, and he was telling her to get them free.

She could hardly do it with Bernard standing over her.

The moment she heard the "dogs," she knew it was her chance. Her head was still reeling, and her body ached all over, but adrenaline gave her strength.

As the angry beasts seemed to race across the living room floor in attack mode, Bernard abandoned her and twirled toward the door. Firing his gun on reflex, he never noticed her grab a pair of scissors from the desk drawer and use them to slice the tape in half.

One swift move was all it took to free her feet.

Cutting through the rope took more effort, but Bernard was already running to the door, firing a second time.

By the fourth shot, Sara heard a surprising *boom!* from the living room. Something clattered across the floor, collided with some unseen object, and made enough noise and confusion to draw more fire from Bernard.

Sara felt the rope fall free from her waist, but she willed herself to stay in the chair. Every fiber of her being screamed for her to run, but she resisted. She wouldn't risk her opportunity to escape until she had a true chance at succeeding. Bernard, she somehow knew, wasn't one to wait for danger to come to him. He would face it head-on, even instigating it if he thought it gave him the edge.

Within seconds, the convicted killer was shooting his way into the living room, ready to take on all challengers, whether they be on two feet or four.

The second he passed over the threshold, Sara was out of the chair and backing her way from the office, into the adjacent bathroom.

Bumping into the warmth of another body, Sara bolted, but a strong arm pulled her back. The hand that quickly covered her mouth stifled any sound she would have made.

Sara squirmed and struggled, until she recognized the voice whispering low in her ear. "Shh," Mason said. "It's me. You're okay now. I've got this."

She sagged in relief, allowing his solid body to hold hers upright. At least until the jelly in her knees solidified again.

When she would have spoken, his hand stayed in place. His words were little more than a breathy thought. “Get out of here. The window’s open. Go to the pear orchard. Stay hidden until Gil or I come to get you.”

She shook her head, ready to protest.

“Please, Sara. I need to know you’re safe. Let me do my job.”

Logic said that once Bernard discovered the ruse, he would peek into the office, find Sara out of the chair, and head to the rear of the house, believing she would have run as far and fast away as possible.

On the off chance Bernard came through this way, Mason ducked in behind the bathroom door.

Bernard, however, took the faster route, lumbering through the main rooms as his anger raged.

Like pawns on a chess board, Mason calculated his moves to counter Bernard’s. While the convict searched the laundry room and its tiny bath, Mason slipped into Sara’s bedroom.

Finding the back addition empty, the windows too challenging for a quick escape, and the only door firmly blocked, Bernard had to believe that

Sara was still in the house. Mason anticipated that the convict would go into stealth mode, gingerly crossing the kitchen to sneak his way into the guest room. Mason waited a few steps behind, just inside the laundry room entrance.

When shadows and a lone squeaky board suggested Bernard moved into the guest bath, Mason hid within the shadows of the kitchen. He hovered there until Bernard's steps faintly echoed in the vacant front bedroom.

Just as Bernard tiptoed back into the living room, Mason slipped inside the fancy guest room.

Bernard silently circled through the west side of the house, going from office to bath to bedroom. He ended up in the kitchen.

Instead of angry, he sounded somewhat amused. His voice had an eerie sing-song lilt to it. Clearly, he thought of it as a game.

"Where are you, Sara? I know you're in the house. The windows are all closed, and the doors are still locked. You can't hide forever. Come out, come out, wherever you are."

He was met with silence.

Some of the amusement slipped. Impatience took its place. "Make it easy on yourself, Sara. If you come out now, I may let you live."

He walked into the dining room, talking into the spooky quiet of the house. "Even if I don't," he continued, "I promise to make it fast."

Still silence.

Impatience gave way to ire. "I never did like playing hide and seek, Sara. You want to know why? One time, some older kids left me and my little brother hiding for hours. They went off to the baseball field and just left us there, hiding behind a stinking old trash can. But you know what? I got revenge. It took years, but I got even. I left the leader, a guy they called Scratch, in a trash can."

Bernard retraced his steps into the living room. With a sickening snicker, he elaborated. "Two or three trash cans, actually, but I finally put him in his place. It was the least I could do for Danny. And when I find you, little girl, I'm going to put you in your place. Now that you've made me mad, I take back my promise to make it quick. I'll take my time killing you, the same way I did Scratch."

Sara was hunkered down in the depths of the old clawfoot bathtub. Mason had begged her to go, but she had made no promises.

Mason assumed she had closed the window from the outside as she made her escape. Even Bernard had missed her during his brief sweep of the room.

But she was still there, and she was ready to defend her home. Bernard may have beaten her in a physical sense, but he couldn't beat her in spirit. Her eye was swollen shut, her face was bloody and bruised, and she thought she might have a broken bone or two. But she still had a will, and where there was a will, Sara swore there was a way.

SJ's Big Dogs was only one of Sara's innovations. A lesser-known gadget was SJ's Echo. By speaking into the mic, the human voice could be altered and projected in all directions, making it virtually impossible to distinguish where the voice originated.

Sara had one of the devices hidden in her bathroom, alongside her palm-sized Ruger LCP 380. Both resided behind the towel rack.

"Will Danny be watching?"

The mechanical voice came from out of nowhere, yet it echoed everywhere.

Bernard all but jumped out of his prison-issued pants and his victim's stained shirt. "Who—Who said that?" he demanded, definitely spooked. He looked around the room, seeing no one.

There was a long pause before the voice came again. "A friend of the family."

"I got no family," Bernard denied.

"Everyone has family," the all-knowing voice said.

"Not me," he claimed, searching overhead but unable to spot the speakers. He aimed at the ceiling and pulled the trigger a time or two, hoping to get lucky.

"No one?" the voice asked, ignoring the pinged shots.

"No one." Bernard's voice was rough. He moved cautiously back to the dining room, still looking for hidden speakers. He kept talking, thinking it would buy him time to outsmart the voice. "Danny died when he was six. My mother, who really wasn't my mother at all, died a few years later."

In a show of bravado, Bernard shot off a few more rounds.

The voice didn't speak right away.

The air stilled, hushed and ready for a reply.

The silent house hummed in anticipation.

Bernard's face, if anyone had seen, paled.

"Your father?" the voice asked at last.

"Which one?" Bernard tried for a nonchalant laugh but failed. "One died in prison. One died of a heart attack. One *not* my father just up and died." This time, he pulled off the laugh. "They couldn't prove it was me."

Bernard made his way into the kitchen, still trying to decipher where the voice came from.

From his place in the guest room, Mason silently cursed. He had told Sara to run. Obviously, she hadn't taken his advice. She was still in the house. And if Bernard searched long enough, he would find her.

To draw attention away from the foolishly brazen woman, Mason tapped the Big Dogs button again.

Bernard jerked a hard left, swinging his gun toward the guest room.

Before he could fire, the voice—Sara's, though it hardly sounded like hers—echoed again from all corners of the house.

"Down, Bruno. Heel, Hondo."

Bernard whirled around. First to his right. Then straight ahead. Then in a wide circle of what had to be fear.

Mason admired Sara's spunk. That was the same bluff she had pulled with him. The echoed voice was a new touch, one he would ask her about later.

For now, there were more serious matters at hand. Protecting Sara, perhaps from her own blind stubbornness, was his first priority.

# Chapter 30

## Sara/Mason

Between anticipating Bernard's next move and keeping one step ahead of him, Mason assimilated snippets of overheard conversations with facts he knew about the convict. Pieces of the puzzle were slowly coming together.

For seven days, Bernard had evaded officials. His escape and sly moves were an embarrassment to the Texas Department of Criminal Justice, the US Marshal Service, Texas Rangers, and to local law enforcement, alike. Basically, he had jerked them all around as he roamed free at his own discretion.

Now, however, he felt cornered.

Thomas Bernard was dangerous enough without adding desperation into the mix.

Police reports said Bernard had taken a Glock 17 off Chuck Dunn's body. While there was a possibility that Dunn already had a bullet in the chamber, most people loaded their first round from the clip.

Mason did the math. Assuming Dunn hadn't fired his weapon yet, and that there wasn't a bullet in the chamber, Bernard had, at most, seventeen rounds at his disposal.

Mason had counted the times Bernard discharged his gun. Bernard had one round left. Two, tops, if Dunn had put a bullet in the chamber.

Either way, Bernard was down to almost nothing, and Mason, with two full clips for his Glock, still had fifty shots. He'd take those odds any day, especially when a civilian's life was on the line.

That's how he had to think of Sara now. She was a civilian and nothing more. There was no room for emotion in the mission he faced.

Before, Bernard thought he needed Sara to lead him to his believed treasure.

Now, he only wanted to kill her.

With slow deliberation, Mason tossed a single bullet across the fancy guest room. It was the one he kept in his pocket for luck. In a pinch, it also served as one last desperate attempt for a shot.

When he thought about it, that, too, came down to luck.

The bullet hit with a dull thud before rolling across the wooden floor.

It was enough to get Bernard's attention.

The escaped prisoner eased across the kitchen, moving sideways so that he kept his back protected. With extreme caution, gun drawn and ready to fire, he stepped into the bedroom.

Bernard did a visual sweep of the room, seeking out shadows and corners. Nothing moved. Even the air was still.

He swept his gaze to the right, so that he had a clear line of sight into the adjoining bath and the front bedroom beyond.

Nothing.

Inhaling a shaky breath, sensing some sort of trap but unable to find its source, Bernard swung his gaze back to the left, gun up.

That's when he saw him.

The lawman had materialized out of thin air, and he had a gun trained on the convict.

It had come down to this. A shootout. Bernard knew he had to make his last bullet count.

Neither man pulled the trigger.

Mason spoke, asking an unexpected question. "Tell me, Bernard. How does it feel to come full circle?"

The distinct, deadly calm of his adversary's voice rattled Bernard. "What, uh, what are you talking about?"

"Put down your gun and surrender. It's over."

"Not yet, it ain't," he said gruffly. "I'll never surrender. If I do, I'm a dead man."

"I can make that happen right now," Mason assured him. His voice hardened as he ordered, "Put the gun down, Bernard. We both know you only have one bullet left."

With a cocky smirk, the fugitive replied, "It only takes one well-placed bullet to kill a man."

"True. But are you that good of a shot?" Mason taunted. "I have two full clips and a loaded gun. A good fifty bullets, ready to fire."

"Maybe I have another gun."

"Maybe you're bluffing. But I can assure you, I'm not."

Bernard was visibly nervous. "Full circle, huh? What's that supposed to mean?"

With a subtle nod, Mason indicated the four-poster bed beside him. "You were born in this room, and if you don't put your gun down, *right now*, you'll die in this room." His piercing gaze bore into Bernard's glazed eyes. "Full circle."

Hearing the voices, Sara had stealthily left her hiding place and slipped across the kitchen. With their eyes trained upon each other, neither man had noticed her.

Her sharp inhale of breath changed all that.

In a flash, Bernard twirled and grabbed Sara's arm.

Mason couldn't get off a shot, for fear of hitting her.

With that evil smile spreading across his face, Bernard jerked Sara to the front of his chest and placed the gun at her temple.

"Hello, little girl. Glad you could join us." His voice sounded almost giddy.

"Let me go!" Sara demanded. Her efforts to get free were futile. She tried twisting. Kicking. Punching an elbow into his gut or, better yet, his groin. But he was too strong, and she was too physically weary. His abuse had weakened her.

Seeing her battered face, with blood smeared across it and one eye bruised and swollen shut, Mason vowed to kill Bernard on the spot. The man had rebuked his chance to surrender, and now he had a hostage. Killing him was inevitable.

"You heard the lady," Mason said, his calm tone belying the rage simmering inside him. "Let her go."

"I don't think so. Like you pointed out, I have one bullet left. And it now has her name on it."

"You can't kill both of us with one bullet," Mason pointed out. "If you shoot Sara, I shoot you. Simple as that. Besides," he reasoned, "if you kill her, you won't know where your inheritance is hidden."

"Or," Bernard said, dragging out the simple word as he cocked his head to one side, "I can tie you both up and still look for the money."

Sara refused to be left out of the conversation. She spoke around a busted lip. "Wait. Inheritance? Full circle?"

Mason was happy to fill her in. It gave him more time to wait for his backup.

"Thomas Ramon Bernard. Did you know he was adopted at birth?" Mason supplied the facts.

"A private adoption arranged by a mutual friend. No contact afterward. A clean break, except for one thing. The baby would take the adopted sur name of Bernard. The birth mother's only request was that he carried his father's first name." He paused for effect. "Ramon."

Another gasp from Sara as realization set in. On some level, she thought she had already known. Her mind was just too scrambled to comprehend it all.

"The mysterious R," she murmured. "Cora's lover."

"So it seems."

"He was the thief!" she blurted out. "He—He stole money and told Cora it was for their future."

Bernard tightened his grip around Sara's gut. "Enough jabber. None of that matters now. Both of them are dead. It's my inheritance. And I plan to collect it, with or without you."

Mason saw the fugitive's trigger finger flex. Bernard was getting antsy.

"I'll kill her," Bernard threatened, squeezing Sara hard enough to lift her feet off the ground. "I swear I will. If you don't want to see her brains splattered against the wall, you'll lay your weapon down. Now."

Mason couldn't detect movement from outside, but he had requested a covert rescue. For now, he had to play along and pretend to do as Bernard ordered.

"Fine." He feigned agreement. Mason bent at his knees, one hand in the air as the other lowered the gun. His eyes were still riveted on Bernard.

"Slow and easy," the convict instructed. "Lay your weapon on the ground and slide it over here."

Mason went through the motions. Hunched at his knees, he pretended to lose his balance. He braced himself with his right hand on the floor as he used his left to slide the gun across the floor.

Bernard's eyes flickered to the gun.

The split second was all Mason needed.

"*Down*, Bruno!" he yelled.

His backup revolver, hidden in his boot leg, was already in his hand.

Despite how dull her brain was, fuzzy and sluggish from shock and trauma, yet somehow painfully aware of each beat of her racing heart, Sara understood.

Bernard had a steel hold on her waist, but her knees went suddenly limp. She bent her body the best she could over his arm.

When the single shot rang out, his vice grip on her slackened. Sara turned just enough to see the small, neat whole in the center of his forehead.

"You're right, Bernard." Mason's murmur was deadly soft. "It only takes one well-placed bullet to kill a man."

With a ragged sob, Sara scrambled to avoid Bernard's falling body. He fell face forward with a leaden *thump*.

"Sara!" Mason caught her as she rushed toward him. "Are you okay?"

"I—I..." She was too shaken to speak coherently, but she managed to nod. She buried her face in his chest, shaking with a sudden frigid cold, despite the warm arms around her.

"Shh. It's okay now. It's over," Mason murmured, stroking her dark hair with a soothing motion. "It's over. He can't hurt you now. You're safe."

He held her for a long, bittersweet moment. He held her until the shaking subsided. Until her sobs lessened and quieted. He held her until her knees finally gave way, and she swayed against him in exhaustion.

Mason backed his way to the bed, dragging her along with him. He laid her there and pulled the quilt up around her, all the while wondering where his backup was. They should have been there by now.

He pulled out his cell phone and dialed for help. In one hand, he held the phone, barking out details and ordering a bus. With the other hand, he gently stroked Sara's back.

Curled into a ball, she was quiet now, except for the tiny whimpers that slipped out against her will.

"I've called an ambulance, Sara," he assured her. "They'll be here in five minutes. They'll take care of that eye. They'll check you out and tend to your bruises. Are you hurt anywhere besides your face?"

When she didn't answer, he gingerly took a seat beside her. The mattress dipped with his weight. Gravity tugged Sara against his hip, but she didn't seem to mind. Or perhaps she just didn't notice. She seemed to be in her own private world right now, a place where no one could hurt her.

Mason had no way of knowing, but it was the same place Sara retreated to each time Shawn beat her.

# Chapter 31

## Sara

Over a week had passed.

After two nights in the hospital for observation and mandatory counseling, Sara was allowed to go home. Her body would heal, but Sara's emotional scars would linger.

The same could be said for the farmhouse. Already, someone had cleaned the blood. They had straightened over-turned chairs, swept up scattered glass, picked up the mess Bernard had slung onto the floor, and righted her slightly-crooked-but-still-somehow-working computer monitor. The bullet holes in her walls and ceiling were still visible, perhaps needed for further evidence. The broken and cracked boards needed repair, but that would come in time. Sara was in no hurry. The scars were proof of her resilience.

If nothing else, Sara was a survivor.

After an endless parade of investigators, detectives, and prison officials, Sara's house was finally quiet. She rejected their offers to relocate her, at least on a temporary basis. She tolerated their comings and goings as they collected additional evidence, dusted for yet more fingerprints, took measurements and trajectory estimations, and asked a thousand and three questions.

Mason, she knew, was on mandatory paid suspension, pending a formal review.

She knew, too, that he would be fully exonerated. His actions that day had been nothing less than heroic.

And each evening, after the steady stream of inquisitions and the well wishes of neighbors, Mason stopped by to check on her.

The first night, she met him at the door. Mason didn't ask her to unfasten the chain. He seemed to understand that she needed time to reassemble the pieces of her life in the only pattern she knew. Reservation.

The next night, she opened the door wide enough for him to see that the bruises on her hands and arms were fading. Puffiness lingered around her eye, well disguised by the deep purples and reds that refused to abate. He returned her coffee mug with an offering of chicken soup, claiming it was a cure-all. The sweet gesture drew a smile from her healing lip.

On the third evening, she joined him on the porch swing. There was a definite chill in the air, a promise of colder weather yet to come. In Texas, temperatures would come and go until winter set in for good—and sometimes, not even then—rising and falling at nature's whim. But this autumn night was cool, so Sara brought coffee and fuzzy, fall-themed throws out to the porch to keep them comfortable.

Two throws, of course. And she didn't sit too close, even though the warmth would have been nice.

On the fourth night, Sara baked cookies and brought them out to share.

And on this, the fifth consecutive night of polite but stilted visits, Sara worked up the nerve to invite him inside.

She had made chicken and dumplings and a skillet of cornbread. Nothing fussy, just comforting. Just a simple meal between… friends? Sara hoped that was what they were working toward. She needed a friend, especially now.

"This is delicious," Mason said in approval. "Perfect for the weather this week."

"I like to make stews and soups and such when it's cool outside."

"The weather's supposed to warm up next week, but it sure hits the spot this week."

Sara wondered if their entire dinner conversation would revolve around senseless talk of the weather and idle gossip. She was relieved when Mason introduced a different topic.

"I have good news, for a change," he told her.

"Oh?"

"I am officially reinstated as a detective. The review board found that I acted in accordance with the law and did nothing wrong. I go back to work, day after tomorrow."

"That's great," Sara said, meaning it. She even offered him a genuine smile. "I knew they wouldn't find you at fault. You were definitely a hero that day."

For a moment, Mason was caught up in the unfamiliar sight of her smile. He spoke without thinking. "You really should smile like that more often, you know. It lights up your entire face."

Uncomfortable with the compliment, Sara squirmed in her chair. "As if I need to call more attention to this purple and black mess." She made a circle around her face with her finger. "A light is the last thing I need."

"You know what I mean, Sara."

"I know I just called you a hero, and here you are talking about lights," she grumbled.

Mason played along. He dipped his head in apology. "I stand chastised. Thank you for the compliment. You were pretty heroic too, you know." He accepted another wedge of cornbread when she offered it. "Headstrong, but heroic."

"Headstrong?"

"I told you to run, Sara. You should have listened."

"I know." She was risking a lot by adding, "But I'm tired of running."

Mason eyed her warily. He wanted to know more, much more, but he was afraid asking questions would only scare her away. He decided to let her set the pace. He placed the cornbread on his plate and wiped his mouth, signaling that he was ready to listen.

Sara averted her eyes, looking anywhere but into his earnest brown gaze. Part of her wanted nothing more than to confide in him, sharing the burden she had shouldered by herself for so long. Another part of her was terrified at letting anyone that close to her, ever again.

In too bright of a voice, she jumped topics. "When we're done with dinner, there's pecan pie for dessert."

"Oh, yeah?" Mason covered his disappointment, inquiring, instead, about her pecan orchard. How soon would the nuts be ready for harvesting? Would she bring in crews to help her? Was it a good crop this year?

They finished their meal, once again covering safe topics like her pecan orchard and the ever-rising cost of hired help. Mason cleared the table as Sara started coffee and retrieved the pie.

"Ice cream?" she asked, poised beside the massive old refrigerator that was once again making a racket.

"Yes, if you're sure it's safe to open that thing."

"Of course."

He eyed the monstrosity with doubt. "So, I didn't help it any?"

"Actually, you did. This is just a little rattle. It will settle down soon."

He looked unconvinced. "Could we have our pie in the living room, where it's less noisy?"

Sara hesitated. This was Mason. Her friend, or something close to that. If she could trust him at the kitchen table, she could trust him in the living room.

She gave a quick nod of consent. "I'll fill the plates. You can bring the coffee."

They carried their dessert into the living room, passing through the dining room with its many battle scars still on display. Mason admired the way Sara drew a deep breath, kept her eyes trained ahead, and trudged on through.

They settled into their seats, almost friends on either end of the couch.

"This is excellent," Mason said, savoring the salty-sweet perfection of her pecan pie. He hadn't even bothered with the scoop of ice cream on top yet.

"Thank you. I found the recipe in one of the Miller family cookbooks." After a few bites, she thought to tell him, "Oh. You know that book you pulled from beneath the refrigerator?"

"The one I risked life and limb to retrieve?" A teasing light was back in his eyes again. Sara realized how much she had missed it.

"I don't recall it quite that way, but yeah, that's the one. It turned out to be Cora's journal."

"The one Bernard made you read from?"

"Yes. One and the same."

"How about that," he murmured. He tried another bite of pie, this one with ice cream.

They didn't talk much as they enjoyed their dessert, until Mason repeated, "And if I didn't say so before, this pie is awesome."

"You did."

He licked the syrupy goodness off his fork. "It bears repeating."

Sara couldn't help but laugh.

As she did, she felt a little crack appear in her armor. For once, it didn't frighten her. Sara wanted to believe the silence no longer felt so uncomfortable. Maybe, she decided, part of moving forward was learning to let go of the past.

"In fact, everything I've tasted that you made has been delicious," Mason said, setting aside his empty plate. "Where did you learn to cook like that? Surely not from a cookbook."

Sara shrugged. "Necessity, I guess."

"Your mom teach you?"

Sara recognized the nudge for more information, but she made a point to never talk of her family.

But because she needed a friend, and because the burden of the past was becoming too heavy to bear alone, she made one exception. Shawn had never been her family.

"Not really. But my ex-husband," she said, trying to sound casual, "liked a hot meal on the table whenever he was home."

Mason picked up on the 'whenever' comment. "He traveled a lot with his job?"

"You could say that." Sara fidgeted with her coffee cup before revealing, "He was a professional basketball player."

To his credit, Mason had absorbed the news of her marriage with little reaction. This, however, drew his attention. "Anyone I've ever heard of?"

"Most likely." With a sigh, she admitted, "Shawn Angelos."

His eyes widened. "With the Golden State Warriors?"

She nodded. "And the San Antonio Spurs, and the Los Angeles Clippers, and then back to the Warriors, before an injury ended it all."

"Wow." Mason was still trying to absorb her revelation. "Shawn Angelos. I haven't heard that name in a while. Were you married for a long time?"

"Too long." She moistened her lips, deciding how much to tell. "It didn't end well. To be honest, it didn't start well, either." She decided to be completely honest. "If I'm being honest, nothing about my marriage worked."

"I'm sorry."

Sara swallowed hard, averting her eyes. *Honesty*, she reminded herself.

"What I said earlier, about being tired of running..."

"Yeah?" Despite the casual reply, Mason went still.

"Shawn knew it as well as I did, but he refused to admit it. He didn't take failure easily." Another hard swallow. "The first time I ran, I knew it was a mistake. I had the papers that said we were divorced, but he refused to accept the fact. If I had just stayed and stood my ground..." She broke off, shaking her head in regret.

"What, Sara?" Mason asked in a gentle voice. "What would have happened if you had stayed?"

"He would have killed me."

Her matter-of-fact answer took him by surprise. Mason cocked his head, unsure he had understood her correctly, even though he knew he had. Words like hers weren't easily mistaken.

And he remembered now, how Angelos' temper had damaged his career. The final blow had been a devastating knee injury.

"Then how was it a mistake to run?" he asked.

"Because after you run the first time," her voice sounded sad, "you can never stop."

"You stopped last week," Mason reminded her. "I told you to run, but you didn't."

"I'm not sure last week mattered."

Again, he let her set the pace to tell her story.

"I can't run fast enough," she continued after a while, "or far enough, to outrun a man like Shawn."

"There are programs, Sara. People who—"

She cut him off before he could finish. "Those people, those programs, can't protect me. I thought I had finally done it. I thought I had finally escaped my past. I took such drastic measures..." She lifted her shoulder in a helpless gesture.

Only half-kidding, Mason asked, "Legal, I hope?"

"I petitioned the court to change my name, if that's legal enough for you. But in the end, even that hasn't worked."

Alarmed, he asked, "Why do you say that? Has he found you?"

"I think so." She shut her eyes before she admitted, even to herself, what she knew was true. "I know so. He's called, even though he never says a word..."

Sara darted a glance his way. She saw understanding dawn in his dark-brown eyes. "The night I called you, about the murder. You were already awake. You said it was a wrong number. That's why you sounded so shaken, even before I told you the news."

She merely nodded.

"If he didn't say anything, how do you know it was him? Couldn't it have simply been a wrong number, like you said?"

"Not at 2:22, it couldn't." Glancing up again to catch his puzzled look, she explained, "Some couples have a song. We had a number."

"That's why you freaked out in town. That's why you didn't want to talk to the reporter or to have your face on film."

Sara was impressed. "Wow. You really are good at your job."

"Did the segment make the news? I didn't have a lot of time to watch the news during that time."

"Oh, yes. And social media. And just about every other format of news and juicy tidbits you can think of. That's when the calls began."

"There was more than one?"

"Yes, until I pulled the cord out of the wall. Thank goodness, he only has my landline number and not my cell."

"At least that's something," Mason murmured. "That's why you're so cautious. I thought you were just suspicious of men in general, but it's more than that. That's why you have the guns and the training."

"And why I invented SJ's Big Dogs."

"*You* invented it?" His eyes widened as a new epiphany hit him. "*SJ's*. Sarah Jennings."

"*SJ Innovations*, to be exact. I don't just work for a computer software company. I *am* the company."

"That explains your obsession with computers," he murmured. "For a while there, I thought you might have some sort of weird technology fetish."

Sara laughed at that. "Hardly. Not a fetish, anyway. Just a love for what I do and a way to support myself."

"I'm impressed. I had no idea you were an accomplished businesswoman. Or a business owner. I thought you were tech support or something."

"I am. As a small business owner, I wear many hats."

"It's a good look on you." He followed the compliment with a solemn note. "But, Sara, I was serious about the programs. My brand of programs, not yours. Programs designed to protect you."

"Mine protect me, too," she countered. "I'd like to believe I've made women everywhere safer. Not just with Big Dogs, but with a variety of security devices, including the Echo I used to throw Bernard off."

"I was going to ask you about that..."

"My money is in designing major programs for retail, like I'm doing now, but my passion is in giving vulnerable people a sense of security. I have several products in development, plus a few more already on the market."

"I'm doubly impressed." His praise was sincere. "You've done a good job protecting yourself so far. But my programs go one step farther. You can rest easy, knowing—"

She cut him off, clearly becoming agitated. "Knowing what, exactly? Shawn isn't the kind of man to bother with the details, like restraining orders. Don't you think I've already tried them? Don't you think I moved a dozen times, until he managed to track me down yet again? Don't you think I knew that the only option left for me was to change my name and re-invent my entire life, hundreds of miles away in an obscure little town in the middle of nowhere?"

"Obscure," Mason murmured, "until an escaped convict made it the center of attention." He surprised her when he reached out to cover her hand and issued a sincere apology. "I'm sorry, Sara. Law enforcement—*my* program, the one I fully believed would keep people safe—failed you. If we had captured Bernard on that first day, even the second, your obscure little town could have remained obscure. You would have remained hidden, and safe."

Sara was pragmatic enough to acknowledge the truth. "Until he found me again," she whispered. She squeezed Mason's hand, oblivious to the fact that their fingers were entwined, and spoke in a stronger voice. "It's not your fault, Mason. I'm not sure where the blame lies. Maybe nowhere, maybe everywhere."

"It definitely lies with Bernard."

"Yes, absolutely. But how far back does it go? To his adopted parents? To his birth parents? From all accounts, Cora Miller was a good person, except when it came to a blind spot with her clandestine lover. She was so hopelessly in love with her mysterious 'R'—Ramon—that she couldn't see he was using her."

"I don't know about any of that, but I do know this. Along with Bernard, someone else is to blame. Someone helped Bernard pull this off."

"Who was it?"

"That's the kicker. None of us have a clue who it is." His voice slipped to a dangerous low. "But whoever it is, God help him or her when we figure it out."

# Chapter 32

## Sara

With her bruises faded and her computer program ready to install, Sara spent the better part of a week in Dallas. It took a few days to get the program up and running, another two to deem it successful.

As a reward for her hard work, she was booked at a five-star hotel. After the project was completed and polished to perfection, Sara pampered herself with an extra day in the city, shopping, visiting an upscale spa, and eating at one of the area's most renown restaurants. After making a few laps in the hotel's extravagant pool that evening, lounging in the hot tub, and sinking into the luxurious linens of her suite's king-sized bed, she could hardly wait to get back home to her farmhouse.

It was amazing, even to Sara, how quickly she had adapted to life on a cozy little pecan farm.

Mason had insisted on meeting her when she arrived back home to make certain the house was secure. He had taken it upon himself to check the property while she was gone. He justified accompanying her inside by citing something about erring on the side of caution.

Secretly, Sara was glad to have him there.

It wasn't just because of Shawn. It wasn't just because of Thomas Bernard. It wasn't just because her house still bore the marks of a battleground. All of those were true enough. After Bernard had taken her hostage there, she knew it would take time for her to feel comfortable in her home again. She knew, too, that Shawn wasn't done with her yet. She had an instinctive sense of pending danger.

But it was more than just those reasons. If she were being completely honest, there was something new brewing inside her. She didn't understand it and certainly didn't like it, but a sense of loneliness had taken hold. She blamed it on meeting Mason during a vulnerable time in her life and realizing how few friends she actually had. Not counting Special Investigator Burleson, the actual number hovered at zero.

"Welcome home," Mason said, opening her car door for her when she pulled under the carport.

She also hated admitting how much she had missed his deep, trust-inspiring voice. They had communicated only by text messages over the past week, and those had been few and far between. Both had been busy with their careers, and suddenly, the parameters of their relationship had changed. She was no longer the victim.

He was no longer the savior riding in on his white horse. Maybe neither had ever been true, but it no longer mattered. They were treading new water, and their friendship was a makeshift raft on a virgin voyage.

*And,* she thought irritably, *does he* really *have to look so handsome?* He wore a crisp cowboy shirt over starched, tight-fitting jeans. The tan shirt was perfect at bringing out the hidden high-lights in his dark eyes. Not that she noticed. It was simply an observation, and a grudging one, at that.

"Thanks," she said, pushing out a smile.

He saw through her obvious effort. "Tired?" he asked in concern.

"Extremely. It was a long week, followed by a long drive. Traffic was backed up on the inter-state."

"Isn't it always? Here, let me get that for you."

"I can get my own suitcase."

"So can I. See? Already have it." His rakish smile irritated her all the more.

"Fine." She knew she was being ungracious. She slammed her car door with more force than necessary, stalking ahead of him to the back door.

His long legs gobbled up the distance, so that he reached it first. He released the suitcase and turned his palm upward. "Keys?"

Rolling her eyes, she handed him the set he requested.

Mason was slow in plunking them from her hand. His fingers skimmed against hers. "Sara? Is something wrong? Are you upset with me?"

She didn't need him going full-on investigator with her. Even she couldn't explain this sudden and undeserved hostility toward him, and she certainly didn't need his help in deciphering its origins.

"Just tired," she claimed.

"Good thing I've already taken care of the dogs for you." He grinned.

Seeing his old sense of humor and his ridiculously, irritatingly, and yes, sexily playful smile, Sara forgot to be angry with him. She had missed him.

There, she had admitted it, if only to herself. She had missed her friend.

"I suppose it is," she agreed, a smile itching at the corners of her mouth.

"Bruno and Hondo have missed you." No longer so playful, he added, "We all have."

His honesty unnerved her. She wanted to say she had missed him, too, but it was still too new to her. The best she could do was hold his gaze and offer a small nod.

Mason turned to unlock and open the door. He went in first, checking the add-on for any signs of disturbance. He asked her to wait at the kitchen doorway as he swept the rest of the house.

"All clear," he said, coming back into the room.

Not unexpectedly, she had disobeyed his instructions and was already at the kitchen counter. He recognized the slight frown on her face.

"What is it?" he asked, already on alert as he glanced around.

"Uhm, nothing."

"We've been down this road before," he recalled. "Last time, you said it felt different somehow."

"It does this time, too."

He had learned to trust her instincts. "You think someone has been here?"

"Yes, but I know that's crazy." She turned her eyes up to him for reassurance. "Right?"

Mason wouldn't insult her by lying to her. "I hope so. But after Bernard managed to get in here, especially when I knew the windows were all locked, it's hard to say." When he reached out to put a comforting hand on her shoulder, Sara surprised him by stepping into his arms.

She wasn't about to analyze her actions. She just knew she was scared. Scared that Shawn had been here, and that he was coming back.

"It's okay, Sara. I'll get a detail out here. We'll check for fingerprints. I'll post someone outside your door at night."

Her face was still pressed against him. "No. We both know your request would be turned down."

"Then I'll do it myself," he claimed. "I'll sleep on your couch."

Sara had the craziest urge to tell him that if he stayed, it wouldn't be on her couch. But that was ridiculous. They were… friends, weren't they? The lines had become blurred and fuzzy, especially while standing within the circle of his strong arms. And Sara didn't do fuzzy.

She abruptly pulled away and stood at the sink, gazing out the kitchen window.

"Tell me what feels different," he prodded.

*Besides you and me?* she wanted to ask. *Do you feel it, too? This crazy pull between us?*

One look into his dark eyes told her that he did.

She turned back to the window, trading one sense of safety for another.

"I can't describe it," she answered. "It's just a feeling."

He nodded in understanding. "I didn't check the attic. You stay here while I—"

"No need. There's a camera and motion detector up there. If as much as a dust ball moves up there, my phone dings."

"Good thinking."

"Like you said. It's better to err on the side of caution."

"Agreed. Is there anything else in your car that needs to come in?"

"There's a box in the back, but I can get it."

"How about if you make coffee, and I get the box?"

She hid an indulgent smile from him as he went back to the car. By the time she put away her purse and briefcase, he had returned with a large box, stuffed with her computer monitor, electrical cords, binders, and such.

"Where do you want this?"

"My office."

"Here, take this from me," he said. Beneath the box, a brown bag dangled precariously from his fingers.

"What is it?" she asked.

"A late lunch or an early supper, whichever way you want to look at it. I ordered from *Bo's.* I figured you would probably be too tired to cook."

His thoughtfulness touched her. She peeked inside, not surprised to see two sandwiches. "You must have thought I was hungry."

"If you don't want both, invite me to stay, and I can take one off your hands." He threw the words over his shoulder as he carried the box through her bedroom door, enroute to the office.

By the time he returned, Sara had plated both sandwiches and placed them on the table.

"I decided I wasn't that hungry," she said in response to his arched eyebrow.

"Then it's a good thing I stopped and washed my hands." Mason grinned, holding up damp palms.

"I don't have any tea made, so you'll have to do with water. Or, do you still want coffee?"

"Water's fine. I'll wait and have coffee with dessert."

She scowled at his presumptuous reply. "I may have a package of cookies somewhere, or maybe some ice cream, but that's about all the dessert I can offer today."

"I guess I left that bag in the truck," he said. "I brought scones from *Read it Again, Sam.* Hope you like orange-cranberry."

"They're my favorite."

As they ate their late lunch/early supper, Mason coaxed Sara into talking about her success in Dallas.

"You're amazing, you know that?" he said in awe. "I had no idea you had such big accounts."

His praise embarrassed her. Sara soon changed the subject, asking about his return to work.

When they pushed away their empty plates, Mason said, "I guess I should go get those scones."

"Before we have dessert... if you're not in a hurry, that is..." Sara stammered, suddenly embarrassed about the suggestion she was about to make, "would you like to, uhm, walk down to the pecan orchard with me? I need to check on my trees."

"I'm in no hurry." He leaned back to stretch, running a hand over his flat stomach. "*Bo's* doesn't skimp on toppings, and we still have dessert to eat. A walk sounds good."

After Mason locked the door behind them, they enjoyed a leisurely walk down to the orchard. In typical Texas fashion, the autumn temperatures had risen again into the eighties during the day. As dusk approached, a cool breeze rustled through the leaves.

Seeing the ready-to-harvest nuts that had matured over the past few days, Sara nodded in approval. "I need to line up my work crew. It looks like it'll be a good crop."

"So, Gil and I are off the hook, huh?" Mason teased.

"Unless you want to pick up thousands of pecans..."

Mason laughed, turning down her offer to become a semi-professional nut harvester.

She hadn't brought baskets this time, so all they did was stroll around the orchard and enjoy its tranquility.

"I can see why you were ready to come back to this," he said, looking around their peaceful setting. "No matter how glamorous they are, city lights just can't compete with what you have here."

"I agree wholeheartedly."

"Ever considered putting a bench down here? It's the perfect place to sit and ponder life's complexities."

It was Sara's turn to tease. "Or, you could do like me and just sit on the ground."

"Nah. My legs would just get in the way."

"Shouldn't have such long ones." She dared to take a peek at the jeans-clad legs striding beside hers.

"They're not nearly as long as Gil's," he reminded her. "Which, speaking of Gil…"

"Yeah?"

"He and I go way back. There's a concert coming up in a couple of weeks, and I'm going to invite him and his wife to go. Isabella's had a hard time with health problems, and this might cheer her up. I thought you might like to join us."

"Oh." She was clearly surprised at his suggestion. At a loss for words, she repeated, "Oh."

"It's just a concert, Sara. Maybe a bite to eat beforehand."

"Okay."

"'Okay,' you agree it's no big deal, or 'okay,' you'll go?"

"Both."

He couldn't resist teasing her again. "You don't even know who's playing."

"Doesn't matter. I need to get out, and Gil seems like a nice enough guy."

"Just to be clear," Mason said in mock seriousness, "he's married. You'll be my date, not his."

"Yeah, I got that part."

A pleased smile replaced the humor. He pushed his luck and took her hand as it swung between them. Sara stiffened for a fraction of a second. Then, without looking his way, she swung his hand in time with hers. They walked back to the house with few words, both content in this new, comfortable silence.

Reaching the house, Sara unlocked the door while Mason retrieved the scones from his truck.

By mutual consent, they took their seats at the kitchen table. Despite their closeness in the orchard and their tentatively scheduled double-date, they didn't head into the living room. It felt too intimate, too soon. Never mind that they had eaten pie in there just over a week ago.

Sara's hand trembled ever so slightly as she sipped her coffee.

Nothing slipped past the detective, but he did misinterpret the cause. "Look, if the prospect of going to the concert upsets you…"

"It's not that," Sara said slowly. "I mean, it does in a way, but that's not what's bothering me."

"Then what is?"

"I can't shake the feeling that someone has been in here recently."

Sara looked around the room. It looked the same as always. Nothing was out of place. She had been through the rest of the house and found the same thing. Nothing seemed out of the ordinary, other than this sense of apprehension crawling over her skin.

"You mean, other than law enforcement?" Mason asked. "I know it had to have been unsettling having forensics and investigators and so many uniforms invading your home."

"Not an experience I want to repeat," she assured him, "but no, that's not it. I can't really explain it. But a pot plant was moved outside by the door—and before you ask, I'm not stupid enough to hide a key there—and there's just a feeling I get in here. Which doesn't make sense. Nothing is disturbed. You came at random intervals to check the house. I have a camera covering the driveway and, of course, the one in the attic. But I can't shake the feeling someone has been in here, invading my space."

"If I can ask, why the attic? Why do you have a camera there and not down here?"

"Obviously, I do plan to put a couple of cameras in down here, after what happened. But the attic... Shawn tried that once before. He shimmied up a tree and crawled in through an attic window. Lucky for me but not for him, he was in the neighbor's half of the duplex where I lived. So, now I have a thing about attics."

"And with good reason," he muttered.

They had just finished dessert and were taking their dishes to the sink when Mason's phone dinged. He read the message with a groan.

"Troubles?" Sara guessed.

"I'm being called in."

She gave him a sympathetic smile. "Never a dull moment, huh?"

"No. But I hate leaving you like this, while you're still visibly unnerved."

"It's probably because I've been gone. Coming home to an empty house can do that sometimes." She lifted her shoulders in a shrug. "But don't worry about me. I'll be fine. Really, I will."

"I'm sure you will be, but I still worry."

Sara put her hand out and gave him a little push. "Go. Do your job. I need to unpack, and then I'm calling it an early night. I'm exhausted."

Mason headed for the door with reluctance. "If you need anything, call me."

"I will," Sara promised, trailing behind.

He stalled at the threshold. "Sure you don't need anything else unloaded?"

"I'm sure."

"Okay, then, I'm headed out."

Sara's laugh was half-hearted. "Go, already. I'll be fine."

For one long, terrifying, hopeful moment, Sara thought he might kiss her. Mason leaned forward, but his lips only grazed her cheek.

"Call me if you need me." He finally made it through the door and onto the porch.

"I will. I promise. And you be careful."

"You, too." He darted his eyes to the door between them. "And—"

Sara rolled her eyes. "I know, I know. 'Keep your doors locked.'"

"That, too. But I was going to say that I'm glad you're home."

"Thank you." With a shy smile, because she knew their words had more meaning than what shimmered on the surface, Sara said, "I am, too."

That night, when the house was dark and silence settled in around her, she had another nightmare.

# Chapter 33

## Sara

A rustling sound awoke her. Sara wasn't as exhausted as she had led Mason to believe, but she was extremely tired. In spite of that, she was sleeping lightly, half-expecting something bad to happen.

The rustling may or may not have been a bad thing, but it put her on alert. She reached for her gun, relieved to find it exactly where she had left it. To be on the safe side, she pulled it under the covers with her.

After a good twenty minutes, Sara detected nothing new. The only sounds she heard were the intermittent groans coming from her ancient refrigerator and the gentle whir of her ceiling fan. Soon, she drifted back to sleep.

Sometime later, she began dreaming.

"Bridddggette."

The fan whispered her name. Her old name.

Sleeping hard now, Sara mumbled a protest. Her head moved on the pillow, making a tangled mess of her hair. Hair that was dark now (toasted chestnut, the bottle called it) rather than honey.

"Bridddggette."

She struggled to come out of the dream. With Shawn's voice haunting her, she knew she was spiraling downward, into a nightmare. "No," she murmured, trying hard to wake up. "No. Not again."

The fan blades whispered back to her, "Bridddggette. Miss me, Bridgette?"

The weight of the nightmare bore down on her. She tried fighting, but her arms were like lead. After a huge effort, she managed to fling one arm aside, pushing back against the terror of the dream.

The flailing movement knocked over the glass she kept by her bed. Water splashed as the glass toppled and then bounced off the mattress on its way to the floor.

She wasn't sure which woke her—the clatter, the splash, or the crash against the floor—but she came to with a gasp. Realizing what had happened, she groaned, reached for her water-soaked phone, and rolled out on the opposite side of the bed.

Turning on the bathroom light, Sara gathered towels to take back to the bedroom, but her first concern was her phone. She took off her protective case, trying to remember whether her phone was water resistant or not. Just in case, she needed to dry it off well and leave it to air. She powered the device off to keep from shorting out the battery.

Sara carried the towels to the bedroom and cleaned up her mess. Glancing at the clock, she saw that it was a few minutes after 2:22.

Her apprehension grew. It had to be coincidence. It wasn't her subconscious playing tricks on her, she told herself. Just bad luck. Nothing good ever happened at that time.

Sara threw the towels into the tub, washed her hands, and dried them off as she debated whether or not to stay up for the day. She could try to catch another hour or two of sleep, or she could catch up on emails and messages.

"You'll probably have bags under your eyes if you don't at least *try* going back to sleep," she muttered, looking into the mirror. "These bags look more like carry-on luggage."

She crawled under the covers, but sleep was elusive. When she closed her eyes, she saw Shawn's face. With each whir of the fan, she thought it was his voice. Her home was over a hundred years old. It was natural to hear a groan or two from its settling joints, but she imagined it was her ex-husband, prying a window open or sneaking into her room.

By the time exhaustion overtook her, dawn was breaking. Three hours of fitful sleep wasn't much, but it was better than nothing.

The first thing she did was call her pickers to set up a harvest date.

Then, lured by the glorious sunshine pouring through her windows, she decided to walk down to the orchard.

She knew it was foolhardy on her part, but she needed the fresh air and exercise. She needed the normalcy of what her life had been like before Bernard's intrusion. It had been three weeks since her cover was blown, and Shawn still hadn't shown up. Surely, she could squeeze in one normal, peaceful day that wasn't shrouded in fear.

She would treat herself to this one indulgence, she decided once she had sufficient coffee in her system.

This morning, it took three cups.

Sara tried relaxing, but even in her beloved pecan bottom, peace eluded her. She couldn't shake this feeling of impending doom.

"It's because of Bernard," she assured herself aloud. "It hasn't been quite three weeks. It's natural to still feel like this. Just breathe and take it easy."

She made a complete round through the trees. She concentrated on the twinkling sounds of Orchard Creek running nearby. Smiled when she heard the twitter of birds flitting from one branch to another. Filled her lungs with clean, crisp morning air.

As the peacefulness finally settled over her, Sara cleared her mind of everything but the beauty of the day. She started back toward the house, thinking of things she wanted to accomplish for the day.

Forgetting, for once, to watch for danger.

In the quiet of the morning, his voice sounded unnaturally loud. "Hello, Bridgette."

Sara stumbled at the unexpected intrusion. Trembled at the recognition of his voice.

"Or, shall I call you *Sara*?" Shawn said the name with disdain.

"Sh—Shawn. What are you—What are you doing here?"

"Is that any way to greet your husband? What's it been now? Two years? Closer to three? And this is all you can say to me?"

Sara found her vice. "Ex-husband, Shawn. We're no longer married."

"That's not what the justice of the peace said. She said, 'till death do us part.'"

He had hit upon a bitter note, one that still sounded sour to her ears. The courthouse ceremony was just one more knot snarled into a long string of disappointments during their marriage. The least he could have done was give her a proper wedding. An opportunity to publicly claim him as her own, where his gaggle of female admirers couldn't possibly ignore her. But no. They had married in a secret ceremony. Shawn claimed the privacy was about protecting her and keeping their love pristine, unmarred by the paparazzi and the press, but she soon learned differently. It was so that other women would still see him as willing, able, and, most of all, available.

Shaking away the memories, she asked in a flat voice, "What do you want?"

"I want to talk to you. Visit. Catch up on what's been happening in your life."

"Why?"

His voice switched to cajoling. "Because I care about you, Bridgette. I've missed you."

It was on the tip of her tongue to say that she hadn't missed him, not at all, but there was no need to antagonize him. Maybe if she were civil, he would go away.

"How did you find me?" she said instead.

"It wasn't easy. But the media was kind enough to help me out. You did a good job of keeping your face hidden, even with cameras all over the place. Naturally, a picture or two leaked to the press. And even with your new haircut and color, I still recognized that beautiful face of yours. Knew every curve of your graceful body."

His smooth praise and seductive tone no longer had an effect on her. If anything, it repulsed her. Shawn repulsed her. How had she ever been attracted to him? How had she fallen for his lies and his manufactured charm? How had she ever been in love with him?

She hadn't, Sara realized. The epiphany dumbfounded her, but she knew it was true. She had needed Shawn. Needed the attention, and the empty praise, and the lure of something more permanent than the upheaval of her military family. Her father had been assigned to so many bases, they had begun to blur over time. The last time she heard, her parents were in Germany again, but they could be anywhere by now. *Home* had been such an ambiguous place that she convinced herself that she would find it with Shawn.

In reality, nothing could have been further from the truth. Shawn was unfaithful and abusive. When she finally saw her knight in shining armor with his armor rusted and peeled away, her love turned into something dark and tainted. At first, she had felt guilty. Hadn't she vowed to love him for the rest of her days? Through sickness and health? Through good times and bad, and through bouts of anger and pain?

She was just now realizing that she had never truly loved him at all.

Sara was so busy making her discovery, wondering if what she felt now was relief or regret, she was slow to notice how his hand slid over the curve of her waist. The gesture was intimate.

Sara stepped aside, making his hand fall.

"And the name threw me off," he continued. Some of the charm fell away, revealing a layer of ice. "Why the change, *Sara*?"

She calculated the risk of telling him the truth, versus making up some claim about doing it for business purposes. In the end, she simply said, "I needed a fresh start."

"From me? You did it to get away from *me*?" She heard the building anger in his voice.

"I didn't like the old me," she said. Maybe, for once, she should try honesty with him. Sara considered the possibility that, before the cheating and the abuse took over, some of the problems with their marriage laid at her feet. She hadn't been honest with Shawn or stood up for her own worth. That stopped now.

"What does that have to do with me?" he asked. "Wasn't being my wife good enough for you?"

Leave it to Shawn to think everything revolved around him.

Sara ignored his selfish outburst and continued, "I needed a clean break from my past. Not just with you, but with my disjointed family. I needed a new name and a new town to find a place where I belonged."

Part of that was true. She didn't add that he was the main catalyst for such a drastic move.

"You belonged with *me*!"

Shawn, as was customary with his narcissistic personality, had started out amiable enough. When she didn't respond to his irresistible charisma, he became belligerent. Who was *she* to deny *him*? He was Shawn Angelos, one of the greatest basketball players of all time!

She had heard it all before. It shamed her now to acknowledge that, once upon a time, his psychological abuse had worked.

Without turning her head, Sara calculated the distance to safety. They were still in the dip behind the house, not far enough along the swell of the hill to be seen from the house, should someone stop by.

But if that someone were Mason, he would know to check the pecan grove. That, at least, was something. The rest was up to her.

Sara belatedly realized she had left her cell phone on her desk when she entered the harvesting memo into her calendar.

When she didn't reply to him, Shawn demanded, "Did you hear me, Bridgette? You belonged with me! You still do!"

Sara met his angry gaze. In a level voice, she said, "Not anymore. You need to leave, Shawn. We're done. I'm no longer your wife. We no longer have a place in each other's lives."

Years had passed since the basketball star had been in his prime, but he had lost none of his speed. Before she realized his intent, Shawn reached out and jerked her to his side. "*I'll* say when we're done! And we, Bridgette Angelos, are not done."

Twisting and turning her way free, Sara jabbed him with her elbow and slipped under his arm. Spying a rock on the ground, she swooped down and grabbed it, hiding it in her pocket.

Shawn was still ranting. "You're still a liar, you know that? You belong with me, Bridgette." The force of his backhand across her cheek snapped her head backward. "You belong *to* me!"

Sara tasted the blood on her lip, felt the echo of the slap reverberate through her brain, but she refused to back down. Not this time. Not ever again. She spat the blood from her mouth, hitting the running shoes that bore his name.

The shoes were old, probably from his coveted stash. There was a time when the name Shawn Angelos meant something, including contracts with major labels. Shawn had bought dozens of each item, hoarding them to be parceled out over time. These shoes looked new, even though Sara knew they hadn't been on store shelves in several years.

As her blood stained his precious shoes, Sara told him, "Just leave, Shawn. I haven't been Bridgette in a very long time, and I swear, I'll never be her again. It's over between us."

"Never!"

This time when he hit her, he knocked her to the ground. When he would have kicked her with his right foot, Sara pulled out the rock. She slammed it into his left knee with all her might.

It was the knee that had ended his career. After two successful surgeries, the third one had gone poorly. There was no recovering from it, not as a professional basketball player. The best Shawn could do after that was to coach, playing his beloved sport from the sidelines. And without basketball, without stardom, without the limelight showcasing him as the team's most valuable asset, Shawn had lost his identity. He had become bitter, and he had taken that bitterness out on his wife. In many ways, his knee had ended their marriage, as well.

The rock was a direct hit on his scar. Shawn's legs buckled. Sara didn't wait for a fall. She scrambled up on all fours and took off, headed up the hill.

Shawn caught her by the ankle and pulled her back. Her shirt rode up, allowing the packed earth of the pathway to bite into her skin. Rocks grated against the tender flesh, but Sara had no time to dwell on the minor pain. It was nothing to what she knew was coming.

Shawn flipped her onto her back and straddled her, his face consorted in rage. His hands were already closing in around her throat.

"You'll be sorry for that, you bit—"

A man's voice startled them both. It came from the crest of the hill.

"Hey! Hey, stop that!"

Sara couldn't turn to see her would-be savior, but she thought she recognized the voice.

Despite the interruption, Shawn's hands tightened around her throat.

"I said to stop," the authoritative voice demanded, coming closer.

"Yeah? And who are you to stop me?" Shawn sneered.

"I'm Officer Gil Ingalls, and I have the authority to arrest you for assault and attempted murder."

*Gil! Sweet, wonderful Gil!* Some of the tension in her body lessened. Gil would save her. His voice came from just behind her now.

"Yeah, well, I'm her husband, and this is between me and her. Butt out."

"Get off her, and maybe I will," Gil countered.

Shawn removed his hands from her neck, spitting in her face. He slowly pushed to his feet, still favoring his left knee.

"You know this man, Sara?" Gil asked. He kept a suspicious eye on him as he waited for her answer.

Sara sputtered out a cough. After clearing her throat, she pushed the words out. "E-Ex. *Ex*-husband."

"I think you should back away, friend," Gil said, sounding affable yet stern.

"Friend? *Friend?* You don't even know me."

"I know you should back up, while I help the lady to her feet." Gil reached down and helped Sara up, all the while keeping his steady gaze on Shawn.

"Lady?" Shawn's laugh lacked humor.

"That's what I said."

Irritated by the officer's interference, Shawn switched tactics. "Sara, tell this man to leave," he ordered. "This is between you and me, not some stranger, law or not."

"Gil's not a stranger," Sara told him. "He's my friend. And if anyone leaves, it will be you."

Shawn's eyes narrowed. His words came quietly, but Sara recognized them as the threat they were. A quiet, distinct-speaking Shawn was far more dangerous than an angry, screaming Shawn.

"Then maybe no one will leave."

Instinctively, Sara edged closer to Gil.

Shawn glared at the other man. "You're the lawman I heard about, aren't you? I heard Bridgette was cheating on me with a stinkin' pig," Shawn sneered.

A beam of sunlight glinted off something metal in Shawn's hand, drawing a gasp from Sara. Her voice warbled. "Shawn. Shawn, what are you doing?"

He brandished the long skinning knife like a sword. "I might just skin me a pig," he said. He swung it to point directly at her. "Or a lying, cheating woman. Your choice."

Before Sara could reply, Gil broke in, "Don't I know you from somewhere?"

Shawn didn't recognize the diversionary tactic. He could never resist an opportunity to talk about himself. "Shawn Angelos," he provided. "Four NBA World Championships. Basketball Hall of Fame."

"Ah, yes," Gil said, his eyes narrowed. "I remember you."

A cocky smile came over Shawn's face, only to fall away when Gil added, "Another bitter has-been."

Shawn's face filled with rage. Knife raised, he took a step forward. He had a height advantage over the officer, but his body had gone soft while his heart had hardened.

Gil, on the other hand, had stayed in shape. As prison guard and now officer, he didn't back down from a fight. He put his head down and rammed into the charging man, pushing Shawn backward. Both men tumbled down the incline, head over heels.

The ground leveled off, giving the men a steady battlefield. Biting back another squeal, Sara scurried down after them, careful to stay beyond their reach.

Amid flying arms and twisting bodies, she caught flashes of the knife.

She heard grunts and muffled cries of pain.

Heard their bodies slam into one another and fall hard against the packed ground.

Heard the sickening thud of two heads bashing together as they rolled off the pathway and into the grass.

Heard twigs and a small branch crunch beneath them as their long legs tangled and fought for dominance.

Sara heard a loud groan, and then an odd sucking sound.

She saw a sudden burst of bright, red blood.

The men were both still now, as blood seeped into the ground around them. Shawn's body was on top.

"G—Gil?" Sara squeaked. She covered her mouth in horror. Shawn had killed him, and now he would kill her.

She knew she should run, but her feet were too heavy, and her knees were too weak. She thought she might collapse as she watched Shawn roll off the top of the other man.

Her time had run out.

Shawn's back hit the ground with a thud. It took a moment for her mind to comprehend what she was seeing. The hilt of the knife buried deep into his belly. Blood poured from all around it. His eyes stared toward the sky.

"Sh—Shawn?" His name was a whisper on her lips.

He gurgled in response, making some incoherent sound that could have been her name, could have been a cry for help. Blood foamed from his mouth.

Emotions rocked through Sara's mind. Fear. Shock. Sorrow.

Relief.

"Gil?" She finally remembered the man beside him. His clothes were covered in blood. She had no idea if it was his, Shawn's, or a combination of both. He was still on his back, his breathing labored. "Gil, are you okay? We—We need to call for help. Where's your phone? I'll call the ambulance." Sara looked at Shawn. There was so much blood.

By the time she glanced back his way, Gil had managed to sit up. He nodded toward the other man. "He's bleeding out. He'll be dead by the time they get here."

"Shouldn't we do something? Put pressure on the wound?" She made a motion with her hand. "Something? Anything?"

"It won't help." Gil lumbered to his feet. He winced and touched his side.

"B—But—But we can't just stand here and let him die!" Feeling helpless, Sara knelt beside her ex-husband. "He's still a human being."

There were times, of course, when she had doubted it. Times when she accused Shawn of being an animal. Yet it was hard to think of him that way now, his face deathly pale and his breathing so shallow, it seemed almost non-existent.

Between the foaming bubbles, Shawn managed to speak. It came out a mumble.

"Br—Brid… gett," he breathed.

"I'm here, Shawn. We're getting you help." She turned to scream up at Gil, who now stood over them. "Call for help!" she implored.

"O—Over." Shawn's voice was so weak, it was hardly a sound at all. "It's… over."

He went still. His eyes glazed over.

Shawn Angelos—her lover/her ex, her friend/her nemesis, her dreamiest love and her biggest nightmare—was dead.

# Chapter 34

## Sara

"Come on, Sara," Gil urged. "Let's go back to the house."

"And—And just leave him?"

"We'll call the ambulance. They'll come for him."

Gently, he took her arm and helped her to stand. Sara allowed him to pull her along, but she kept looking over her shoulder.

Shawn never moved. Never came after them.

Shawn was truly dead.

The reality sank in as they trudged up the incline and toward the house. After years of abuse and fear and running, Shawn could no longer hurt her. She was finally safe.

She expected the knowledge to bring her more peace than it did. Right now, all she felt was a deep, bone-weary sadness.

At the house, Gil led her through the front door and encouraged her to sit at the kitchen table. He brought her a glass of water, set it before her, and took the chair across from hers.

"Shouldn't you call someone?" she asked, motioning to the phone in his pocket. Hers was still in the office. "The sheriff? Mason? The—The ambulance?"

"I will. In time." He was clearly in no hurry. "First, I want to ask you some questions."

Sara supposed it was common. He was the first officer on the scene. He would need to gather information to pass on to the investigating officers. Obviously, since he was involved in the fight and the resulting death of the perpetrator, he wouldn't be involved with the case. It never occurred to her that, being with TDCJ, he had no jurisdiction here.

With her mind and nerves still in turmoil, Sara belatedly thought to ask, "Do you need an ambulance? Were you cut?"

"Minor flesh wound," he assured her, looking down at his side. "Now. Those questions."

Sara fingered her water glass. "I know. I never talked about Shawn. Mason knows part of it, but I don't like bringing up my past."

"I don't want to talk about your ex-husband. I want to talk about Thomas Bernard."

Thoroughly confused, Sara's forehead wrinkled. "Bernard? Can't that wait? Shawn's body—"

"Isn't going anywhere," Gil interrupted. His voice lost some of its compassion.

"But—"

"But nothing. Do you still love the man?" he seemed to challenge.

"No. No, I haven't in a long time, but his body is just lying out there..." She flung her arm toward the orchard.

"Dead. It's laying there dead, and there's nothing you or I can do to change that. What I need right now is for you to focus."

Sara was confused by this side of Gil's personality. His demeanor was unnerving. He sounded so cold. So unfeeling.

Something nibbled the edges of Sara's mind, but it was too vague. Her brain still felt scrambled. Her face hurt from Shawn's assault. Her body ached all over. Her emotions were all over the place. Isolating a single thought or a single feeling was too monumental of a task.

On some level, Sara knew she was in shock.

"Okay," she agreed, wanting to help Mason's friend. Her friend. Gil had saved her life. Of course, he was her friend.

Pleased with her compliance, Gil nodded. "I need to know what you told Thomas Bernard."

Sara blinked. Once. Twice. "I'm sorry," she said, assuming her mind was worse than she thought. Or maybe it was her ears that had the problem. "What did you say?"

"I need to know what you told Thomas Bernard before Mason killed him."

"What does Thomas Bernard have to do with Shawn?"

"Nothing."

"Then why—why are you asking me about him? I know the investigation is still open, but surely… surely, it can wait!"

"This is off the record, so to speak," Gil told her. He leaned over the table, so that his face was closer to hers. "This is just between you and me. Did you tell Bernard where the money was hidden?"

"Money? Wh—What money?"

His palm smacked against the kitchen table, causing Sara to jump. Her eyes widened when she saw the look on his face.

"You know what money I'm talking about," he told her coldly. "The money his old man stole from all over the county. It's somewhere in this house, and I mean to find it."

His determination could be based on the dedication of a good and devoted officer. Gil worked for the exact prison the inmate had escaped from. There had to be immense pressure on the officers there, trying to right a wrong and find the weak link in their protocols. They had made a commitment to the general public to keep them safe, and they had failed. Dedication like that was commendable.

Yet, somehow, Sara knew that wasn't the case with Gil.

Gil Ingalls wasn't a good man. Sara would stake her life on it.

Judging from the look in his eyes, she might be doing just that.

Her mind cleared just enough for one uneasy thought to leak out. She had locked the door when she left. Gil hadn't needed a key when he escorted her inside just now.

There was still something more, she knew there was, but it couldn't quite break through the surface...

Sara chose her words carefully. She tried to keep fear from creeping into her voice. He couldn't find out she knew the truth, not if she wanted to find a way out of this latest nightmare.

"Like I told the others," she said slowly, "he kept talking about money hidden in the... in the walls." To cover the nervous quiver in her voice, she put a hand to her forehead. "I don't feel so good. I think I need to lie down."

"Not yet. First, you need to tell me where he looked. Where the investigators looked."

"You, uh, can see the broken boards. There was nothing there."

"And the investigators? Where did they look?"

Her confusion was real. "Nowhere."

Gil stood so quickly, he knocked the chair out from beneath him. It clattered to the floor, stretching Sara's taut nerves ever tighter.

He paced a few feet, then whirled back toward her. "You're telling me they didn't search the house?"

"That's right."

"Why they hell wouldn't they?" he raged.

"Why would they?" she countered.

"Because there's a small fortune hidden here! Somewhere in this house, Ramon Garcia hid his life savings, and it was enough for his son to risk his life for."

"Bernard thought there was money, but he was wrong."

"How do you know that? How could you possibly know that?" Gil demanded.

She had used it as an excuse a few moments ago, but now she truly did feel ill. Her stomach roiled with nausea. Her head was pounding. She saw flashing lights and zigzags quivering in her line of vision. Her heart was beating too fast.

"I—I really need to lie down now. Please, Gil. I don't feel right."

"I'll have the medics check you out when they come for Angelos," he told her, not unkindly. "Right now, I need answers." His voice firmed. He walked over, bent down near her, and looked her in the eyes. "Tell me what you know."

Sara looked at him, seeing two faces. All four of his eyes looked evil. She gagged, trying to hold down the bile.

The projectile of her vomit spewed directly into his face. Repulsed, Gil jumped back, but not before he slapped her.

"Look what you did!" he shrieked. He was already at the sink, wiping away the mess with one of her best towels. The smell of vomit was one thing he couldn't tolerate. It reminded him of how sick Isabella had been during chemo. He had gladly cleaned up after his wife when she was sick, but now the smell never failed to remind him of that dark, helpless time during their lives.

"I—I told you. I need to…" Sara slumped in her chair, her head hanging limply from her neck.

"Oh, no, you don't," Gil said. He grabbed a nearby glass, filled it with water, and flung it upward into Sara's face. She came to with a sputter. "You don't get off that easy," he told her. "Tell me where the money is!"

"No money," she said, fighting off another bout of unconsciousness. Water dripped from the hair framing her battered face. Blood dripped from her busted lip.

"There is! I know for a fact that Ramon Garcia stole over two hundred thousand dollars during a period from 1965 to 1974. And he gave it to Cora Miller to hide, here in this very house. He told me so himself."

If she had had the strength, Sara's head would have popped up in surprise. Only her eyes managed to look up at him. "H—How?"

"He was a prisoner in the Walls Unit while I worked there. He was an old man by then, staring death in the face. He mostly babbled, half-senile at the time, but I did my homework. His stories checked out. Everything he told me—every robbery, every break-in—was documented in newspapers and police records. I knew he had to be telling the truth."

"But... Bernard. How...?" Full sentences were too taxing, but Gil filled in the spaces for her.

"Ramon said he had a son. A midwife helped Cora with the birth and with finding a home for the baby. Garcia was in prison by then, but he kept tabs on her. Or maybe it was the money he kept tabs on." His laugh sounded brittle.

"I still don't..."

Before going on, Gil tossed her a wet cloth. "Here. Clean yourself up. You look pathetic."

Thanks in part to him, but Sara didn't say so. She could hardly speak at all.

"He knew a few details about his son. He knew that once a year, Cora sent money to his adopted mother. He wanted me to locate him, so that he could meet him before he died."

Sara found enough energy to wipe her face. The cool cloth felt heavenly against her bruises and helped to revive her somewhat. As she attempted cleaning her clothes, she asked, "Did he?"

"No. He died before I figured out that Thomas Ramon Bernard was his son." Satisfied with his own hygiene, other than the blood already soaked into his shirt, Gil tossed Sara a second towel.

"By a stroke of luck, I was transferred to the Roscoe Unit, the same unit where Thomas Ramon Bernard was serving out a life sentence. I saw the resemblance immediately, even before I heard his name."

"Luck?" Sara asked.

Another slippery thought wandered through her mind. Twice now, she had the sensation that someone had been in her house. The last time, it was after returning from Dallas. The first time, it was after Mason and Gil had thoroughly checked her house, making certain all windows were locked and secured. What if...

"I was a guard," Gil went on, "before I became an officer with OIG. Bernard was a prisoner. With nothing else to do, we sometimes struck up a conversation." He shrugged his shoulders. He pushed away from the sink counter and wandered around the kitchen, studying boards and trim work, much the way Bernard had done. "I knew he was serving life. I saw no harm in telling him about his old man."

"So, you cooked up the plan to help him break out of jail."

Gil sent her a hard look. "To be feeling so bad, you're still sharp enough," he noticed.

"The water in the face helped. Thanks," Sara said with sarcasm.

He ignored her sassy reply. "We didn't come up with the plan right away. I'm not a dirty cop." The look she sent him put him on the defensive. "I'm not!" he insisted. "Or I wasn't." He ran a hand along the back of his neck. "But Isabella was so sick. And her hospitable bills were staggering. I—I didn't have a choice. Faced with my wife's health or breaking a few laws, I had to choose Izzy."

Sara had revived enough to send him a scathing look, matched only by the tone in her voice. "A *few* laws? You helped a dangerous criminal break out of prison. He killed a man. That's on you, Gil. You did that, as surely as if you pulled the knife—or bottle, or whatever it was—yourself."

For the first time, a look of remorse crossed his face. He looked downright sick at heart. His lanky body curled inward with shame. "That wasn't supposed to happen, I swear it wasn't. He promised."

"You trusted a criminal to keep his word?"

His voice stiffened, along with his posture. "It doesn't matter what I did or did not believe. It doesn't matter why I did what I did. Not really. All that matters is that I find the money. I can pay all of Izzy's bills and still have enough left for us to start over somewhere."

"A person can never outrun their past," Sara told him. Her voice was ripe with sorrow. "Today was proof of that."

"But I can try. And you're going to help me. You're going to tell me where the money is."

"Gil, there has to be another way. Loans. Relief programs. I can help you find—"

"Don't you think I've tried all that? I can't pay the loans I already have!" He ran both hands over his head, cradling the back of his neck. "I took out a second mortgage, and that's fallen behind, too. So don't talk to me about help."

Clearly distraught, Gil paced in place. When his hands dropped back to his side, they were curled into fists. "No more talking. Just tell me where the money is!"

"I told you. There *is* no money!" Sara immediately regretted raising her voice. The throbbing in her head returned, and she felt woozy.

"You're lying."

"Why would I lie?"

"Maybe you want it all for yourself. Maybe Bernard found it, but you hid it again." His eyes roamed around the room as the idea galvanized in his frantic mind. "Yeah, that's it. You hid the money for yourself."

When his eyes came back to settle on hers, Sara knew he was too far over the edge to reason with. Any argument on her part would only ensure more pain and suffering.

Sara had to think fast. To buy herself more time, she let her head droop forward again.

"Oh, no, you don't!" Gil responded. He yanked her hair to jerk her head back up. "You're going to tell me where my money is!"

Sara kept her eyes shut, but she could feel his hot breath across her face. He was so close, bits of his spit splattered on her cheek. It was all she could do not to flinch, but her life depended on this. She had to convince him that she was one step away from unconsciousness.

She uttered one word. It came out in a faint whisper. "At—Attic."

Gil pounced on the word, clinging to the hope that all his sins hadn't been in vain. "Attic? That's where you hid it?"

She heard the uptick in his voice. Knew his eyes glowed with newfound optimism.

She made no reply.

"Get up!" he demanded. "Show me where it is!"

When she made no move—when she didn't utter a single sound—Gil kicked the rungs of her chair. Sara fell forward on the table, willing her body to go limp.

"I said to get up!" he demanded. He yanked her hair again, harder this time, trying to get a reaction.

When Sara remained motionless, he dropped her head back onto the table. She swallowed back a cry of pain as her cheek smacked against the scarred wooden surface.

"Forget you," he muttered in disgust. "I'll find it myself. You're useless."

For good measure, he kicked the chair again. Sara prepared herself for a hard landing, but it never came. The chair didn't move far enough to unseat her.

Seeing her inert form still sprawled over the table, Gil made another sound of disgust and stalked away. He obviously knew exactly where to find the attic stairway.

Sara waited until she heard him stomp up the steps before making her move. The chair threatened to tumble at her fast departure. She didn't bother to stabilize it, but luck was with her. It stayed in place as she dashed for her hidden gun.

Gone.

It came as no surprise, but she had held out hope that he had forgotten to remove it before coming down to the pecan grove. With no gun in sight, Sara grabbed the sharpest knife she could find and raced toward the front door. Her hands fumbled with the lock when she heard him roar in frustration from above.

# Chapter 35

## Mason

Mason pulled into the long driveway leading up to Sara's house, wondering why Gil's truck was pulled over to one side. It was parked before the curve, just out of view from the house.

Some sixth sense told him that something wasn't right. Mason parked behind his friend and stepped from his truck. Drawing his gun, he approached the house with caution, wondering if Sara's abusive ex-husband had finally resurfaced.

A strange vehicle in her driveway seemed to confirm that notion.

As he neared the house, he heard the screen door open and saw Sara stumbling from inside. She held what looked like a knife in her hand, and her choppy movements set off all kinds of warning bells in his head.

Crouching low, Mason eased his way closer.

To his surprise, it wasn't a stranger who came barreling through the front door. It was Gil. Were they both running from Sara's enraged ex? He crept nearer, trying to get a good read on what was happening.

"Get back here, you liar! There was nothing in the attic! You lied to me!" Gil bellowed. His tirade was aimed at Sara.

More incredulously, so was the pistol Gil had in his hands.

Mason cursed beneath his breath, disbelief warring with what his eyes were seeing.

Looking over her shoulder, Sara stumbled as she ran. Her foot snagged on the grass, and she fell to her knees.

As she scrambled to get up, Gil's voice taunted her. "There's no place to run, Sara. No place to hide."

Mason had never heard his friend's voice sound so cold and dispassionate.

"I have a gun," he threatened, "and I'll shoot you if you don't come back here and tell me where the money is."

Sara hesitated, before slowly turning back to face him. She wielded the knife at shoulder's height, warrior style.

"I told you, Gil—" she said, her voice surprisingly strong, given the circumstances. There was a healthy dose of defiance in it, as well.

Mason couldn't help but smile at her spunky reply. His smile evaporated when he crept closer and saw the bruises on her face. Her lip was swollen, her hair was tangled, and her clothes were a mess.

"—there is no money," she insisted.

Mason didn't understand the conversation he had stumbled into, but he couldn't barge in right away. Not until he knew the dynamics of the situation. There had to be a better explanation than what his eyes told him: one of his most trusted friends and brother in arms was holding a woman at gunpoint, threatening to shoot if she didn't do as he said. Worst of all, it wasn't just any woman. It was the woman Mason had developed feelings for, no matter how much he denied it.

"You're lying!" Gil grated out. "Get over here."

Mason saw Gil tighten his grip on his gun, but his hands looked unsteady. When he stopped to study his friend, he realized Gil was unsteady, as well. Not physically, but emotionally. Mentally. Somewhere along the line, Gil Ingalls had come unhinged.

The gun bobbled. "Over here," Gil repeated. "Take me to where the money is, or I swear, I will drop you in your tracks."

Mason stood and stepped slowly into the open. His gun was trained on his old friend.

"No, Sara," Mason urged, not daring to look her way. He kept his eyes steady on the other man with the gun. "Don't go near him."

Gil jerked his head, glaring at his unexpected presence. "Stay out of this, Mason," he growled. "This is between the woman and me."

Mason moved steadily forward. "I know what you're doing. You're de-humanizing her. But this isn't a suspect, Gil. You can't be dispassionate about her. This is Sara. My friend. Your friend. She made us that pear cobbler, remember? You don't want to hurt her. Put down the gun, and we'll talk this all out."

"No! There's nothing to talk about!"

"Sure there is. Tell me what's going on here. Maybe I can help."

"I don't need your help. I just need my money. Tell her to give me the money, and we can all walk away from this."

"What money is that?" Mason asked, slowly easing his way toward Sara. She still held the knife, even though it did little good against Gil's gun, especially at such a distance.

"The money Ramon Garcia hid here fifty years ago! The money his son came here to get."

Trying to keep up with the unfolding chain of events, Mason frowned. "You mean Bernard?"

"Of course Bernard! We were going to split the money, fifty-fifty. But you killed him before I could get my share, and now *she* has it all!" Gil accused, shaking the gun at Sara.

Mason absorbed the latest blow with surprise, but his expression remained neutral. *Gil* was the insider? His old friend had helped Bernard escape and wreak havoc on the community, and on Sara? Shock gave way to sorrow. Sorrow turned into disappointment. Disappointment morphed into anger.

He couldn't let his anger show. He had to keep Gil calm. "Put your gun down, Gil, and we'll figure this out."

Speaking in an even tone, Mason edged closer to Sara. He needed to place himself between her and Gil before Gil did something incredibly stupid.

"It's too late for that. Izzy needs another treatment. I need this money to save my wife's life!"

"Then we'll find another way. Just put down the gun."

"No! Don't you see?" Desperation ravaged his friend's face. His voice was panicked. Tears welled in his red-rimmed eyes. "I can't get the money. This is my last chance. If she doesn't give me the money, my wife dies. I won't let that happen."

Gil gripped his gun harder, switching his attention back to Sara. "If you don't tell me where it is, I'll kill you. I swear I will!"

Mason answered instead, his voice matter of fact, "And then I'll kill you."

"Stay out of this, Mason. It's none of your business."

"I made it my business. Back off, Gil, or I'll shoot first."

"You wouldn't do that," he argued, glancing at his friend. "You wouldn't let Izzy die!"

"I won't let Sara die, either. Put down your gun, Gil. Now."

"You're bluffing." Gil shook his head, confident in his frantic denial. "You won't shoot me. I'm your friend!"

"Don't stake your life on it, Ingalls. Put your gun down, right now, or you'll find out just how serious I am."

Mason saw Gil's gaze jerk back to Sara. Saw his shooting arm tremble. Saw the madness overtake him, and the resolution set in. Money or not, Gil would shoot Sara.

That left Mason with two choices. He could shoot his mentally disturbed friend, injuring or possibly killing him, or he could take the bullet meant for Sara.

He chose the latter. Diving her way, he used his shoulder to push her roughly to the ground, never letting Gil out of his gun's sights.

"I mean it, Gil!" he yelled. "Drop it!"

Gil looked around in panic.

His eyes went to Sara, who lay motionless on the ground.

His gaze shifted to Mason, and he found himself staring down the barrel of a stainless 1911.

He knew he was out of options.

"I did it for Izzy," Gil said in a ragged whisper. With a desperate gulp, he bent his elbow, holding the gun to his own head. "Tell Izzy I love her."

Mason's reaction was instantaneous.

His bullet pinged off the side of Gil's revolver. The sheer velocity of the shot knocked the gun from Gil's hands and sent him reeling backward. Mason rushed forward, kicking the useless weapon aside and flinging himself on his friend, wrestling him into a face-down position. Using his own belt, Mason quickly secured Gil's hands behind his back.

Only then did he turn to check on Sara.

This time, she wasn't faking unconsciousness.

# Chapter 36

## Sara

Some days, Sara swore her life played in a loop, like a video snippet stuck on auto-play.

For years, her life had been stuck in the chaos that surrounded Shawn and his moods.

She did something, he lashed out.

She bore the marks of his anger, he begged for forgiveness.

Repeat.

When she finally found the strength to leave him, it was a short-lived reprieve, playing out in much the same way.

She ran, he found her.

Repeat.

Taking more drastic measures, she changed her name. She changed her life. She moved away from everything and everyone she had ever known, and she started over.

And it worked just fine, until the nightmares came and pulled her back into the same cycle of madness.

And then a different kind of nightmare entered her life, when a man named Thomas Bernard escaped prison.

It set in motion a new yet painfully old pattern. Living in fear. A resurgence of nighttime horrors. The feel of a man's imprint on her cheek. A fight for her life.

Repeat.

The cycle was the same; only the villains changed. Shawn. Bernard. Shawn. And then, to her utter disbelief, Gil Ingalls.

Even the visits to the ER were on a loop. Two nights in the hospital for observation and mandatory counseling. Instructions on how to care for a concussion and bruises to her face. The sad look of the doctors and nurses who thought to themselves, *Will this woman never learn?*

Media attention was something Sara never wanted any part of, yet that, too, played like a broken record. At first, it was all about the amazing Shawn Angelo. Then, as the shining star crashed and burned, the media obsessed over that. Just when Sara thought she was free of the meddlesome reporters, Thomas Bernard escaped from prison. And somehow, even that looped back to Shawn. His death brought on a new batch of reporters, all clamoring for another story. She breathed a sigh of relief when some big-name athlete created a more newsworthy scandal and drew the cameras away.

There was a reason Mason had warned her to keep her doors locked. Opening them led to nothing but danger.

Then, there was Special Investigator Mason Burleson. He posed a danger all his own. Somehow, the lawman with the trust-inspiring voice and the teasing smile had gotten past her defenses. Somehow, he had made her lonesome for a friend. He forced her to set aside her preformed judgments and self-denials, so that she could actually trust a man again. He gave her hope in finding a normal life for herself.

But the biggest and most frightening danger she faced was the danger of falling in love with him.

In the six weeks since her horrific ordeal, the two of them had spent increasing amounts of time together.

With her pecans harvested and the tree leaves turning a vibrant yellow before falling to the ground, Sara and Mason often strolled through the orchard arm in arm. They were careful to avoid the spot where Shawn had died, but Sara refused to allow her ex-husband to ruin the beauty and tranquility of this special place. With Mason's help, she found her beloved orchard peaceful once again. She even added a bench for quiet contemplation.

Some evenings, she cooked, and he came for dinner.

Other times, they went on day excursions. Sara had lived the past year in a shell and knew so little about her new community, but Mason made it his mission to change all that. Several of the places they explored were new to them both.

Sara's landmark job in Dallas had led to other major accounts for *SJ Innovations*. Some days, she was too busy with work to see Mason, but he understood. He had another case that took him to Mount Pleasant for several days.

Slowly but surely, they were building the foundation for a solid relationship. Sara was the first to admit it frightened her, but Mason would smile that once-irritating, now extremely sexy smile at her and assure her there was no hurry. He wasn't going anywhere. He wanted theirs to be an equal, honest relationship built on mutual respect and trust. It would take however long it took, he said.

Next week was Thanksgiving, and Sara would be having turkey and dressing with the Burleson family. It made their relationship seem so much more serious, and yet it felt right, somehow. For the first time in more years than she cared to count, Sara would be spending the holiday amid a family. It was something she was looking forward to. She had already committed to bringing pecan pies as her contribution to the meal.

Tonight, they had attended a black-tie fundraiser for Isabella. The entire law enforcement community had rallied around her, offering her the much-needed emotional and financial support to fight her battle against cancer. Gil's fate was still undetermined, but not hopeless.

And after weeks of Mason's polite, hands-off approach to earning her trust, Sara had made the first move. She wound her arms around his neck during a slow dance and had all but forced him to kiss her.

All the stars in Texas had never been as bright as they had been that night.

Sara was proud to be seen with the handsome Special Detective Burleson and wanted him to be equally proud of her. Judging by the look in his eyes, and how difficult it was for him to leave after a very heated good-night kiss, she thought she had succeeded.

Sara was honest enough to admit, if only to herself, that Mason was everything she had ever wanted in a man. It was only a matter of time before she was hopelessly, completely in love with him. Perhaps she already was. She wanted a future with him. She craved her happily ever after, but one thing stood in their way.

Sara still had one secret tucked away for safekeeping, and she feared she could never reveal it. Not to Mason. Her dream man was an upright, law-abiding officer. She hadn't intentionally done anything wrong, but he might not see it that way, not in light of recent revelations.

Mason was still reckoning with the knowledge that Gil, the friend he had trusted his life to—had trusted Sara's life to—wasn't the man Mason thought he was. Despite Gil's obvious mental illness, Mason was having trouble understanding how his old buddy could have broken his moral oath to his office and to mankind. Sara's lawman lived by a strict code of ethics, where black and white left little room for gray.

Sara's secret was definitively gray. Too gray to share with him now, but perhaps in time, when their relationship was more solid...

And that night, when she crawled into bed, still warm from Mason's kiss, she had her favorite dream of all. It was really another memory, one that never grew old, and one she always welcomed.

> She had been in the farmhouse for less than a month, and she still hadn't decided where everything would go.
>
> To avoid leaving a trail that Shawn could trace, she hadn't bothered with a moving company. She only brought what she could fit in her car. She sold the rest and would re-buy when she reached her destination.
>
> Sara had stacked most of her boxes in the front bedroom, appointing the other front room as her office. Her bedroom would be at

the back. She liked the idea of having her office and bedroom on the same side of the house, separated only by a bathroom.

For now, she would stay in the only room with furniture, the one with the fancy bedroom set in it. Later, when she had the time, she would go into one of the nearby larger towns (anything had to be bigger than Maypole) and buy a queen-sized bed for what would eventually be her bedroom.

The fancy room, as she called it, was pretty enough, but it didn't suit her style. And the mattress was horrible. It was lumpy and stained, and after only a few nights of sleeping on it, she had a backache. She would buy a new full-sized mattress for it, too, she decided.

She ordered two memory foam mattresses online, the kind that could fit into a compact box on wheels. After carving out a day she could pick them up, she prepared their spaces for arrival.

Getting the mattress off the four-poster bed was a feat in itself. Sara had tugged and pulled, succeeding only in getting it stuck on an angle. It was a mattress with coils and springs, so the metal frame wasn't as forgiving as the foam mattress that would replace it.

When she tugged again, this time more aggressively, she heard something rip.

"Great, Sara. Look what you've done. Now you'll have cotton batting floating all around the house."

She looked with dread, wondering how difficult it would be to clean up. Could she just use a vacuum?

It wasn't cotton batting that spilled from the torn mattress. It was something green, and about the size of a dollar bill. Sara grabbed it for closer examination.

It *was* a dollar bill!

More accurately, it was a fifty-dollar bill. And it was by far not the only one. Almost the entire mattress was stuffed here and there with bills of every denomination, from one dollar to one hundred dollars. Sara stared at the fortune in amazement, wondering exactly how much was tucked inside. No wonder the mattress was so lumpy! Most of the original stuffing had been pulled out and replaced with money.

Sara had heard stories about old-timers who didn't trust financial institutions and chose, instead, to hide their money at home. This had to be the life savings of several generations, she surmised.

With all of the Miller family deceased or having relinquished all claims to the property, she was reluctant to call the real estate company. No matter how nice the realtor had seemed, who was to say he would attempt to find Cora's next of kin? He might just keep the money for himself.

Sara eventually man-handled the mattress off the bed and propped it against one wall. She would debate her options of what to do with the money while she drove.

On the way, fate whittled down her choices. First, she had car trouble and had to call a tow truck. After she forked out three hundred dollars to the truck driver, the dealership said it would take almost a thousand dollars to repair her vehicle.

The real clincher, however, was the phone call she received while picking up the mattresses in her rental car. A small hotel chain based in Houston was interested in seeing her software programs for the hospitality industry. Could she bring several computers down and show management what she had?

Sara jumped at the opportunity, even though she only had two computers. One of them was on its last leg and was literally held together with duct tape. Not exactly the image she wanted to project for her up-and-coming little company.

Then and there, Sara decided she would use some of the money to repair her car and to buy two new computers. She would need monitors, too, and a few new drives and computer modules. It wouldn't cost more than a few thousand dollars, and she was confident there was that much in the mattress.

Once back home, Sara pulled all the money out of the mattress, counted it, and piled it into neat stacks. The needed purchases would barely make a dent in the cash.

Feeling a nibble of guilt, Sara made up an excuse to call the realtor and ask if Cora had any known relatives. She had found some letters, she claimed, and wanted to forward them to some of her family. The realtor assured her there was no one close enough to the old spinster to want anything in the house.

An internet search assured her there had been no bank robberies in the area. There was mention of a grocery store heist in Apple, but in a town so small, she doubted it could have amounted to much. Certainly not the small fortune she had been sleeping on for two weeks!

Her conscious clear—mostly clear, at any

rate—Sara's mind had spun with possibilities. She could expand her business. Develop more programs. Experiment with new ideas and new prototypes.

She would have to use caution, of course. She knew she couldn't deposit large sums of cash in her bank account without setting off red flags. Instead, she would need to make small, discreet deposits over a period of time. She was already paying with cash whenever possible, for fear that Shawn might find her.

If Sara were smart, she could make the money last for several years, the same way Cora had undoubtedly done, and her family before her.

From that night forward, Sara had slept on her comfortable new mattress and never once doubted her decision to move to this sleepy little town. She had been looking for a miracle, a chance for a new beginning, and she had found it.

Sara had hit the jackpot when she bought the old Miller homestead. Not just with the found money, but in every way imaginable. She couldn't put a price on peace of mind. She had a cozy little farmhouse where she finally felt like she belonged, and she had her beautiful, serene orchards. She had a home, not just a shoebox on a military base or in an apartment complex, and it came with a history. She didn't know it all, but that was fine. She had plenty of time to uncover the story behind the money-stuffed mattress and so much more. For the first time in her life, Sara felt blessed.

And each night when she counted her blessings, she remembered to count the money stuffed inside her mattress.

One wrinkled, crumbled bill at a time.

# Note from the Author

Thank you for reading my book and for indulging my love of writing.

If you enjoyed this tale, please take a moment to write a brief review on BookBub, Amazon, Goodreads, and/or the platform of your choice. Reviews play such a pivotal role in an author's career. Reviews are how readers find us, how sales charts rate us, and how we know if we've met your expectations.

After leaving your review, please feel free to drop me a personal note. (This is the best part of being an author!) Email me at beckiwillis.ccp@gmail.com or visit www.beckiwillis.com.

## Becki Willis

Best-Selling Author Becki Willis loves crafting stories with believable characters in believable situations.

When she's not plotting danger and adventure for her imaginary friends, Becki enjoys reading, spending time with her family, unraveling a good mystery (real or imagined), dark chocolate, and a good cup of coffee. A professed history geek, Becki often weaves pieces of the past into her novels. Family is a central theme in her stories and in her life. She and her husband enjoy traveling but believe coming home to their Texas ranch is the best part of any trip.

Becki has won numerous awards, but believes the real compliments come from her readers.

Made in the USA
Thornton, CO
07/24/23 10:04:47

ddd57c1b-26c8-40a7-91b5-da964356a41bR01